Showing Up

THE GEG SERIES
BOOK FOUR

I0629266

JACQUELYN AYRES

Cover Designer: Robin Harper, www.wickedbydesigncovers.com

Editor: Claire Almendinger, www.bnwauthorservices.com

Formatting: www.champagnebookdesign.com

Promotional Company: Bare Naked Words,
www.bnwauthorservices.com

Personal Assistants: Wendy Shatwell

Dedication

In loving memory of my dad, who always showed up but never got the appreciation for doing so. He operated like a single parent even though he wasn't. I don't know how he did it; he had at least twenty years on all the other parents and two ungrateful kids.

We didn't always see eye to eye, and he'd always say, "you're gonna miss me when I'm gone." He was so right. I've missed him for almost half of my life now.

I wish I could go back in time to tell him "I love you" and hug him once more. Most of all, to finally say "Thank you."

Chapter One

Julie

Today's Topic

RED'S GOT THE BEAT
Putting it out in the universe blog post:

Love isn't always about finding the right person and building a life around that discovery. We all know that there are many different levels to such a big emotion. But we're all different when it comes to this word, aren't we? Why? What makes our tickers tick differently?

Sometimes you have to go back to the beginning . . . to the first person you loved. And you may realize you didn't love that person exactly the way you should have. But, it's not because you made the choice not to, it's because you were never given the choice. Not only that but the very person you were supposed to feel this amazing bond to ends up being the culprit. You are left to ask the question why? And no matter how many answers you get, it never quite fills the void.

My mother has this amazing ability to constantly make me feel like that five-year-old little girl on stage, in a school play or dance recital, searching the crowd frantically as far as her eyes can see, thinking maybe this time, she'll show up!

    I'm thirty-five now and . . . I'm still waiting for her to "show up."

    She was my "first love." And I'm pretty convinced that she is the reason I have been cynical for so long when it comes to that emotion.

    Until I met him (Insert dreamy sigh).

    And strung him along . . .

    And hurt him . . .

    And acted like I didn't care . . .

    Then, I looked into the mirror, and I saw her instead of myself. Nothing puts your ass in check quicker than realizing you're turning into your mother.

    This self-discovery happened in a flash when he almost walked away. Had I not been surrounded by my friends, or verbally slapped by the fiancé of my friend (who put him through the same ringer), I may not have broken the chains that bound me to my protective wall. The very same wall I erected years ago because of my mother. She encouraged me to build it. I wish this were metaphorical, people, but it's not. My mother has always told me—trained me to believe—that I am the only one I can depend on. "Never put the key to your happiness in someone else's pocket," she'd say. That is great advice, though. There's only one problem: I feel that, as children, the key to our happiness is in our parents' pockets. They are supposed to keep it safe and warm there until we are old enough to have it placed in ours. What if the parents didn't fulfill their duties?

    I had a long chat with my best friend (you know—the therapist I often quote on here) about this key idea and why people turn out the way they do. I won't blow up this page with psychoanalytical bullshit. I will only share my opinion. We are all products of our upbringing whether it was a good or bad one. So, how do good people come out of bad situations and vice versa? I think some of us are just born with the ability to work through anything life throws at us. We're strong enough not to blame things whole-heartedly on one or two fucked up issues in our life. Sure, we all have shit in our life that we want to grab the crutches for, but if you've ever used crutches in real life, you know the added discomfort they entail. It's the same metaphorically, I think, so why bother?

Some people just can't help it; they don't have that "I'll show you!" attitude. Luckily, I do have that. Mine is accentuated with a "fuck you," as well.

Then, I'm left with these thoughts: why can't that person see that they are holding themselves back, blaming others for their misfortune? And, what are their thoughts on someone like me who seems to be able to keep their shit together?

I know I seem to have gone off course here, but I haven't. You see, my mother seems to fall into both categories, though she never lays blame on anyone or anything, so I'm miffed. For years, my friends and I diagnosed it as narcissism. I don't believe that now. There are moments when I can see her feeling so deeply for what others are going through and yet struggling to say something. When she says nothing, that's when I know she wants to take the pain away. It's when she goes to verbalize that she ruins it; she tries to relate every situation to one of hers . . . where she was magnificent in the moment, of course.

My mother showed me how to build a wall. The moment I let it begin to crumble, we stopped talking. I shut her out. We haven't talked in months. All I have to do is pick up the phone, and it will be as if nothing ever happened.

That's the problem.

I need something to happen. I need for things to change. At the end of the day—I love my mother. But, I need to know that she really loves me, that I am important in her life and not just for show, not just for a title. I'm tired of looking out in the crowd to see if she's there waving. For once, I want to just know that she is.

Out into the universe this goes, along with hugs for anyone else going through something similar.

Goodnight, peeps!
XXX Red

I CLOSE MY LAPTOP and take in a deep, cleansing breath before glancing over at the lump of hot Brit, snoring away in my bed. He was with the guys tonight way past closing time. It was only twenty minutes ago when he warned me that he was going to have me every which way tonight and that it'd be best for me to just *"shut it and take what's coming to you."* I agreed but asked for a few minutes to finish my post. "A few minnents . . . thash all . . ." he slurred as he pulled off his clothes and got into bed. Not two minutes later and the snuffling symphony began. God, I love him. Besides my friends, he is the best thing to ever happen to me.

Instead of waking *Casanova* up to fulfill his promise (because I like taking what's coming to me), I head into the bathroom and do my usual routine before climbing in next to him. I snuggle up close enough to solicit a stir from him. He turns onto his back and wraps his arms around me as soon as I lay my head on his chest. We both release a contented sigh before drifting off.

"What's on your agenda today, love?" Blake asks, glancing over his shoulder at me.

"Blogging, homework, spending approximately three hours mindlessly watching the *Home Shopping Network* because today's special may just be the thing I need in my life. Then, I will organize my office, have lunch with Judith, all while trying to fit in a good dose of procrastination. You?" I reach out as he approaches me with my cup of tea.

"Well, not quite as busy as you, I dare say. I may not be able to fit procrastination in at all."

"It really is an art form to be able to squeeze that into any pressing agenda."

"Clearly, you're a master," he admonishes. I huff on my nails and rub them on my shirt.

"Incidentally, I read your post from last night." He sits across from me. I just stare down into the piping hot liquid in my mug. "I hate to see you like this, love. I mean, your mother is not my most favorite person in the world, but still . . . it breaks my heart to see you hurting so." His forefinger lifts my chin so that he can look in to my eyes.

"Get used to it, Blake; my mother makes me feel this way whether she's in my life or not," I reply, fighting my tears off.

"Let's clear the board today and do something jolly!" he says, almost too enthusiastically.

"Didn't I just help you get your jollies off?" I quip.

"I mean it, Red. Let's just get in the car and find an adventure!"

"Why is it that when you say that, I see us on the side of the road with an overheated car and a flat tire?" I raise my right eyebrow.

"Because your glass is half empty at the moment. Let's fill that baby up, aye? C'mon!" He grabs a hold of my upper arm, squeezes it and shakes me a bit.

I stare at this handsome beast of a man: trimmed beard, twinkling hazel eyes, full head of wavy black hair, a smile that could make you "come to Jesus." He's a good man; he treats me better than anyone ever has, he makes me laugh, he makes me feel safe, he makes me feel like it's okay to be in my skin. I don't know how or why I got so lucky to have him in my life, but I no longer waste a moment to tell him how I feel about him . . . *ever.*

"I love you," I simply state.

"Good. Let's go on now and make more reasons for you never to stop." He leans up out of his chair, his face an inch from mine, and he lays the gentlest kiss on my lips. A little "love peck," if you will.

"Where are we going?"

"Wherever our love takes us," he almost whispers before leaning in for another kiss.

"You're such a dork."

"And you. Are. Completely. Charming," he says between kisses.

Chapter Two

Cynthia

Lost Moments

Present Day

THERE ARE THINGS I DON'T TELL ANYONE. THINGS I'M ASHAMED of. I put on quite the act. But "woman who has it all together" has been the hardest role I have ever played—I've been playing it for over thirty years now. I have received no applause, only tomatoes (or an occasional pie in the face) thrown at me when there is an audience. She is not a character you love to hate; they just plain hate me. *She* hates me. I did everything all wrong. No, this is not a new revelation. I've always known. You must know how it is, though; old habits die hard.

Once upon a time, I was liked by everyone. I still am. That is . . . by people who don't know me very well. I am finally taking the initiative to change that. I *can* get back to the person I used to be. She's still in there; she's just buried. Maddie has been helping me.

It's a slow process, but I'm making progress. Do you know how I know? Maddie. She hasn't come out and said it; it's in her demeanor toward me. The tension seems to have let up between us. Her smile is genuine now when I show up for my appointment. She's more relaxed. She even laughs with me. Sometimes she tilts her head and studies me a little with a peculiar smirk on her lips. I don't ask her, but I think she wonders why I've hidden this side of myself from the world. Or maybe I'm projecting my own thoughts and questions onto her.

I read Julie's post this morning. She doesn't know that I follow her. I do this under an alias, of course. I cried. No—I sobbed.

I spent most of her life, shaping her into a woman who doesn't need to depend on anyone. Somehow, I added myself into that equation when I should've always been her "go to." Just to give myself some kudos, I succeeded. I have only recently realized this. However, even though Julie can stand on her own two feet, she has an army of people who really love her, behind her, ready for whenever she needs them. As you may have figured out, I'm not part of that club. Don't get me wrong; I love her too. But, my efforts in the way I raised her only pushed her away from me. I worry that I will never be able to pull her back again. Too much damage. Too much hurt. She doesn't even know the half of it . . .

Maddie had me starting a list. She calls it a "Re-boot Agenda." Every day, I write down something in my life I would like to fix— whether it's a relationship with someone (besides Julie) or a situation that has happened because of my behavior. Her feeling is that Julie is not only the biggest piece, but she is the last one for me to set back into place in my life. That I won't have the strength and patience it will take to rebuild a relationship with her until I've gained the confidence from fixing all other important factors on my list. She should be the last part of the journey back to me. It's quite a long list, but she's helped me prioritize it to the things that are still relevant. Shannon is the only other person I have hurt the most.

The only one besides Julie that matters.

We'd known each other most of our lives, but it wasn't until middle school that we became best friends. This sudden leap in friendship happened over the love of a lesser popular boy band at the time: The Four Seasons. Everyone else was gaga over the Beatles. We, of course, thought this was great because it gave us a greater chance of having one of the guys fall in love with us. Gosh, we were so silly. Now that I'm thinking of this, I wonder if she ever reached for the phone to call me while our girls were heavy into their New Kids on The Block phase to reminisce with me about ours. So many times, I did, but my stubbornness got in the way.

The irony is not lost on me; our girls have been best friends their whole lives. They have what we had. Only, they still have it as adults. I have nothing. I wasted thirty years pushing my best friend away from me because I was ashamed of myself. I haven't been there for her at all during her illness. I've said *nothing* but awful things about her daughter. Truth be told, I love CiCi. She's so much like Shannon, I want to hug her and cry.

How can my best friend ever forgive me? I'm not worthy of her forgiveness. But I have to try. I just have to.

1962

"*Attention class!*" *Mrs. Belmont calls over the ruckus of our chorus class. Poor Mrs. Belmont; it's going to take her about five more times to get this class to quiet down.* "*Attention!*" *she says with a little more gusto . . . in a meek, mousy sort of way.*

"*Jesus Christ—she never learns,*" *huffs Shannon Donovan. She huffs again but adds in an eye roll at another attempt by our chorus teacher, then gets up and turns off the lights.* "*Shut your traps, everybody!" she yells out, and the room instantly quiets down.*

Mrs. Belmont clears her throat slightly as if she's a little uncomfortable with the fact that she requires the assistance of a thirteen-year-old girl to help her get her class under control. "Thank you, Shannon." She gives her a curt nod as Shannon re-seats herself next to me. "This year we will be having a winter talent show," she informs. "We will be doing group performances, so you will need to find buddies to work with. You can have anywhere from two to five in your group. Because you will be working as a group, you must pick a song from a group. I would like you to stay current, please," she adds.

"Um . . . like there were any popular singing groups twenty years ago," Shannon says under her breath.

"The Andrew Sisters," I mumble.

"What?" she snaps.

"The Andrew Sisters were huge twenty years ago," I clarify.

"Oh . . . right," she says thoughtfully. "They're pretty cool. My mom listens to them a lot. I forgot about them. I was thinking of all the big band music."

"Ugh. My dad listens to that. It drives me crazy. I need stuff with words," I whisper so not to get caught chatting.

"Some of it is alright, but I know what you mean. Are you going to do the show?" she asks quickly.

"I don't know. Not sure who I'd pair up with. I'm pretty sure everyone here will be singing The Beach Boys or The Beatles. I like The Beatles, but I think that will make for a boring show if everyone is going to sing the same group."

"Lame-ohs," she agrees. "I'd rather sing stuff by the Four Seasons, but I don't think anyone in here is into them."

"Are you teasing me?" I ask her, pushing down my gleeful hope.

"What do you mean?" She crinkles her brow like she's confused.

"They are my favorite group," I admit cautiously.

Shannon stomps her feet on the floor excitedly, but quietly. Suddenly, she stops. "I have two questions for you, Cyn—what song should we do and when are we going to have our first practice?"

"Me? You want to pair up with me?" I'm shocked. Shannon and I have known each other since elementary school, but we've never hung out before. Cyn? No one calls me that because . . . well, it sounds like sin.

"Hell yeah! We're gonna knock their effin' socks off! What do you say?" She swats my arm.

"You cuss a lot."

"Congratulations on your ability to hear. Now, are we doing this or what?" Her face is so serious, I can't help but laugh. I slap my hand over my mouth when Mrs. Belmont clears her throat, looking in our direction, then quickly nod "yes" to Shannon when Mrs. Belmont looks away. Shannon tears a piece of paper from her notebook and rips it in two. She quickly scribbles something down then passes both pieces to me. One has her name and phone number, and the other is blank. I jot mine down on the blank one and hand it back to her as we stand up to do our vocal warm-ups with the rest of the class.

Shannon turns her head to me and crosses her eyes, shaking them a bit, and a laugh rumbles up from my belly that I try to stifle. It turns into a loud snort. I cough to try and cover it up. Shannon's shoulders shake, and she brings her focus back to Mrs. Belmont. I smile, knowing we just had one of those connections that friends have without ever saying anything. See, I instantly knew she was making fun of Pauline, who, when she gets up in her higher register, sounds like a dying cat.

I've never had that before—a friend connection. I mean, I have friends; I'm friends with everyone. I just don't really have one that I can communicate to with a look. That is . . . until today.

Chapter Three

Julie

What's Up, Doc?

"Yes!" I groan as I walk through the door, getting hit with a scent of deliciousness. No, I am *definitely not* at my place. I have just arrived (a half an hour early—shh, don't let anyone know I'm capable of being early. I've got a reputation of being late to uphold!) at the St. Claire's for my weekly lunch date with Judith. She's Maddie's mom and one of my surrogates. Oddly, she's the one I'm the closest to. I say oddly because she's so reserved and classy and I'm so . . . not. We're like polar opposites, but, somehow, she gets me. She values me, encourages me, and just makes me feel good about myself. She's the mom that "shows up."

It's funny . . . all the things that Maddie complains about, I cherish. Don't get me wrong; Maddie loves her mom and is very close to her, but we all have a list of things that annoy us about our mothers. Okay, I may have a book. It's just that, I love how Judith frets over us like we're still little kids. It makes me feel loved—important.

Maddie is over it, of course. She doesn't need that anymore. I do. Luckily, my best friend not only knows this, but she welcomes me to it. God, I love that girl. She's so selfless.

"Is that my favorite jewel?" Judith calls out from the kitchen. See the wordplay there and how she makes it sound like I'm priceless?

"Yes, Mom! Just taking off my jacket. I'll be right there!" I answer as I hang it up in the closet and deposit my flips flops as well. We had one warm day of seventy degrees last week, and that was my invitation to be in flip flops until early October now. It's forty-nine today (just a slight chill for us New Englanders) which requires a light jacket or sweatshirt, but my piggly-wigglies will freeze for all I care; once the flip flops are out, warmer footwear is gone!

I head out to the kitchen. "What are you making? It smells fantastic!" I groan again as the smell hits me full-on.

"Oh, thank you, honey!" She pulls me in for a hug. "I've never made Jambalaya before, so I thought I'd try it. I don't think Dad will be too happy about it. It's spicy," she adds apprehensively.

"Well, it'll give him a good excuse to spend extra time in the shitter." I shrug.

"Julie—language!" She smacks my arm but gives into a giggle. "Would you and Blake like to come for dinner tonight?" She turns back to the chicken salad she's making us for lunch. She puts grapes in it. *It makes me love her more.*

"I don't know. Blake promised me that the take-out will be off the hook tonight."

"You need to learn how to cook." She shakes her head disapprovingly. "I told you I would teach you. My offer still stands."

"I wouldn't want to step on Charley's toes." Charley is one of my best friends. She's CiCi's younger sister, who is my number one. We won't discuss the fact that in my thirties I still number my best friends according to how close I am with them, so don't even try it.

"I highly doubt she will feel that way." She moves onto cutting the celery.

"She won't until my food tastes better, and with you as my instructor . . . well, you know that will be a given." I pop a grape in my mouth.

"Flattery will get you everywhere, my dear." She winks then pushes me over with a shove from her hip.

"I'll see if the Brit can break away from work to come for dinner. What time?"

"Six?"

"Sounds good. Is Maddie still joining us today?"

"Yes. She'll be here in twenty-two minutes."

"And thirty seconds," I add because Maddie is always on time. Like . . . it's not normal.

"I read your blog this morning." Judith wouldn't know subtle if it bit her in the ass. If she wants to dig—she hits you over the head with the shovel to tell you.

"And . . .?" I grab a handful of grapes and slowly make my way over to the small kitchen table.

She presses her lips together, but her chin still twitches. She looks up from cutting the celery, tears pooling into her eyes. It signals my own to start—damn it. "I hated it," she announces. I suck in a quick gasp of disbelief. "It was well-written and thought-provoking; don't get me wrong. I just hated that it's real . . . that you hurt so much, and that there's nothing I can do to take away your pain." The tears win their battle. "I love you, Julie. As if you were my own daughter—I love you. And," she takes in a deep breath, "I can't, for the life of me, understand how *any* mother could . . . Never mind. It isn't my place to say anything, and it's certainly not okay for me to speak ill of your mother. I'm sorry." She shakes her head and wipes her tears with the back of her hands before continuing with the (now slaughter of) celery.

Wait for it . . .

Wait for it . . .

.

.

.

"It's really *fucking shitty* of her!" Judith suddenly gasps, drops her knife, and then slaps her hand over her mouth in shock at herself. I practically suck in my lips trying to hold in my laughter. "It's not funny, Julie!" Her eyes widen as she tries to collect herself, adjusting her apron and whatnot. "The lengths this woman's actions bring me to," she admits breathlessly.

"I bet you're a freak in the bed," I state matter-of-factly. I live for this shit. Maddie would die a thousand deaths before she'd ever say something like this to her mother, but I do it every chance I get. I'm probably the only one to get away with it, too.

"Julie!" Judith gasps as if in shock. Completely unbelievable, though, when she's trying to hide her smile. "You're not too old for me to take my wooden spoon across your bottom!"

"Is that what you say to Dad when he spends too much time playing with his trains downstairs instead of pulling into your station?" I bite my lip playfully.

"Well, I never!"

"You've have two kids, Mom. I'm sure you have."

"You! You!" She starts laughing, losing all the authoritative composure she was trying to have. "I don't know what I'm going to do with you; you're so bad!" She throws a piece of celery at me. I catch it with my mouth and chew victoriously, smug smile in place.

"Thank you."

"Don't thank me until you get the rest of the food that goes with that piece of celery."

"I'm not thanking you for the celery," I inform her, my chin quivering along for back-up.

Her eyes connect with mine again . . . knowingly. "You should've been *my* daughter," she says.

"I am."

"You are." She nods in agreement, a small smile caressing her lips.

"The milkman must've been a real hottie." I click my tongue. She laughs and wiggles her eyebrows. Just then, Maddie calls out a hello as she walks in through the door.

"In here, sweetie!" we both yell together. Judith laughs at me again and throws another piece of celery my way. I miss this time, and she does some weird dance over it that cracks me up. God, I love her.

"Hey, guys," Maddie sighs as she walks into the room.

"What's up, doc?" I waggle my eyebrows.

"I read your blog today," is her reply. The apple does *not* fall far from the tree.

"Did I use any big words that made you proud of me?" I widen my eyes.

"It was a very healthy post." She ignores my comment.

"I try to stick to the pyramid to keep my dysfunction balanced. How are things down under?" I try to change the subject.

"Nice try."

"I don't want to talk about it, Captain."

"Captain?" Judith asks. Maddie widens her eyes at me to let the daggers out. You see, Maddie doesn't want her mother to know that she is Captain of the asswhores. I don't understand why; it's quite the honor.

In case this is your first time tuning in (if it is, thanks for letting me be your first. I hope it is as good for you as it is for me. You know . . . you *always* remember your first . . . *blows air kisses at you*), we've been calling Maddie "Captain" for over a year now because we decided we needed capes since we called each other asswhores like we're a bunch of Superheroes. Maddie claimed the colors red, white, and blue, stating it was because she was the captain. We haven't let her live it down since.

"Just an inside joke that we barely understand now," I inform as if it's unimportant.

"Well, I agree with Maddie," she goes back to the real topic. "We were just slightly talking about this."

"Slightly?" Maddie asks.

"I lost my composure, and I don't want to talk about it."

"You? You lost your composure?" My friend seems taken aback.

"She cussed," I say in a hushed voice.

"You didn't!" Maddie gasps.

"Shh! Shh!" Judith throws her finger up to her lips. Maddie and I combust into laughter.

"Are the voices listening, Mom?" I ask because there is—sure-as-shit—no one else in this house.

"Stop picking on me!" She seems to be getting pissed.

"I'm sorry," I say quickly.

"Let's just eat." She waves her hands, pushing at the air.

I get up from the table and head over to the counter separating the kitchen from the nook and grab the plates before leaning forward to kiss her cheek. She smiles at this and quickly places some chips on each plate before I head back to the table. Maddie and I wait for her to come over with her plate before we start.

"How's Hunter?"

"You just talked to him last night," Maddie reminds her.

"I know. I just . . . I like having a grandson." Judith blushes.

Maddie stares at her mom thoughtfully for a moment. "I don't think I've told you this, Mom, but I really do appreciate how quickly you've taken to Hunter. How accepting you've been of him really means the world to me."

"Oh, Maddie, he's so easy to love. I don't feel like I've had to put any effort into it at all. He's a great kid. I'm really proud to call him my grandson." She tears up.

"He's really happy to have you and Dad. He really loves you, Mom." Maddie reaches across the table, grabs her hand and squeezes it.

My heart squeezes, too. I'm happy for all of them. But, I'd be a liar if I said the little green monster I try to not acknowledge isn't fighting its way to the surface.

I'll never have this.

Mother and daughter moments.

I should be used to it by now, right? I'm always an extra wheel to mother and daughter moments: CiCi and Shannon, Charley and Shannon, Maddie and Judith. I used to be an extra wheel to Ava and Ivy's moments, but Ivy passed away about ten years ago. So, sadly, Ava and I connect over this extra wheel business. We cling to each other when it happens. The only difference between her and I is that she's been on the receiving end of these moments where I have never been.

I feel like a fucking orphan.

The irony? I have red hair.

If only my name were Annie.

I digress . . .

"Julie?" Maddie squeezes my forearm. I bring my attention to her. "Where'd ya go?" She tries a chuckle, but her and I both know where my thoughts went.

"Sorry. What were we talking about?" I shake it off.

"Wooden spoons and trains, dear," Judith says nonchalantly as I attempt to take a sip of my drink. "Attempt" is the key word here, people. My chin and shirt would disagree with me.

"Did I miss something?" Maddie laughs a little, watching the two of us give into ours.

"Inside joke," I inform her. She rolls her eyes, smirking before she attacks her sandwich. Judith reaches across the table and grabs my hand, squeezing it. Her smile hits her eyes, and they aren't just filled with mirth, they are filled with love, reminding me that the sun will come out tomorrow. Well, I think we all know what movie I'm picking out for Blake and me to watch tonight . . .

Chapter Four

Blake

Sexy and I Know It

Wiping down the bar, I glance up and see my friend, Dec, walk through the door. His eyes meet mine and he gives me a nod before heading over. *Fuck all that is holy!* Did I just say *his eyes meet mine*? Julie blogs about the books she reads. Quite often, I'm her listening ear when she falls in love with a passage. I can now confirm that she is making me sound like one of her romance novels. We'll just keep this between us, of course. No need for me to lose my man-card, right? That would suck; I'm British. Apparently, according to Julie, that places me higher on the male hotness chart. You don't want to help pull my card. By the way, what is it with you women? We Brits are just normal blokes. Never mind. I agree—we're much sexier.

"Blake! What is wrong with you?" Dec yells, and I bring my focus back to him. I didn't even realize he had walked up to the bar already.

"Do you realize that we have a tighter lock on our man-cards for having an accent?" I ask him out of bloody nowhere. He stands there, staring at me as if the music in my bar has stopped and everyone has shut up, soaking in the awkwardness of what I just said.

"I trump you," he finally says.

"Huh?"

"I'm Australian, yet no one is ever sure if I am or if I'm English, so I'm intriguing. My man-card is platinum, dude." He smiles.

"I'm gold. And, in saying that, gold is more valuable on the market these days." I hold my hands up like I hate to be the bearer of bad news.

"Whatever gets you through the day, brother." He slaps my shoulder.

"Yeah, yeah. So, what brings you in tonight?" Dec usually doesn't come in on Tuesday nights unless we have something planned.

"Maddie wants me to check on you, but I didn't tell you that." He grabs the beer I offer him.

"Julie's post?" I ask.

"Yeah. I read it, and I can honestly say that I don't understand why Maddie is making a big deal out of it."

"Tell me you didn't say that to her," I almost beg. He directs his bottle to me as a "cheers," indicating that he did, indeed, do that. "Fuck, mate," I sigh disapprovingly.

"I'm still learning, what can I say?" He shrugs before taking another gulp of beer.

"So, she sent you down here?"

"Why do women think we wouldn't figure something like that out?"

"They're hopeful." I laugh.

"They're nosy."

"You have a list of questions for me?" I shoot a brow up.

"You okay? Are you two okay?"

"Yes."

"Alright. No other answers needed, my friend." He shifts his beer at me again. "I do feel like she is being ridiculous. However, I did *not* say that to her."

"I'm proud of you." I laugh. "The thing is, this has been going on Julie's entire life. I mean, you got a taste of her mother's behavior last Thanksgiving," I remind him. That was epic, by the way. Kyle's mom threw a pie in Cynthia's face. It would've made Jerry Springer weep with joy.

"Yes, but I also saw how supportive she was trying to be when we lost Hope. Even Maddie has let up on her criticism of her since then. Maybe she's ready to change, mate." He takes another sip of beer.

"The problem is, every time Julie gets hopeful of that, Cynthia pulls the rug out from under her." I open the latch and come out from behind the bar.

"I understand that." He nods . . . more to himself, I think, and glances over at the band setting up. Of course, Dec would know; he went through something similar for most of his marriage to Renee. She really screwed him up as far as relationships go—Maddie had her hands full. But, she was the right girl for the job. "New band?" He jerks his chin in their direction.

"Yeah. *Bliss.* They are friends of one of my regulars, visiting up here from New Jersey for the weekend. I checked them out on-line before booking them. They're spot on." I turn at the sound of glass breaking. "Fuck all that is holy!" I snap. "I swear this new girl breaks more glasses than she fills!"

"Why don't you let her go?" he asks.

"Every time I try to, she starts crying and I lose my balls. I hate to see a woman cry. She's just a klutz. I'm wracking my brain to come up with a job that she's qualified for and will keep her away from anything breakable." I raise my hand in a dismissive way when Willow mouths sorry to me, her chin quivering.

"You need to get Mitch or Kyle to do it for you; those two are all business."

"You may be right," I agree.

"What else is new?"

"Conceited much?" I ask.

"What? Oh," he laughs, "I actually meant what *else* is new . . . as in your life."

"Ah! Sorry," I laugh. "Actually, my godfather rung me up before. He's coming here for a holiday. He retired last year and has been a traveling gnome since. I think it's getting a bit boring for him; he wants to be around family for a while, and I'm all he's got," I fill him in as I watch more and more people walk through the door. *Damn, I've got a long night ahead of myself.*

"How long is he staying?"

"About a month, I'd say. He'll get along famously with our crew; no worries there. Listen, mate, unless you can jump behind this bar with me, I've gotta get back to it." I jerk my thumb in the direction of the—suddenly full—bar.

"Go on, then. I have a few errands to run before I go home. I'll catch up with you later." He hands me the rest of his beer and gives me a fist bump before heading out.

I turn the key and quietly open the door. It's 4 a.m., and I'm trying my hardest not to wake my lovely lady up. After I walk in, I turn to close the door and lock it. With a deep, tired sigh, I turn back to head down the hall. Suddenly, I trip over some sort of box on the floor and go flying into the half table thing she's got against the wall, holding a lamp that has now crashed with me onto the floor as I yell, "Bloody *fucking* hell!"

"Blake? Is that you?" Julie calls out.

"Who the feck else would it be?" I groan.

"Be careful. I left a few things in the hallway," she warns me. Seriously?

"Right . . . I've come across them, love. Thanks for the warning," I call up to her as I sit up and feel my forehead for any blood. I wince; just a large goose egg. Bet that'll look attractive in the morning.

The stairway light comes on and I hear her pitter-pat down the stairs. "What are you doing?"

"Just disposing of the lamp you detest so much." I really do have the patience of a saint.

"Shit, Blake, I told you to look out," she huffs when she finds me.

"You certainly did. Though, it may have been more useful information had I received it about three minutes earlier." I grab her out-stretched hand.

"I'm sorry. I forgot I left these here. They are donations for The Salvation Army." She leans in for a kiss once I'm standing.

"Do you think I can donate this concussion I've just obtained?" I'd like to say I'm joking, but that lamp is heavy as all fuck.

"Did you cut yourself?" A look of concern crosses her face and she grasps my hair gently, pushing it around to find any injuries. See, I thought when I left for work, about twelve hours ago, I couldn't possibly love her more than I did then. But . . . I've just fallen a bit harder at this very moment. I know, I know; I sound like a pansy. If you only knew how badly this woman used to break my heart, you'd understand why it leaps so now.

"Why are you up so late, love?" I palm her left cheek and caress her lips with my thumb.

"I'm not up late; I'm up early." She smiles and purses her lips against it.

"Will you come back to bed with me?"

"I can't. I have my exam this morning. I need to study."

"Is it Anatomy and Physiology? I can help greatly with that subject, as you know . . ." I lean into her neck and trail kisses up it. Her breathing changes tempo and she lets out an airy version of an explicit four-letter word. It makes me smile as I nip at the sensitive area beneath her ear, then work my way back down.

"It's English," she mutters and tries to push me away.

"Ah! Well, that's my native tongue . . . and I use it properly. You should let me help you with your studies on that." I run my tongue up her neck slowly before pulling her lobe into my mouth and sucking on it. She whimpers.

"You have a concussion, remember?" She tries to pull it together, so it seems, as she is a little more assertive with the pushing.

"You win, Red, due to the fact that I'm actually so exhausted, I don't believe my performance will be up to par." I finally give in. Of course, the throbbing pain in my head helped me come to that decision.

"C'mon, I'll tuck you in." She smiles and gives me another kiss.

"Look, love, I told you I'm tired; there'll be no tucking me in anywhere tonight . . . no matter how much I love being tucked inside of you."

"Let's go, *Casanova.*" She shakes her head, grabs my hand, and pulls me along to follow her upstairs.

"As you wish . . ." I trail off, mesmerized by her lovely arse climbing the stairs in front of me, in those Wonder Woman panties she fancies. I fancy them, too. I know—you're shocked by this revelation.

Chapter Five

Cynthia

Best Friends Forever

I WAIT PATIENTLY FOR MY APPOINTMENT WITH MADDIE. I STILL have another fifteen minutes, so I decide to do something I know I've been avoiding, despite how much I've told myself I've just been too busy to reach out. Maddie will have my head if I didn't get this done. Okay. I can do this. It's just a text. An olive branch, if you will. I'm a chicken; a text is too impersonal for this. But . . . it's all that I've got at the moment.

Me: Hi Shannon! ☺ When you get a chance, I'd like to meet up with you.

I want to talk to you about a few things. Whenever you can.

Me: No rush.

Me: Okay, thanks.

Me: Hope you're doing well.

Me: Bye.

I look back at my text. God, I'm such a spaz! Why did I put

a damn smiley emoji? Why did I send multiple texts? My phone tweets.

Shannon: Are you okay?

Me: Yes.

Shannon: Cuz you never text me . . .

Me: I know.

Shannon: Are you dying?

Me: Dramatic as ever . . .

Shannon: I spend my afternoons watching soaps.

Me: ???

Shannon: In the soaps, when somebody from your past suddenly contacts you, they're either dying or they are your long, lost sister.

Me: Our daughters are best friends. I didn't randomly show up in your life again.

Shannon: That all depends . . .

Me: What??!

Shannon: Is this Cyn or Cynthia?

Me: I'm one in the same.

Shannon: Nope.

Me: Nope?

Shannon: I haven't seen Cyn in 30 years.

I let out a slight sob and slap my hand across my mouth to cover it up. Looking around, it seems no one has noticed my behavior. I get up just the same and make my way to the bathroom. Once inside, I let my body shake with grief before I answer her.

Me: Cyn

Shannon: I'll be home all day tomorrow.

Me: Okay.

I wait another five minutes. No other reply. That's it. It's something, though, right?

I make my way back out to the waiting room only to hear Maddie call me from down the hall. I stop to change course, greeting her with a smile. Her head tilts, brows furrowed in concern. I wave it away as I walk into her office.

"You were crying," she states as I take my seat.

"Yes."

"Why . . . what happened?" She sits across from me.

"I talked to Shannon, that's all." I adjust my skirt and avoid looking at her.

"Just now?"

"Yes. I . . . uh, didn't have the chance to contact her before today," I throw out there.

"Bullshit."

"Okay." I shake my head in agreement.

"How did it go; happy cry or sad one?" she inquires.

"Happy. Relieved. Confused." My tears pool into my eyes again as I fight the emotions.

"Confused? Why?" Maddie always gets right to it; she doesn't believe in easing into stuff. At least, not with me.

"I tossed away our friendship!" I practically yell. "I've dismissed our friendship for thirty years like it didn't mean anything, but it was *everything* to me!" I sob. God, I really wish I could pull it together.

"You're mad?" she asks as she pulls a few tissues from the box and hands them to me.

"I'm pissed!" I almost scream. And then, I do something I haven't done in a long time—I cry for Cyn. And Maddie, God bless her, she stays silent, letting me have my breakdown.

"You're grieving. Let's talk about that," she finally tries to pull me to shore.

"I don't know how to explain it. I don't know why I'm so emotional today. I mean, I know why I'm emotional. I just don't understand why I can't control it at the moment." I grab a few more tissues.

"You're mourning a great loss; there are no rules," Maddie offers.

"It's not like she died." I shoot her a disbelieving look.

"You're mourning the friendship you had with her. The same friendship that has been dead for thirty years because that was what *you* wanted."

"I didn't *want* that. I had no choice."

"We all have choices," she replies.

"Oh, Maddie! Life isn't that cut and dried!" I raise my voice.

"Isn't it, though?" She raises a brow.

"No. No, it's not. You don't understand."

"Help me to."

I lean my head back and look up at the ceiling as I take in several deep breaths. "I was embarrassed," I simply state.

"And . . .?"

"And . . . she was right. She was right about everything. I didn't want her to be. I didn't want to admit that she was. I wanted to make it all better, so I could be the one who said, 'I told you so.' But, it never happened." I bring my gaze to her cactus. Such an odd, random plant to have in an office, especially in New Hampshire.

"I've known Shannon most of my life. She's not the 'I told you so' type," she says. I know she's right, but I feel my stubborn pride sticking its nose in. "Tell me what transpired in your conversation," she says after a few minutes of silence. I pull my cell out of my purse, pull Shannon's text up, and show her. I watch Maddie as she studies it. "This is good!" She looks up at me and smiles.

"I don't know."

"Cynthia, you're still her best friend."

"No, I'm not. How could I be?" I wave off this nonsense.

"Look, I don't know how your relationship was with Shannon, but I can tell you that if I didn't see Julie for thirty years, she would still be my best friend. There are some bonds that cannot be severed by time, neglect, or distance. Those are the very strongest bonds, and by the way this text went, I'd say you two have that bond." She hands my phone back.

"You think she feels that way?" I'm taken aback. I've always thought of Shannon as my best friend even though all of these years have gone by.

"It's pretty clear to me." Her smile is encouraging. "I think this is really good, Cynthia. Yes, I would have rather you done this earlier than today, but the old saying rings true—'better late than never.' We both agreed that she is the biggest key to you getting back to Julie, right?"

"Yes. She is." I let the waterworks run rampant. "She's the key to getting back to me, which is most important of all."

"You're wrong." She shakes her head.

"What?" I jerk back.

"*You're* the key. And, you're turning, unlocking, and letting things—yourself—out. I'm so proud of you. I don't know who you were before, but I think I'm starting to see glimpses of her. I have to tell you, I really like her."

"You would." I laugh through my tears. "I was you. I was Julie. Okay—no." I laugh again. "I was you, Ava, and probably Charley. Shannon was Julie and CiCi."

"That's awesome." She tears up with me.

"It really was." I hiccup gasp. "Oh, Maddie," I shake my head, "I've missed so much. I've missed so *very* much—not just with Julie, but with all of you girls. I've missed the experience of watching you girls grow up with my best friend by my side. Nothing will ever replace that, no matter how much work I put in."

"The point is—you won't miss any more. Keep your focus on that; the rest will fall into place," she encourages. That's the great thing about Maddie—she *always* encourages. I don't think there is a situation this girl can't see the bright side of, and I love her for that.

Chapter Six

Julie

The Golden Girls

I TYPED THE LAST WORD OF MY ENGLISH ESSAY, SAVED IT, AND sent it this morning. I don't mind writing papers. I like the challenge of making myself sound like I'm interested in the bullshit I'm writing about. I love writing in general. There's something to be said for the escape you experience and the therapy it provides. No, I don't want to write novels—become an author in that way—but I do love to freelance, work on my blog, and review books. How cool would it be to get a job reviewing books professionally for a magazine or something? I would so open the eyes to the rest of the world on indie writers. They have written some of my favorite books. Anyhow, that's one of my aspiring dream jobs, my other is to be a Creative Writing professor.

"Jules, can I get an ETA on when you think you'll stop massaging that dog's ass cheeks? I'm getting a little nervous you might slip a pinky in and start talking dirty to her, calling her your bitch and whatnot," CiCi bombards through my thoughts of the future.

"As if I'd do that to anyone but Blake." I huff.

She smacks my right forearm. "Seriously—*stop!* I see it all going down in my peripheral, and it's wigging me out!" She shakes a shiver off her body.

"Sorry." I stop. I turn the water off and cover Meely with a towel, picking her up to bring her to the drying station.

Today is Lindsey's day off. She's CiCi's future sister-in-law and her right arm around this new mobile bathhouse for pets. She doesn't actually like to take a day off but today is doctor appointments day. Lindsey has Down syndrome. She fucking rocks it, I'm telling you! That girl is amazing. It's funny; I can relate to her a lot. No, nothing has been deemed medically wrong with me (though my friends may disagree), but I get a lot of the same sort of treatment that she does. People see her and automatically think she's not that intelligent, doesn't have much to offer besides awareness of her condition. They judge her by the way she looks. I fall victim to that, too. I'm a model (though I've recently given it up). People look at me and think I'm not intellectual . . . that I don't have much to offer besides my looks. It doesn't matter that I'm three classes away from my Masters in English or that I could run mathematical circles around them. I'm just a dumb model, and she's just a kid with Down syndrome. That's okay. It makes it that much more enjoyable when we blow their ignorant asses out of the water.

"So, what's really going on with you?" she asks.

"Oh God, please don't ask me about the blog post." If one more person mentions it to me, I may have to throat punch the lucky winner.

"No, no! Your mother is an asshole, no question about it. What's going on with *you* today?" she emphasizes.

"I was just thinking about school. Only three more classes till I'm a straight-up nerd." I start to groom my client.

"I know. I'm really proud of you . . . learning English like that.

Has it been harder to understand with Dumbass being your native tongue?"

"I don't think so. Does it sound harder to you?"

"Sometimes . . ." she trails off then nudges me with her hip, letting out a little laugh. "Not to bring it up but . . . how *are you* doing with the whole mom situation? This is the longest you've gone without letting her back in," she reminds me.

I shrug my shoulders and offer a whole lot of silence. I don't really want to talk about it. "How are things going with wedding plans?" I opt to change the subject instead.

"I love Kyle, but this would be one area in life where he is completely in touch with his feminine side." She offers me an eye roll before rinsing off her fur-client.

"So, he's into the planning. That's good!"

"No. No, it's not. He's driving me nuts. I don't ever want to have a front row seat to him planning out the details of a major life event again! I'll need knee replacements by the time I'm forty, for Christ's sake!"

"Knee replacements?" I tread. If you've already met CiCi, you know how her brain sort of functions. Normally, I know how it functions best, but this time, I'm clueless.

"I choke on his cock several times a week just to get him to shut up about the plans," she states nonchalantly, causing a guttural laugh from me. "I think I'm developing TMJ," she adds.

"Too Much Jizz?" I inquire with mirth.

"For reals, yo."

"You're disgusting." I laugh. Totally going to use that on Blake!

"What about you and Stuart?" Often (even more so since our encounter with those pale chicks with the blonde hair and crazy gorgeous eyes), my friends refer to Blake as Stuart because they say he looks a lot like the rugby player/model, Stuart Reardon. He hasn't caught on as to why they do this yet, and I, of course, keep him in the dark because it's more fun that way.

"What about us?"

She stares at me as if I'm the dumbest person in the world, and it irritates her.

"I don't know. It's too early! I mean, give me credit for accepting that this is the real thing. No need for me to lose my shit, too. I don't want to screw things up. I'm taking things as they come," I lay it out.

"It's taking a lot out of me to have this adult conversation with you, you know? And then, you have to go and say some shit like *you taking things as they come?* You're setting me up for failure and you know it!"

"Shut up!" I laugh and place Meely in her crate, then turn the fan on to dry her.

"I hate this . . ."

"What?" I look over my shoulder.

"I mean," she huffs, "It's like all of the sudden, shit is getting real and we're all growing up. I feel like I have way too many adult conversations lately."

"Ceese, we *are* adults." I turn to her.

"Yeah, I know out in the world we are . . . you know—sort of, but, I feel like it's happening more with us. I don't like it. I hate it. I feel like we are going to lose who we are because we're too busy dealing with grown-up shit. I sound like an idiot." She waves me off.

"No. No, you don't. I get what you mean. It's been a crazy fucking year. I mean, one of us should write a book about it," I admit. *Suddenly, awkward silence happens as we both turn to you and raise a brow . . .*

"The thing is, Ceese, it's good to know that when shit goes down, we're there just as much as when times are slightly easy. It shows our strength."

"You sound like Maddie." She gives me a half smile.

"Well . . . she is our captain."

33

"Aye," she says in a pirate voice. When it comes to friendships, it's all about balance, people.

"How's your mom?" Shannon's no longer in remission from her MS.

"We finally ordered her one of those scooter chairs for when she's out to places like flea markets or amusement parks."

"Did you get yourself one?"

"I mean, I had to, right?" After a moment, she starts laughing so hard she's crying.

"What?"

"I . . . um . . . I souped Mom's up," she says through her tears.

"What do you mean?" I begin to laugh with her.

"It plays music after she gets going." She snorts.

"What music?"

"I changed the words to 'I'm Too Sexy.' It plays my version of that song whenever she moves. *I'm too sexy for my walker, too sexy for my walker, move your ass, or I'll run you over . . .*" she sings, and I about piss my pants. Only CiCi could do this to her mom and get away with it. The only thing that Shannon will be pissed about is that she didn't think of it herself.

"How the hell were you able to do that?" I wipe my eyes.

"Trent."

"Duh," I sigh because I should've known. Trent is Ava's husband and the only man who's lasted the longest with the GEGs. He's some sort of computer wizard. I never remember his title, but I always remember his phone number for when my shit breaks down.

"By the way . . . have you seen Ava, outside of us all getting together?" she asks, suddenly serious.

"Um . . . no, actually. Why, what's up?"

"I don't know. Just getting a weird vibe from those two. It's probably because of the babies, though." She blows it off and places her client into a crate, turning on the blow dryer.

"Remember how fucking weird Charley was after each kid?" I

remind her.

"Yeah, which is why I never told her when I dropped them."

"You dropped the kids?"

"No."

"You just said you did."

"No, I didn't."

"Dude?"

"Shh. Let's save that story for when we're tired of our old ones."

"No."

"Hungry? I think we should get lunch." She races to the front of the bus and takes off out the door. *Hooker.*

I follow her, knowing we won't have to go too far for lunch. CiCi has an obnoxious habit of watching every reality show known to man. Her latest obsession is about food trucks. She has an app for it. We parked this bad boy right next to a Mexican food truck she's been following. She then advertised where we were to her customers and to bring their appetites. She calls it cross-promotion. I'm sure the owners of the Mexican food truck call it *annoying*.

"Speaking of Kyle . . ." she leads as I walk up next to her.

"Were we?"

"Yes. We just had this conversation in my head. You showed up; I thought I should share."

"That may help. I wouldn't want to mess up my lines." I humor her.

"Exactly. That shit slows down production. Anywho, I just realized that he'll be home tonight, and I forgot to get together with you girls for the makeovers and shit brides do with their bridesmaids." She moves up in line.

"When are we supposed to get together?" I ask as I eye the menu.

"We got together two weeks ago. We had a blast . . . as usual."

"Yes, if I pretend real hard, I can remember the awesome time we had." I shake my head.

"Look, he knows when I bullshit him. That's what I love about him. But, he also knows that I will do whatever it is I'm supposed to do to keep the façade up. So, whatever you're doing tomorrow, it's going to involve our posse and the mall," she informs me.

"I have plans."

"You do. You're going to meet us at the mall at 2 p.m."

"Why do you pull this shit on us?" I half complain. I don't really have plans outside of sitting in my yoga pants, doing jack shit.

"Puh-lease! Your yoga pants called me yesterday. They need a day off from your ass." She rolls her eyes, then orders.

"What are we doing?" I concede.

"Make-overs and you know . . . shit bridal people do at the mall." She shrugs.

"Are we doing your registry?" I ask with excitement. Oh, the power of that registry gun . . .

"Sure," she says then goes to pay the guy. "Hey, do you want me to groom your Chihuahuas today?"

"Ceese!" I yell in a hushed tone. "That's so racist! I can't believe you!"

"They actually have Chihuahuas, dipshit, put your politically correct crown away."

"Oh." I laugh lightly, kind of embarrassed. I glance up at the menu, trying to move on from that.

"You should order the Dipshit Special," Ceese offers.

"Ha-ha," I say.

"It's right there." She points to it with irritation. Sure enough, they have a special called *Dipshit*. "They let me name it." She smiles with pride.

"Why would you name it that?"

"Because if you eat the whole thing, you will blow your ass out later in the day."

"Who would eat that then?" I look at her like she's crazy. Well . . . she is.

She stares at me like she's willing me to grow a brain cell. "A Dipshit," I finally say when a cell blossoms.

"A dipshit," she agrees.

"Thanks for recommending an ass blow-out meal to me; you're a true friend," I praise then turn to Juan (I think that's his name. His t-shirt says, "I hate tacos, said no Juan ever"), "I'll have the number two."

"You sure will," CiCi quips.

"Guys, I have two hours only," Ava announces as she walks up to us.

"Hello to you, too," Charley pipes up.

"Sorry." She shakes her head. "Hi. Hi. Hi. Hello." She kisses us all. "My boobs will leak in two hours and fifteen minutes."

"Should we call in the boob squad?" CiCi asks.

"I didn't bring my pump," Ava adds.

"We'll milk you—no problem." CiCi shrugs, and we all agree with this statement.

"Thank you for being a friend, Blanche." She chuckles.

"I'm Sophia, Rose. Get that shit right!" she says as she leads us toward the make-up counter. "If one of you bitches spray me, you're going down," she warns the perfume girls, standing in our way, with a bottle ready to make us smell like cheap hussies.

Pah . . . like we need perfume for that!

We make it to the counter of our destination and plop into the few open seats. Maddie and Charley stand behind us, waiting for their turn. CiCi gives the lady our names. When the lady asks CiCi what look she's thinking about for her wedding, we all collectively hold our breaths. "Wholesome," she says, seemingly embarrassed. "But . . . with a slight hint of 'I fucked all the groomsmen,'" she adds. Ah, there she is.

"She's kidding," Maddie says quickly when the woman stands there speechless.

"Fucked them senseless," CiCi adds.

"She didn't. Most of them are our guys," Charley ensures.

"Yup." CiCi winks at the girl.

"Ummm . . ." the girl says.

"Don't mind her, please. Make her look like class and not the trash she speaks." Ava waves off at the girl.

Looking bewildered, the girl pulls it together and grabs some palettes.

Three hours later . . .

"Fuck the wedding. Let's go on the road as *Jem and the Holograms*," Charley states as we stand in front of a long mirror in the scarf section. Seriously, she's spot on; we look totally "outrageous."

Just then . . . "Picture it . . . New Hampshire . . . two-thousand-who-the-fuck-cares . . . five best friends get their make-up done for the upcoming wedding of one of the girls. The make-up artist does a shit job, transporting them back to the eighties when hot pink, angled eyeshadow was all the rage. They could've gone home and washed that crap off, but did they? No! They stayed in the 80s and headed right over to the wig department to rock this look out Golden Girl style," Maddie gives her best Sophia Petrillo story. I should mention that she is wearing an old lady wig. I don't think I need to mention that we are now beelining it over to the old lady wig department. I mean, it's a given, right?

"I look like Carol Brady with a curly mullet," I announce, studying myself in the mirror.

"Please buy that and wear it for Blake," Charley begs.

"Done. I'm also going to play "Young & Beautiful" by Lana Del Ray when he walks into the bedroom.

"Solid plan," Maddie agrees.

"Trent would probably be glad for anybody but me," Ava mumbles.

"What?" we all yell.

"Nothing."

"See?" CiCi nudges me when Ava turns away.

"Yeah." I nod in agreement. This is very odd behavior . . . very unlike Ava. Normally, sunshine beams out of her ass for no particular reason. The last time she behaved this way, she was playing *Press Your Luck* with Clomid shots.

"Big bucks; no whammies." Ceese's eyes stay on Ava as we walk.

"Can you get the fuck out of my head, please! You always do that." Well, when you've been friends this long . . .

"No, I won't. It's crazy as fuck in there. I like it." She grabs a leopard print scarf off an endcap without missing a beat and covers her wig like a babushka.

"At this point, we may have to sing our theme song ourselves," Charley declares.

"With all of these people staring at us, you would think it would randomly start playing over the intercom," I add as I acknowledge the many people staring at us. I look over at CiCi, and she is waving and flipping the bird simultaneously at all the onlookers.

"Stop!" Ava whisper-yells, noticing CiCi too.

"I'm an old lady. Old ladies don't give a shit. This is me—not giving a shit."

I'd say her speech makes me want to join her, but I joined the revolution before she uttered the first word. It was the right thing to do. I'll tell you why: old lady wigs are empowering. I'm serious. No, really. Next time you're having a bad day, put an old lady wig on and flip off random people. *It's life altering!*

Chapter Seven

Blake

Family Ties

I usually don't request a slow night but I've been secretly begging for one all day. It's great to be busy—packed, even—but when you don't have the staff to help or to have a night off, it's rough. Lately, it's as if I have a revolving door with these new hires. It doesn't matter if it's a bartender, waitress, or cook, I can't find any bloody decent help! I've been reduced to placing near nasty ads to get good people in. I really don't understand it. There's good money to be made here.

I take in a deep breath and rub my hands over my face, trying to wake myself up a bit before I get back to the inventory. Suddenly, it occurs to me—this is just the type of challenge that Kyle would love to figure out. I pull my cell out of my back pocket and proceed to text him.

Kyle, I need your bloody fucking help!
Dude, I have my own battles trying to figure out CiCi.

What?

I can't solve any Julie issues. CiCi brings her own level of exhaustion.

Agreed. However, that's not what I need help with.

What's up?

I need to get able, not-afraid-to-work-a-day-in-their-life bodies in here. I'm sinking, mate.

What position?

That's what he said.

Dude . . .

Can't help it. I need every position.

That's what he said.

Fecking GEGs. Lol.

We're all victims in this, Blake.

I'll feel around (shut up!). But I do have one person in mind.

Send them here, please! I don't care what the experience level is, as long as they work hard and have a bloody care in the world!

I wouldn't send them your way if they didn't.

Also, I'm forwarding my employment advertisement to you.

Please fix it!

Sure thing, boss!

Do you ever sleep?

Do you?

Fair enough! Later.

Ciao!

Fancy arse!

Stop checking out my arse . . .

I must. It's completely inappropriate . . .

With a gleam of hope in my heart, I carry on with the inventory so I can go and relieve Willow at the bar. Yes . . . Willow is tending the bar for me at the moment—*desperate times.*

"All right, Willow, you're free to go," I announce as I come out from the back.

"I was twenty-two when I walked through this door and ordered me drink! Look at me now; I've got grandkids I ain't never met! What kind of lazy-arse bloke runs this place?"

"Uncle Rupert! You told me you'd be in on Tuesday!" I shout, making my way over to him. Boy is he a sight for sore eyes!

"I *was* here on Tuesday! I've been sitting here for five Tuesdays since, waiting on me drink!"

"Ah shut it!" I lift the bar hinge and pull him in for a hug.

He pushes out of my embrace, holding my arms steady. "Look at you! Just as ugly as ever!" he teases.

"Good thing I'm only your godson."

"Why do you say that?"

"Because if I were your son, I'd be a hell of lot uglier!" I hit him back and laugh as he tries to wrestle me. *This man.* I owe everything to him. Not material stuff; heart is what he gave me.

"You're the *only* son I've got, and I love you, you ugly bastard!" He holds my face tightly and plants a big kiss on me. You know . . . the embarrassing sort parents like this do?

"Where are your suitcases? I'll have my help—that being me, of course—bring them up for you." I look around.

He huffs sarcastically. "Your guess is as good as mine!"

"What do you mean, Uncle?"

"They lost me bloody luggage—right bastards!"

"Only you!" I laugh. Honest to God, my godfather has had his luggage lost so many times, it should be in *Guinness Book of World Records*. "Where've your underpants flown off to now?"

"I hope somewhere tropical." He shakes his head.

"Well, I still have a few things in the drawers upstairs for when I crash here. You can borrow them till we get to the shops."

"I fly commando. You sure you want me junk free ballin' in your trousers?"

"I haven't much of a choice, now do I? Thanks for the visual of your wrinkly balls bouncin' about, though." I shake my head in disbelief. My godfather is the king of TMI.

"Jealous? They are quite big, ya know?" He raises his brows.

"No, I don't know. I don't want to either. But thanks for the share! Can we move on now?"

"Yes! When do I get to meet this Julie person? I need to tell her what a silly lass she is for involving herself with such a git."

"Don't be blowin' my cover now." I smack his back. "Get yourself a seat, if you think you can behave, and I'll grab ya the drink you were griping about." I give him a slight push, guiding him to a seat at the bar. Throwing a bar towel over my shoulder, I let the hinge door fall, and grab him a glass. "What's your poison?" Though I don't know why I ask; my uncle is a Scotch—neat.

"You know what I fancy, and don't be giving me cheap shit either." He shakes an authoritative finger at me.

"Yeah, yeah . . ." I trail off, grabbing a bottle of Macallan. "Here . . . thirty-year-old Macallan," I offer.

"Your arse!" He huffs.

"Oh yeah? What year is it then?"

He brings the glass up, smells it, then takes a swig. "Eighteen," he announces.

"How the hell do you know that?" I'm impressed.

"I know me whiskey. I also know how to subtract. Brilliant, ain't I?" He holds the glass up to cheer me before taking another gulp.

"No way you saw that label, old man." I laugh in disbelief. He shrugs indifference. I roll my eyes before heading off to the customer waving me down at the other end of the bar.

"Shhh!" I try to hush him as we walk through the door, but it's no use. He's on his third run through of "Whiskey, You're the Devil."

"Blake?" Julie calls out as she runs down the stairs.

"Aye, there she is!" he booms, making his way to her. He grabs her hands, pulling her off the last step. "Whiskey, you're the Devil . . . you're leading me astray . . ." he sings again and twirls her around the living room in some sort of old drunken man dance you only see in the movies. God bless her; she laughs, joining him with not a care in the world.

I love her.

"Don't worry about me toes, lass, I've got ten of um!" he says mid-chorus as she tries to keep up with him.

"He's clear out of sense, though!" I laugh as I clap along. Uncle Rupe loses his footing and they fall back onto the couch, laughing.

"I'm Uncle Rupert, lass, in case yer wonderin."

"Thanks for telling me. I thought you were just another drunk-en stray Blake likes to bring home."

"What are you doing with the likes of me ugly godson, any-ways?" He holds his hand out towards me as if to prove his case.

"Well, his ugly godfather didn't get here soon enough to straighten me out. Tis' a shame!" She gives it back, imitating his accent, no less.

"She'll do, lad." He laughs.

"I agree. Now," I clap my hands together, "let's show you your room so you can sleep this off, yes?"

"I just assume sleep right here. With the room spinning and all, it may be best." He grabs a throw pillow and fluffs it before letting gravity pull him down. Julie jumps up in time for him to stretch out. Instantaneously, Uncle Rupe begins to snore.

"How was that for a first impression?" I throw my arm around her shoulders as we stare down at him.

"The best ever. However, lucky for him he did that this week and not last."

"No truer words spoken," I agree. I may have caught nonsensical hell a few times from her last week.

"I thought he wasn't going to be here for another week or two?" she mentions as we turn to head upstairs.

"You'll learn soon enough that you can only guestimate with my uncle. He's a fly-by-the-seat-of-your-pants sort."

"How long is he staying?"

"I think at least a couple of weeks," I say as we reach the top step.

"What's the *at most* amount?" She turns to stand in front of me.

"Life?" I shrug and widen my eyes to indicate I haven't a clue.

"He's pretty fucking hot. I'm sure I can find a few old ladies who would like to bang him," she states thoughtfully.

"Believe me, darling, when I tell you that man needs absolutely no help in that department. I'm half surprised his willy hasn't fallen off yet." I place my hands on her hips and encourage her to start walking backwards to our room. "I can tell you about another willy that hasn't fallen off yet, either, but would love to *get off*." I give her a cheeky smile.

"Do you need me to free Willy?" she asks coyly as her hands find my belt buckle.

"You're the only one who knows how to get me to jump over that bloody wall." I lean in and attack her neck.

"I think we just created a new sick-fuck category: children's movie pornography. I think we should stop and put some serious thought into what kind of road this thinking will lead us down." She stops.

"I think we should take the 'shut-the-fuck-up-and-kiss-me-road," I inform her.

"Legitimately a better idea," she says against my lips.

I continue to lead her back toward our room and kick the door shut with my foot once we enter.

"Well, somebody's feeling a little extra enthusiasm tonight." She pulls away from me, playful smile intact as she grabs the hem of her tank top. She takes her time pulling it up and over her head. I lick my lips as I take in the site of this gorgeous creature in front of me. "Do I have to undress you, too?" She reaches forward to start at the buttons of my shirt.

"Apparently." I breathe, staring into her eyes. "There are moments when your beauty stops me dead in my tracks. I'm incapable of doing anything but soaking it in," I admit while attempting to free her hair from the clip that's keeping it hostage.

"If you don't stop talking to me like that, you will surpass all of my book boyfriends in the hotness department. Then who will I fantasize about?" she asks as her hands glide up my chest and onto my shoulders, pushing my shirt off them.

"Eh, this may sound a bit crazy, but you could fantasize about me. I promise not to tell anyone, what with the shame of it all," I add.

"That's a lot of pressure, sweetie. I mean, the expectations of a book boyfriend are just," she pauses as she reaches up way above us, "pffbbt," escapes through her lips.

"I have full confidence in myself." I bring her hand down from her level demonstration. "For instance, if I were a book boyfriend who, perhaps, would like to reel his woman back in, I think I would be expected to do something like this," my left hand glides to the back of her neck, and I grasp her hair, pulling her closer to me, "before I shut her up like this." I slam my mouth against hers. She gasps but gives in quickly, allowing the intrusion of my tongue. Just when I feel the tension in her body dissipate, I break the connection abruptly. Nose to nose, the sound and heat of our rapid breaths only heightens the air of urgency that has been reignited. "I'm correct, yes?"

"Yes," she pants.

"And, if I were one of those selfish, alpha book boyfriends

women hate that they love, I would inform you that I'm going to take what is mine, whether you are ready for me or not, right?" I drop my hands, making quick work at my belt. "Right, Julie?" I ask her, impatiently.

"Yes. Only—"

"—Only . . . she always is ready, right, love?" I nip at her bottom lip before sliding my hands under the band of her PJ bottoms and guiding them down. "If I were the gentle book boyfriend," I start as I come back up after she steps out of them, "I would do this, just to make sure." I slide my two fingers through her lips, only to find her drenched. "Christ, Julie," I groan and push them deep inside of her.

"Blake!" she gasps, clenching onto my shoulders, her forehead falling onto mine.

"Am I meeting all expectations, so far?" I ask. I believe she would answer me if I wasn't working so diligently at making her combust. Not another second goes by and her legs are shaking, causing her to lose the ability to stand without my arm around her lower back, holding her up. "That's it, love," I encourage her as she wraps her arms around my neck for extra support. Her head falls back, her mouth open, letting out the most beautiful sound as she milks my fingers. A few more twitches and all the tension releases; she practically collapses in my arms, breathing heavily. I pull out and quickly grab under her knees to carry her to our bed. She already has a sated look on her face, but I am nowhere near done with her, yet.

Only . . .

I'm not really a book boyfriend, so if I don't get inside of her this moment,

I'm going to be the poster child for Pre-Mature Ejaculation.

I place her on the bed and stare at her with (what I hope looks like) a smoldering, alpha male-ish stare as I take my time unzipping my trousers. She licks and bites her lip at the same pace.

Puppies . . . fishing.

The catch.
The release.
Feck!
Cars. Engines.
Revving.
Shit!
Otters.
Otters? Where the fuck did that come from?

"Blake . . . please, baby," she coos. *Right!* I crawl over her, grabbing her right leg to wrap around me as I situate myself. "I need you." She threads her fingers into my hair, pulling me to her and attacking my lips. A small, magnificent maneuver on my part, and I'm deep inside of her. "Oh, God, yes!" she cheers. "Hard and fast, please," she requests.

Oh, it's going to be fast . . .

I reach down, sliding my arm under her left leg to pull it up higher, giving me better leverage as I unleash the beast inside. Too quickly, the surge begins. "That's it; don't stop!" she cries.

Otters!
Otters working on their den.

"Oh, Blake! Harder!" She rakes my back.

Otters . . . enjoying a leisurely swim down the river, on their back.
Otters, greeting other otters, joining the swim, with fist bumps.
What?

"Ohhh . . ." Julie cries as she comes again.

Thank Christ!

I slow down, letting my release finally happen (otters, be damned). I flood her. Seriously, I may be dehydrated now. "I love you," she whispers once I collapse. "I've missed you."

"I feel the same way . . . the missing you. Love, too!" I lift my head to her smiling face.

"You're definitely way better than any book boyfriend out there." She kisses me.

Chapter Eight

Cynthia

Coming Home

I RAISE MY HAND TO KNOCK ON SHANNON'S DOOR, BUT JACK opens it before my fist falls to it. "Hi, Jackie," I greet him in the old familiar way.

Oddly, it feels good, like I've come home.

"Cyn . . ." he trails off, stepping back, holding the door open wide for me. I step inside. "I'm going to do a few errands, give you girls some time."

"Okay." I smile. "Where is she?"

"In the kitchen. Tea's ready," he informs me. It's funny how the strangest things can tear you up. Shannon is the only one I ever drink tea with. I'm a coffee; she's a tea. I nod and focus on making my way in that direction, trying to pull myself together.

I am *still* her best friend.

I stop at the threshold to the kitchen, noticing her trying to put sugar in her tea. It's like she's drunk. Except, she's not. It's her MS.

"I'm doped out on pain pills," she announces out of nowhere. *I knew it!* I stay quiet, trying to think of what to say. I try to focus on our friendship from thirty years ago.

"Can I have some?" is what I come up with.

"Sit down. I put it by your cup and saucer." She points.

I walk over and sit. "There are two pills here." I look at her.

"Good job; you remember how to count." She stabs her spoon into the sugar bowl. "Get your spoon. Between the two of us, we can manage for you to have a little tea with your sugar." She retrieves her spoon, a quarter of it filled with sugar.

"I'm still sober; I can manage the rest." I smile as she pours it into my cup.

"Good because this focusing shit is not working out for me at the moment." She closes her eyes as if to meditate or regain strength.

"How high are you?" I try not to laugh as she quietly makes popping noises with her lips.

"Lake Winnipesaukee, 1965," she answers.

"Well . . . shit—you are completely baked," I announce. We had gone camping that summer with a group of friends. To this day, I'm not actually sure we ever made it to our destination or if we hallucinated the entire trip.

That's all I'll say about that.

Well, it was the 60s. So . . . you know, free love and all . . .

With the amount of drugs we consumed, it probably was.

"Twice . . . like the potato." She laughs. "Join me," she adds, shuffling an uncoordinated finger towards the pills next to my saucer.

"What the hell?" I mumble. I pick them up and pop them into my mouth, chasing them down with my tea that I haven't fully doctored up yet.

"How long do you think we should wait?" Shannon asks with her eyes closed.

"For what?"

"For that stick to fall out of your ass so I can talk to my best friend."

"You still see me that way . . . your best friend?" I choke up.

"It's hard to explain, but yes." Her voice falters as well.

"I don't know where to start," I suddenly blurt.

"Well, let's fly right past the *I'm a selfish fucking bitch* portion because everyone has received that memo more times than they care to mention." She brings her cup up to her lips.

"Okay . . ." I hesitate, "I guess I'll start by thanking you for wrecking my opening line. I mean, I've been working on those specific words for a long time." It's like slipping into an old pair of comfortable slippers. How can something so hard be so easy? Shannon's lips curve into a small smile. "I guess I'll start with I'm sorry. You were right. I hated the idea of being wrong. It's taken me thirty years to figure out that no matter how much time passes, I'll never prove myself right. That the only thing I did was waste thirty years by being stubborn and pushing away the people that I love till I figured everything out."

"So, you haven't figured everything out?" She raises a brow.

"Apparently not," I huff in a small laugh.

"If it makes you feel any better, none of us have. Oh, we think we have. But, then, life throws its many curveballs and we are left to sit there, dumbfounded by it all."

"You're right."

"Well, some things never change," she quips. I smack her hand in jest. "What brought you to your 'Come to Jesus' moment?"

"Losing Hope. You know, the baby—not actual hope," I clarify.

"That was . . . that was a tough one." Her chin quivers. My eyes fill up, and I quickly grab her hand to hold. "My girls . . . the pain was crippling, watching them go through it. Watching all of the girls going through that." Her voice shakes as she gives in to her tears. "I . . . I've been questioning God a lot, Cyn. What kind of

God does that to people? What kind of God lets me suffer like this? I'm a good Christian woman!" Her anger stands in the spotlight. "I mean, I'm not a poster child, but I'm still a good one. I don't understand it." She shakes her head. "I'm so mad," she says through her teeth.

"I don't have those answers. The only thing I can say in God's defense is that he has surrounded you with people who love you dearly. Focus on that part of God's job." I try to encourage her. It's not easy when I'm weeping along with her.

"How's your brother?" she asks, changing the subject.

"Same as ever—trying to grow up." I roll my eyes. Years later, this is still a sore subject.

"If it hasn't happened by the age of seventy-five, I think it's safe to say he's a fucked-up version of Peter Pan."

"Pretty much," I agree.

Soon enough, we're catching up on each other's family gossip and scandal. The pills are slowly creeping up on me, saying hello. I feel like maybe a countdown should happen to lift off. "I'm getting high," I announce randomly, as one does when they are getting high.

"I don't think you're moving."

"What?" I say as if I just ran five miles.

"You're in your seat."

"Yes. Yes, I am. But, we're floating." I know I'm not, but I am.

"Don't worry; just enjoy it." Shannon smiles toward the ceiling.

"Why is this working so fast?"

"Because you didn't eat."

"How did you know I didn't eat?" I try to stay focused.

"You never eat."

"I eat," I argue. She raises a brow at me. I give in to a little chuckle. She's right . . . as usual.

"Okay now, I'm sorry I had to take pain pills but I'm having a tough day pain-wise. In saying that, I'm sure Jack isn't going to stay out long because he knows when I take these puppies, he's going to get lucky. So, let's get crackin' here." She lifts her teacup up to her mouth.

"You and Jack still . . .?"

"Christ, Cyn, we ain't dead! Of course, we do!" she scoffs.

"I mean . . . regularly?" Holy crap, what the hell is wrong with me? I can't believe I am asking her this.

"As regular as a bowel movement," she replies.

"You just compared your sex life to defecating."

"No, I didn't. I compared the regularity of it." She shakes her head.

"It doesn't matter; you lined it up next to taking a shit."

"Well, as long as I don't shit where he eats, then it's all good." She brushes it off.

"You mean, shit where *you* eat," I correct her.

"Honey, I can't bend like that." She winks before taking another sip.

"What? Oh. *Oh!* Good God!" I laugh.

"Speaking of being *regular*," she pauses to make air quotation marks, "you keeping the cobwebs away?"

I clear my throat and look everywhere but at her. "That's personal," I finally say.

"How long has it been?"

"We're not here to discuss my sex life." I bring my attention back to her then take several moments to widely blink the intoxication away.

"It's a good thing. Otherwise, we would've just said hi and bye at the door."

"Screw you." I laugh.

"I know it's desperate times, but I'm already taken." She laughs with me. After a few minutes, we finally settle down. "C'mon, Cyn, what's going on?"

I take a deep breath before going into most things. Not

everything, of course. I'm not ready to tell her *everything*. I wasn't ready to tell Maddie, but for the sake of wanting to succeed at turning things around with Julie, I did. That hardly went over well with Maddie. Maddie is one of her very best friends. I understand what a burden I've placed on her. On the other hand, it was so therapeutic to tell *someone*.

"I could never understand it," Shannon states, pulling me out of my thoughts.

"What?"

"Why you pushed Julie away so much. It broke my heart . . . for both of you. Also, at various times over the years, I've wanted to beat the hell out of you for it. Goddamn it, Cyn! What were you thinking?" She slams her teacup down.

"I was thinking I didn't want her to be like me . . . to turn out like me!" I let my frustration fuel my words. "And I succeeded, didn't I?"

"No. No, you didn't." Her eyes fill up. "She's so much like you that I hate to be around her at times." She wipes at her eyes. "It made me miss you. Miss who you were before David."

"She's not like me."

"She is!" she yells.

We sit in silence, staring at each other. Both of our eyes are filled to the brim with tears. Hers seem like angry tears. "Why are you here, Cyn?" Shannon finally asks.

"I'm trying to find the woman . . . the person I used to be," I confide.

"So, you came here?"

"Yeah, you were the last person to ever see her."

The stubborn tears finally lose the battle and trickle down her cheeks. "She was a great friend, and I've really missed her."

"She's really missed you too." I choke on the lump in my throat. "And, I'm really sorry about Grandma. I know how close you two were."

Shannon's shoulders start shaking violently. Just when I think she's sobbing, a huge belly laugh rises out of her. "You're such an asshole," she says through her laughter.

"What?" I'm completely miffed.

"Grandma died twenty years ago!"

"Well, I know. I just . . . I've been meaning to say something," I try to defend myself but give in to the absurdity of my condolences.

"In that case," she tries to pull herself together, taking in a few deep breaths, "I'm really sorry about Whiskers," she says then starts laughing again. Whiskers was my cat. She died over a decade ago.

"Whiskers? You do know my mom almost died from a heart attack, right?"

"Yeah, but she was always such a bitch. Whiskers was a sweetheart."

"God, she was so old . . ." I pause, thinking about her—my cat, that is. My mom? —complete bitch.

"She was always old." She rolls her eyes.

"I was talking about Whiskers. But you're right, my mom has always been her age going on ninety."

"I always ask Julie about your dad. I visit him from time to time. You know, when I'm able to."

This stops me dead in my tracks. "You visit my dad?" I didn't know this. And my dad, well, with the Alzheimer's, he wouldn't remember to tell me.

"Your dad is a great guy. He was always like a second father to me. Of course, I visit him. You know, you just don't turn off love for someone because things in life change. I've always considered him family. Are you mad that I visited him?" she asks with a little hesitation.

"No. I'm floored, really. How is it possible?" I ask as my eyes are invaded again.

"How is what possible?"

"That you could remain such a good friend to me behind my back? That I could come to you after thirty years and still find my best friend sitting in front of me? I don't deserve this." I grab a napkin and blow my nose.

"There you go again, making this all about you," she teases.

"Well, I am the resident narcissist!" I announce.

"I'm so happy your birthday is next month."

"I'm scared to ask why." I bite my smile back and shake my head.

"You'll see." She rubs her hands together.

Just then, we hear the front door open. "Shannon, I'm home!" Jack announces.

"Told you." She looks at me pointedly.

"I guess that's my cue." I smile on the outside. Inside? I'm panicking. *I can't drive!* First of all, I haven't taken any sort of narcotics in years. Secondly, I'm not exactly in my twenties. Thirdly, why the hell would it matter that I'm not twenty? —intoxicated is intoxicated! *Pull it together, Cyn!* I just called myself Cyn! "I just called myself Cyn!" I alert Shannon.

"Congratulations on knowing your name. I'm so proud of you."

"Did you hear me?" I ask excitedly.

"I heard you. I didn't hear the voices in your head, though. Are they as excited as you are?"

"If you ever question where CiCi gets her personality from, I may have to commit you." I poke at her.

"Shannon, sweetheart, how are you feeling?" Jack asks from behind me. I look over my shoulder at him and note the anticipation in his eyes. I control myself. Some things never change. When your best friend tells you something about anyone and you are only able to notice what they are talking about, it's very hard not to start laughing or hi-fiving them for being spot on. Also, I'm jealous. I can't remember when I last had sex.

"I'm really happy for you guys." I bring my focus back to Shannon.

"You were my maid of honor, so we're all caught up there." She teases.

"Oh stop!" I wave nonsense at her. "No, I mean, you guys are really lucky to find the right one to have your *happily ever after* with. Your relationship is a diamond in the rough. I'm envious," I admit.

"It's not too late for you." Shannon reaches across the table and grabs my hand. "Jack has plenty of single friends he could introduce you to. But since I love and care about you, I won't let him try it."

"Thanks. I have another problem you may be able to help me with."

"What's that?"

"I can't drive," I admit.

"Yes, I believe the entire state of New Hampshire is aware of that. It's actually part of the rush hour traffic report; they inform us when you are on the road," she states straight-faced before looking over at Jack. "Is her ride here?"

"Yes, and he's not happy about it."

"He who?" I look back and forth at them.

"He—me." I hear someone say from behind me. I turn to see Kyle, CiCi's fiancé, there. *Oh boy.*

"Hi, Kyle, it's nice to see you." I try to smile.

"Ready?" he asks with a stoic expression.

"Yes. Thank you for picking me up." I grab my purse as I stand up and slide the strap up and onto my shoulder. "Can I call you later?" I ask Shannon.

"Yes. *Much* later," she emphasizes, widening her eyes.

"Why don't you call me," I say slowly and give her a wink.

"That's a better idea," she agrees then waggles her eyebrows at Jack.

"Okay! I'm going to leave now!" I try to take off, but my feet aren't as assertive as my brain, and I fall into Kyle. "Sorry." I look up at him.

"Yep." He grabs my arm and helps me along.

I follow his lead. "Do you know where I live?"

"Yep."

"I'm sorry for inconveniencing you," I offer as we make our way out the door. "My car's gone."

"Yep." He guides me into his.

"Are you just going to say 'yep' to me the entire time?" I huff.

"Yep."

"Where's my car?" I demand.

"Mitch is driving it to your house."

"How did he get the key?" I ask before he slams the door. I wait for the answer, watching him round the car before opening his door and climbing in.

"Happy."

"No, I'm not," I snap.

"Happy . . . *Jack* gave him the key," he clarifies.

"Oh, how did he—oh, never mind." I wave the question off. Who cares? "Thank you for driving me."

"You said that already." He brings the engine to life and sets it into gear.

"Yes, but you didn't say *you're welcome.*"

"Don't push it, lady. The only reason why I'm doing this is because I'd do anything for Mom and Dad." He takes a quick left.

"You call them Mom and Dad? Already?" I'm taken aback.

"Yes. Well, I love them already. Besides . . ." his lip curves up on the right in a smirk, "they don't really give you a choice; once they decide you're family—that's it."

"You're right." I glance out of my window, willing my emotions to stay at bay. I would love nothing more than to have this same type of dynamic in my family. Even if Julie and I find our way to the relationship we should've already had, I've alienated Blake more times than I can count. I was wrong about him. Of course, that's not shocking since I never gave him a chance in the first place. All I saw was David. That wasn't fair of me. He's not David, and Julie is not me.

"Cynthia! Where am I turning?" Kyle asks with a large dose of irritation as he plays around with his phone. I guess his GPS isn't working right.

"Oh, I'm sorry. I was lost in my thoughts. Go down two blocks and make a left," I answer quickly then fall back into silence. I really don't know what to say to Kyle. I don't dare ask him how his parents are doing. Last Thanksgiving, his mother threw a pie in my face and told me off. I hope that someday everything works out, and I can give that woman a hug for what she did. It was humiliating—Christ Almighty was it humiliating, but I needed it. Well, not the pie in the face. I didn't need that. Okay . . . maybe I did. But still, I'm certainly not going to ask about her.

"What brought you to visit today?" He brings our awkward silence to a screeching halt.

"I'm trying to right a lot of wrongs," I simply state.

"Does that mean we should expect you soon? Is this like an AA step or something?" He makes the left turn.

"I'm not an alcoholic."

"Drug addict?"

"No! Why would you think that?" I turn to him in shock, then close my eyes to wait for my brain to catch up with the rest of my body.

"I'm not sure. It can't be that I'm driving you home because you're too high to do it yourself. No. No, that's not it." He stops at a red light and takes in a deep breath.

"Shannon slipped me them. This is not my norm." I turn back in my seat to face the light.

"I'm well aware of your norm," he says almost under his breath.

"You don't know me, Kyle. Oh hell, I don't even know me anymore." I look away as my chin begins to quiver.

"You're right. I'm sorry. Is the AC too much on you?" He reaches forward and dials it down.

"I'm okay."

"You know, Blake is a really good guy," he informs me out of nowhere.

"I believe I've come to that conclusion all on my own. I just wish I had sooner. I'd have one less cloud to simmer down in my shit storm. Turn here," I direct before rubbing my temples.

"I've never heard you curse before."

"Shh . . . don't tell anyone. They'll think I removed the stick from my ass. And don't tell her I said this, but CiCi is the best thing that could've ever happened to you. She's smart, funny, beautiful, loyal, and just has the biggest heart of gold I'd ever seen in anyone. You make sure you take good care of her." My voice is shaking. I feel so overwhelmed by everything. I notice Kyle doing a double take at me in my peripheral vision. "What?" I demand.

"Nothing. Just that . . . I think you should stay on the drugs," he advises in a calm, yet, stupefied fashion. I whack his arm and allow myself to laugh. It is pretty funny. Suddenly, I feel a slight shift inside me. *Well, I'll be damned!* Maddie told me a moment like this might happen out of the blue—the beginning of acceptance. She's reminded me time and time again that I cannot change what has happened. I can only accept it as a chapter in my life, learn from it and move forward. That's what that just felt like—acceptance. It was very euphoric. Then again, I am higher than a motherfucker. *Holy shit—I just said that!*

"Why are you laughing?" He shoots me a strange look.

"I just said motherfucker." I laugh again.

"Um . . . no, you didn't."

"I did. You didn't hear me because I said it in my head. I said I was higher than a motherfucker. In my head, though. I would never say that out loud!" I widen my eyes at him in horror.

"Of course, you wouldn't." He smirks. "I have to say, Cynthia, I feel like Julie and CiCi have been cheated out of this moment with you. I'm pretty sure they have fantasized about what you'd be like high."

"Are you suggesting I get high with them? Oh my God! Kyle, do they get high? I've always been so worried about them doing drugs.

Are they smoking the Kiefer, Kyle?"

"I'm pretty sure that Kiefer is an actor and they are definitely not smoking him, or anything else for that matter. Wow, are we on to the paranoia portion of our drive?"

"I feel like it's getting worse." I turn up the air and lean into the vent. "What the hell did that bitch give me? I meant that lovingly, of course," I add.

"Is this your house?" He pulls into a driveway.

"Any house is good—I just need to lie down." I open my door. "Can you stop the car, please?" I place my foot out the door and tap on the ground to help slow the car down. *Oh my God, what did she give me? This can't be right. Who stops a car like this?* "Kyle! Stop the car!"

"I wish I had some music to go with your *Lord of the Dance* moves." He sounds amused. I don't know what the hell is so amusing. "Cynthia, open your eyes."

I open my eyes to find him standing in front of me, holding the door open wide. I can see he's trying really hard not to laugh. At least, I think he is.

"What took you so long?" Another man asks. I slowly bring my attention to him. Slow, as in, bionic sounds should accompany my movement. *I'm going to kill her. Maybe she's trying to kill me.* "And what the hell is she doing?"

"Michael Flatley has nothing on her, man!" Kyle states to . . . uhh . . . to-uhh—Mitch!

"Mitch!" I yell.

"What?"

"It's you! You're Mitch."

"Wow. What the hell did she take?"

"Shannon gave her some of her *Dr. Feel Good* pills." Kyle laughs again. They both lean down and each grab an arm. And then, umm . . .

Chapter Nine

Julie

Mama, can you hear me?

(Think Yentl)

I OPEN MY EYES TO THE SOUND OF MY NEW NORM: UNCLE RUPERT banging a pot at the bottom of the stairs, and yelling up, "Come and get it!" Uncle Rupert loves to cook a huge breakfast . . . at 7 a—fucking—m every damn morning!

"Who knows he's here?" I look over at Blake who is staring blankly at the ceiling.

"I'm not sure we'd get away with it, love."

"We'd at least have a few months of quiet. We could buy a ticket for him, using his credit card and act as if he left, that we have no clue as to what happened." I turn toward him.

"What would we do with the body?"

"Okay, we'll buy a boat with his credit card, wait a few days, take care of the situation and place his body on the boat. He'll sail off into the sunset. He'll love it." I snuggle in closer and place a kiss on his shoulder.

"I don't know whether to be afraid of you or turned on." He turns his head and kisses my hair.

"Maybe I should help you with that decision, Mr. Spencer." I lift my head to look into his eyes before leaning in for a kiss.

"Get your lazy arses down here!" Uncle Rupert yells again.

"A boat it is," Blake agrees, laughing against my lips.

We both give in to the requests of his lovely (read: pain in the ass) godfather and climb out of bed to head downstairs.

"Bloody hell, you two are like a couple of teenagers!" Rupe states as we walk into the kitchen like the ensemble of a zombie apocalypse.

"Everyone has a spirit animal, ours is the sloth," I inform him.

"Actually, I think mine may be the otter, love," Blake corrects me before bringing his attention to Rupert. "Unc, how is it that you can party late into the night and still get up before the bloody rooster as if you've had ten hours sleep?" Blake asks as we make our way to the table.

"It's simple—I'm Irish!" They both say the last part together.

"That's the reasoning behind everything he does," Blake says under his breath just before his godfather places our plates in front of us, commenting on how big and fat our sausages are.

"Just the way I like them: big and fat." I wink at the brit.

"You best sleep with me tonight then, love," Uncle Rupert says as he sits down with his plate.

"Manners, Uncle." Blake's voice is laced with impatience.

"Oh, come off it, now. I've been here a week; if she don't have me number by now, she's a lost cause." Rupe takes a hearty bite, smiling through his chewing.

"Well, it's just . . . I joined you last night, but all you had for me was a breakfast sausage and two little dried up tater tots." I sigh and grab the ketchup to drown my eggs.

"See—she's fine. I'm not insulting her." He throws his hand out at Blake.

"I don't like it." Blake turns to him with a look of steel. *Damn.*

"Sorry, son." Rupe pats Blake's shoulder.

"Blake?" I reach for him. He abruptly puts his hand up for me to let it go without making eye contact. Very odd behavior on his part, if you ask me.

"Alright, I'll be off then." I swear his godfather swallows his last egg whole as he says this. "I've got me own redhead I've been eyeing the past two days. I don't want to miss her." He wipes his mouth and gets up from the table, bringing his dish with him.

"The woman at the coffee shop?" Blake asks.

"Yes. I've narrowed down the timing of her arrival. She's never a minute late; wound up that one is. I'd like to unwind her." He waggles his brows at us.

"Have you said anything to her, yet?"

"I said good morning to her yesterday."

"Did she fall at your feet like all of your other conquests?"

"She gave me a small smile and a nod. I nearly busted out of me trousers accepting her challenge. It's been a while since I've had me one of those, what with me good looks and charm." He throws his hands out as if he can't believe this is happening to him.

"One of those, what?" I interject. What the fuck? This is my house—I should know everybody's business without having to ask. They should just tell me as a courtesy so I'm up to date on all of the gossip.

"A challenge, lass. Oh, she's a beaut, that one!" He sighs like cupid bit him in the ass—*hard.*

"What's her name?" I probably know her.

"Haven't a clue."

"How old is she?" If he says twenty-something, I'm going to puke. That shit just grosses me out.

"Oh, I must have at least ten years on her. She's beautiful." He gets that far-off, I-think-I'm-in-love look again.

"As long as she's not in her twenties, I approve." I grab my coffee and take a swig.

"Oh, I can't do the girls in their twenties anymore—it's exhausting. Everything's about the future . . . and kids, for Christ's sake. Do I look like I want to be bopping a toddler on me knee or changing a nappy? Look, I want to sow me wild oats. I don't want to be plowing that field for the next eighteen years because of it. Nah, I stick with me age group; shops are usually closed." Rupe gives himself a pat down. "Alright then, how do I look?"

I give him the thumbs up. It's all I can do after the overshare. The rest of my energy is going toward pushing out the images of Uncle Rupe sowing his wild oats. I don't have to tell you that once you get an image like that in your head—it's permanent.

"Good. See you kids later!" And with that, he's gone.

I wait till I hear the front door close before turning to Blake. "Okay, what's going on with you?"

"I don't like him flirting with you or making comments like that."

"Okay, but you know I'm not into old man dick, so you're safe. What's really going on?"

"I'm just tired, Red. I can't get any decent bloody help at the pub. Kyle's trying to help, though. He's sending a guy to me today. I don't understand it. I have a successful business!" He suddenly explodes. "I pay well. Why do people look down on this kind of work?"

"Whoa—wait a minute. That's not people, babe, that's your dad." I correct him.

"Well, it seems *Dad really does know best!*" He pushes his plate away.

"Where is this coming from?" I grab his hand.

"Ugh, I don't know. I just need a bloody break; a feckin' day off!"

"Let's work on that together. I'm all done with school this semester, so I can help," I offer.

"Yes, but I want my time off to be spent with you, love."

"We'll figure it out." I lean in and kiss him.

"What's on your agenda today?" He grabs my hand and kisses the back of it.

"Well, I'm going to start my day out by fucking a hot Brit senseless. Next, I will shower and get ready for my lady appointment, where I will have to pretend like I don't know my vaginer is full of semen as she is poking about. After that excitement, I will go to a yoga class and think about the review I have to write today while I'm supposed to be clearing my brain of all thoughts." I pop a piece of toast into my mouth, happy with the agenda I've laid out.

"I'll wear a condom."

"For what?" I ask.

"For when you are fucking me senseless."

"Oh, I said a *hot* Brit. According to your godfather—you're ugly."

"Ugly is the new hot. Keep up with the trends, Red." He steals my bacon and chomps into it.

"I guess you'll do," I concede with indifference then turn my focus back on breakfast. One thing I'll say: Uncle Rupe can be a pain in the ass for waking us this early for breakfast, but it's always groan-worthy. I look up, noticing Blake smiling to himself. "What?" I inquire.

"I was just thinking about how I'll miss these funny conversations we have when there are toddlers about, causing us to be more G-rated."

"Are we opening a daycare?"

"I mean later . . . you know, down the road a bit."

"A daycare?" I'm not sure how I feel about that. Don't be daft—of course I know what he's talking about. I'm just . . . I'm not ready for all that talk. I don't want kids.

"Sure, we can have enough to look as if we're running one. I've always wanted a big family." He gives me a toothy grin.

Shit.

I give him a slight smile and bring my eyes back down to my plate, willing this moment to leave as quickly (and rudely) as it came.

"Julie?"

"Hmm?" I scarf down another bite.

"Can you bring your eyes back up here, love?"

I take in a deep breath and slowly bring my eyes back up to his. We sit in silence for a millennium (shut up; that's what it feels like!). "Right," he sighs. He takes in a deep breath. "I'm gonna go ahead and put this out there, in case you're not sure: you are the center of my happiness. *You* are the most important—above all else. Understand me?" He reaches for my hand and squeezes it.

"Yes." I agree. *It's bullshit.* He wants a family.

I don't.

I can't.

"Don't push me away because I said something that freaks you out," he says in an accusatory manner. *Boy, does he have my number.* "Julie . . . please," he pleads.

"Do you think they will come out British or American?" I ask in my usual smartassy way. *Why the fuck did I ask that?*

"I suppose we won't know till one of them calls me "Guvnor."" He laughs. I laugh with him, relieved. I don't want kids, but I don't want to lose him. I'm happy to have dodged this bullet at the moment, but I know I can't dodge it for too long.

"We should go practice." I smile.

"Indeed." He licks his lips, staring at me as if I'm a steak.

Slowly, keeping my eyes trained on his, I get up. Brushing any crumbs off my PJ's, I suddenly take off for the hall that leads to the staircase. I don't have to look over my shoulder to know he's hot on my trail. As soon as I begin my run up the stairs, I feel his arm encircling my waist, lifting me. I yelp, laughing at his overzealous behavior. He continues up the stairs quickly, keeping me airborne. *God, that's hot.* I love his body. He's so strong and muscular but in a lean way. I'm not one for the bulky muscle sort. He's got a full head of hair, too. I don't think I have to tell you what a hot commodity this is for a girl in her mid-thirties, or mid-anything, for that matter.

He places me down as we enter our room and quickly grasps my face in his palms. "I love *you!* A life without you would be no life at all. I need you to understand that." His eyes are pleading with me. I'm so overwhelmed; all I can do is nod in agreement before he attacks my lips.

I got in my car to head to yoga. Ava's expecting me. I've changed my mind, though. I'm sure my phone will be pinging or buzzing an hour from now, after class. I'll answer her as soon as I can.

I cut the engine and close my eyes, trying to collect myself before I get out. A minute or two goes by and my door is opened from the outside. "What's wrong?" Judith asks frantically. I open my eyes to look over at her. Suddenly, without an ounce of control, I start crying a cry I haven't heard come out of me since I was a little girl. "Let's get inside, honey." Judith grabs my hand, pulling on me to encourage. I climb out and into her open arms.

I sob.

I finally follow her lead inside. We sit on the sofa, her arms still around me—protecting me. "Just blurt it out. Whatever comes to your mind—say it," she encourages.

"Blake wants kids, and they found a lump." I cry.

"You're going to be a fantastic mother. Don't let what happened to you set the course of your life; it will make you a better mom.

Who found a lump? In your breast? You had your appointment to-day? I thought that was next week. It could be benign. Did they give you a mammogram? Is there a history in your family? I'll be here—whatever happens—kids or lumps, you have me," She spurts out with minimal oxygen.

I sob, clutching onto her even tighter.

"Julie! I need answers!" she says frantically.

"I . . . just need a mom," I reply through my cries.

"Okay. Okay," she agrees quickly, holding me tighter, rocking me. "I love you. It's going to be okay. I will be here. I'm with you," she continues her encouragement.

This is just what I needed.

Only . . .

I want *my* mom.

Old habits die hard, what can I say?

This, of course, makes me cry harder.

I can't begin to explain to you the devastation in knowing that you can't turn to your mother in times of emotional need. It's one thing if she is gone, it's another when she is alive and well. The pain is unbearable compared to anything you are going through that may require her extra support and guidance. And suddenly . . .

I'm five again . . .

On a stage . . .

Looking out to see if she showed up.

My grief rocks through the core of me. It's like a caged animal, screaming to be heard . . . to be set free.

"Please. Please tell me what they said," Judith cries. "You're scaring me, Julie." She kisses my head.

I try to calm down, taking in a few deep breaths. "I don't know. They won't know anything till I get a mammogram and the radiologist looks at it. I'm just extremely emotional." I try to pass off my behavior.

"Listen, I don't want you to do anything rash."

"What do you mean?" I lift off of her to look into her face.

"Don't push Blake away," she says sternly.

"I can't give him what he wants." I shake my head.

"You can. You want it too, you're just too stubborn to acknowledge it."

"No. No, I don't." I pull fully out of her arms.

"I know you better than you know yourself, trust me. Don't do anything rash."

"You don't know me. You don't know what's in me . . . what I want!" I argue.

"Okay. Let's focus on the next step first. Did they take a biopsy?"

"No."

"When do you expect a phone call?"

"I don't know."

"Julie."

"What?"

"Everything is going to be all right." She squeezes my shoulders.

"Bullshit."

"Language," she reminds me.

"Bullshit. This *fucking* sucks!" *Fight the power!*

"You're right—this fucking sucks." Judith St. Claire just cursed with me as a united front.

She's the mom that shows up.

I fall back in her arms, remembering that she is *not* the enemy. I'd be lost without her.

The worst thing you can do, when there is a possible diagnosis floating about above your head, is make *Google* your bitch. I've been slapping the keys on that whore for three hours, obtaining—at least—four other legit illnesses. Seriously, if I don't have cancer, I'm still doomed. The good news? I'll totally get medical weed for my glaucoma. Yes—yes, I do have glaucoma! I just only have it when I'm drunk. That's most likely a pre-cursor to having it without drinking. I read that in one of the articles. No, I don't remember if it was a medical professional who said it. Wait—no! I get cataracts when I'm drunk. Same thing, though, right? I can't see shit. I should get some medi-mari. Hah! Medi-Mari! I'm copyrighting that shit!

Suddenly, my cell phone rings. It's a ringtone I'm not familiar with. This is not unusual, as Blake changes my ringtone for him quite often. Apparently, this one is telling me to not bite the dick that fucks me. Thank you, *Zedge*, for bringing my boyfriend hours of entertainment with your little app. I slide to accept and put it up to my ear. "I don't want to hear another word about you needing a break. If you have time to fuck with my phone, you don't need a break."

"That one had me laughing for a good ten minutes," he admits through a laugh.

"I'm glad it brings you so much joy. What's up?" I ask as I shut down my laptop.

"First chance I've had to see about your appointment today," he says before commenting to somebody about something. "Fuck, we're slammed," he adds in a huff.

"My doctor forwent the lube for the last part of my exam, you champ." I smirk on my end.

"Did she ask you if I would come in to be studied?"

"I'm sure she would've, but she had mentioned that their research was just full to the brim—wink-wink—of men with superhero complexes. Maybe next time, stallion." I sit back in my chair and debate on whether I should tell him or not.

"It's their loss, really."

"Too true." I smile. *I love this guy.*

"Everything else check out all right?" he asks hurriedly in the midst of a lot of clanking about.

"What are you doing?"

"What *aren't* I doing should be the question. Just trying to re-plenish glasses before the interview I have in twenty."

"The guy Kyle is sending?"

"Yes. Bloody hell, I hope it works out, and he can start today." He groans in an exhausted state.

"I doubt he'll want to start today, babe, but I do hope he's a keeper. I hate to see you so stressed. Do you want me to come down and help today?" *Please say no. Please say no.* Though, I guess it would take my mind off things.

"No, love. Stay put. I need you to be my oasis when I get home."

"Well, when you put it like that . . ." The wheels start to turn.

"I'm going to come home to coconuts covering your tits, aren't I?" He laughs.

"Damn it—you're quick!" I complain.

"Not really, love; I just know you. And . . . I love you. And miss you." He sounds lost in thought.

"Blake?" I sit up quick. *What* is going on with him?

"Sorry. I just . . . can we think about a weekend away? I'll close the bloody place down to do so." His irritation rings through the phone clearly.

"Sure," I say quickly. "Are you sure you don't want me to come down there?"

"No. Definitely not! I'm a right bastard with everyone tonight; you don't need that. Stay put. I love you. I have to go."

"Love you, too," I reply before he hangs up.

Sheesh! I'm glad I didn't tell him about my appointment.

Chapter Ten

Blake

Slow It Down . . .

TODAY HAS BEEN ONE OF THOSE DAYS WHERE I WOULD LIKE TO just hit pause to place all of the issues in order and deal with them accordingly. However, we all know that life is like the Road Runner and we are all Wile E. Coyote, getting the shit kicked out of us while we're trying to catch it.

My day started off with my godfather being too familiar with Julie. You and I can both sit here and come up with a list of all the reasons I'm being stupid, but I know my uncle Rupe. I also know how he manages to sweep women off their feet without them realizing it. Given Julie's past, or at least the past she wants me to believe, makes it a little harder. I may have moved on from the way she used to hurt me, but I haven't forgotten.

Next, I get a call from Judith, Maddie's mom, about Julie's appointment. Yes, I know. The thing is, I'm not supposed to know. Julie is supposed to tell me herself. Now don't be getting on about

Judith breaking code or whatever you'd call it. She, like me, knows Julie very well, and she wants her to remain happy. She happens to think I am the keeper of her happiness. I stand a bit taller knowing her confidence in me is strong; she's Julie's go-to for all mother-ly needs. That aside—I'm worried out of my mind. Obviously, I'm worried about Julie and her health, but mostly, I'm worried she'll push me away. This is why Judith called me; she feels the same way. Terrible timing, though, me asking while I was busy at work. It gave us both distraction. I am hoping that she will tell me on her own. Soon.

Thirdly, I'm short-staffed. But, we're all aware of that as I have been bitching about it every chance I get. God, it's making me a bitter shit! And this leads me to now. Well, five minutes ago, really. You see, Kyle walked into the pub with my interviewee, Jonathan. Jonathan is a friend of Lindsay's. I know this because Lindsay is also here, beaming her beautiful smile my way, barely able to con-tain her excitement. Jonathan, like Lindsay, has Down syndrome. This is *not* the part that has put me off. Nope. No, Kyle decided to pull me to the side for a "quick chat."

"Look, I think I know you well enough to know that you won't be a douchebag about this," is how he started our conversation, "but, I feel the need to make sure. You've got to trust me on this, man, Jonathan will be an asset here. He's hardworking, friendly, and determined. He won't fuck you over."

"I've had a shit day, mate. I don't need you coming in here to make sure I haven't suddenly turned into an arsehole! You do know me well enough, Kyle!" I yelled.

"I'm sorry, man." He held his hands up in surrender. "I'm over-protective when it comes to Lindsay, that extends to her friends. I'm sorry. You have to know I wouldn't have sent him here if I didn't think you'd give him a fair shot. I'm just being a big brother; it has nothing to do with you."

"It's alright." I slapped his shoulder. "Just to reassure you, though, I can tell his IQ is higher than half of my employees just by saying hi to him." I smiled.

"I feel bad that I have to agree with you." He smirked.

And now, here I am, sitting across from Jonathan in my office. "So, you're currently working at Stop & Shop in Manchester?" I ask.

"Yes, but my hours have been cut," he answers quickly. I don't ask him why; hours are being cut everywhere. Except here, of course . . . "Tell me, Jonathan, if I hire you, what can I expect from you? What are your strengths?"

"I'm not afraid to work, Mr. Spencer. I like to make sure I do a good job. I like to make people happy, so I'm good at customer service. I'm reliable. I hardly ever call out. Don't let my condition fool you; I'm very smart. I can do many things." The determination on this kid's face gives me the urge to bow to him. I'm guessing that Kyle vetted him for this interview, but I wouldn't be surprised if I were wrong. I like this kid.

"Well, Jonathan," I start off, "having a disability can be a tricky thing in life, but there is only one disability that causes me not to hire someone."

Jonathan looks down as if he's been defeated again. This breaks my heart and enrages me all at once.

"Would you like to know what disability I'm completely against?" I ask him. He looks up at me and nods versus saying yes. "Ignorance," I state. "It's the worst disability any man could have, and I just can't bring myself to hire someone who suffers from it."

"Oh," he looks up. "So . . .?"

"You've got the job!" I cheer.

"Really?" His eyes light up.

"Yes, really." I reach across my desk to shake his hand.

"Which job, though?" he asks while shaking my hand.

"Every bloody fucking one you can handle," I say cheerfully. "I'm swamped; when can you start?"

"Tomorrow?"

"You just earned yourself a fifty cent raise for saying that." I stand up. "Come, let's go share the good news." I smile, before opening my office door.

"I already like working here!" he states excitedly as he jumps out of his seat to follow me.

"Wait until tomorrow; you may change your mind." I slap him on the back as I guide him out of my office. We manage our way through the crowd to find Kyle and Lindsay staring in our direction. Lindsay's face is lit up like a Christmas tree. "He'll do!" I announce with another slap on his shoulder. Lindsay screeches and runs into Jonathan's arms excitedly. I can't help but smile looking at them. I shoot a glance over towards Kyle and notice him trying to look happy. However, his sister is being hugged and kissed; it's easy to see he's struggling with this, as most big brothers would, I imagine. I bump his shoulder with my fist in an encouraging way. He looks at me and shoots me a shy smirk and a shrug. "Want a drink?" I shout.

"No, man. I have to get these guys home. Thanks, though. I'll catch up with you later. I think we need to get the guys together."

"Sounds good to me! I better get back at it." I thumb over my shoulder then turn back to Jonathan. "Can you be here at two tomorrow? That will give us time to start training before it gets crazy."

"Yes, sir!" He straightens up as if he were in the army. Yeah, he'll definitely do!

Every night, except when I have someone booked, my band closes out with a high-energy rock song. I like for people to walk out of here feeling pumped. I guess the locals like it too because they always come back. Tonight, we are closing out with "Drunken Lullabies" by Flogging Molly. Fitting, aye? Oh yeah, I should mention that most times, it is an Irish rock song. Hey, it's what I grew up on, what can I say?

I scan the crowd as I yell the words into the mic, and I see my godfather singing along cheerfully. I motion for him to climb up on the stage. Uncle Rupe—God love him—heads up at the first motion. *Not a shy bone in that man's body.* He makes his way over to me and takes on the vocals with me. I can't help my smile. Some of my most favorite memories are jamming with him and my father. My dad is wicked at the bagpipes. Unc's poison is the fiddle. And me? —drums, piano, and guitar. *God . . . those were the best times.* Then, my mother left, and suddenly Dad felt like he should grow up. That's when the drift between us began. He dropped everything fun that meant something to him. He dropped me, more or less. He hasn't remarried. Mum was the love of his life.

I have a great mum. She's very supportive. Very optimistic. Very happy; remarried and all . . . My stepfather, well, he's alright, I suppose. Sort of boring, straight-laced, and very predictable. *Don't really like or trust him; spotty sort, really.* My dad tries to tell her this every chance he gets, which, after ten years, looks a bit ridiculous. *Poor bastard.* I've decided that he takes it out on me because it's easiest to do. He was not happy when my grandfather bestowed his business upon me. He did offer it to my father, at first. I think Dad thought once he'd declined that'd be it for the Spencer control of Mick & Marley's. He's not happy I took over. Probably even less happy that I've made it more successful than Granddad.

Before I know it, the song comes to an end. We bow to the crowd. Several last catcalls ring through the air. "Thank you for spending your evening with us. Don't forget to head over to the bar to cash out your tabs and collect your credit cards. I really don't want to chase any of you down tomorrow. I may be known to buy myself a coffee on the patron when that happens. Call it my inconvenience charge, if you will. Drive safe! If you're drunk, don't drive at all, please. I've got a bunch of *Uber* drivers outside like the paparazzi, waiting for you."

Just when I go to say something else, Uncle Rupe intercepts me, "Will ya shut the feck up now, and let them leave, me boy? Christ, you've got them nearly sober now with your carrying on about."

"Ah bugger off, old man! I'm just being a responsible business-man." I roll my eyes with a smile.

"You're being a bloody bore!" He turns back to the slow-moving crowd. "Listen, anyone have the sniffles? Me nephew will make sure you have a hankie before you go; he's a responsible business-man, ya know."

"Oh, fuck off with ya now!" I laugh, shaking my head before making my way off the stage. Grabbing a bin full of dirty glasses, I head into the kitchen where my crew is working diligently to call it a night. "Carlos! Head home, mate!" I bark at my sous chef. This guy hasn't had a day off in three weeks; could be longer.

"No, boss, I finish," he says in his broken English and continues at his steady pace. I wish most of my staff had half this guy's heart. Carlos has been with us for twenty-plus years. He fled here from Cuba. Somehow, he found his way to New Hampshire, and land-ed on my grandfather's doorstep, asking for work. He was barely a man then, but Grandad always said he could see in Carlos's eyes the great man he would become. So, Sean Spencer did something he'd never done before (and never did again): he hired Carlos to clean up his yard. It got my grandmother off his back, and it gave him the chance to see if he was right about Carlos. He soon discovered that he was right; his yard had never looked so good before. He paid Carlos extra, and then asked him if he would like to work on the "honey-do-list" my grandmother never seemed to let end. Carlos accepted eagerly. The following weeks, they got to know each oth-er pretty well. Soon enough, Carlos confided in my grandfather about how he got here. That was a huge leap of faith when you think about it; my grandfather could've called immigration on him.

Instead, he offered him a job here—with one condition: he had to become a legal resident. Carlos, of course, was overwhelmed. He didn't know where to start and was afraid to do so. I don't blame him. My grandfather assured him, though, that he would help him in every way. And he did. He hired an immigration lawyer who set Carlos in the right direction. As soon as he obtained his Green Card, Granddad put him on the books here at Mick & Marley's. He's been with us ever since, busting his arse. Several years ago, he finally obtained his citizenship. My Grandfather wept with joy. I think that may have been only the second time I ever saw him cry. The first time was when Grandma died. He said something to me that I will never forget, *"The best and most rewarding investment you could ever make is one that you put into another life. Like any investment, it could turn out good or bad, but when it's good, there is nothing in the world like it."* I learned a lot from that man. "Carlos, I think your wife may have forgotten what you look like." I slap his shoulder.

"Except on payday!" he jokes then rolls into his contagious laugh. It's contagious because he sounds like a little girl giggling; you can't help but laugh at his laugh.

I leave him to finish his work, and head into my office to sort out tomorrow's deposit. Soon enough, my door opens, and Uncle Rupe strolls in. "Still at it?" he asks

"Didn't you leave?" I look back down at my register.

"No. I was helping out in the bar. Look . . . what's going on with you? You seem a bit off." He seats himself in the chair across from my desk.

"I am off. Sorry, Unc. I've got a lot on my mind." I offer him a small smile and try to get back to my numbers.

"Do you need me to leave?"

"No! Don't be silly! But, we could do without the breakfast wake-up call a few mornings a week," I add in.

"Nonsense! If I didn't feed you two breakfast, you'd go the

whole day without eating!"

"Look at you with your hankie out for my sniffles!" I tease.

"Just don't be expecting me to wipe your arse, too." He gives it back.

"How was your *coffee* this morning?" I ask, wiggling my brows with the word coffee.

"Brilliant!" He slaps the top of my desk for emphasis. "The café was full. She had a table with an empty chair just waiting for me. I got me coffee and sat right down. She looked up at me as if she was shocked. I suppose she was, though. I says to her, 'Somethin' going on in town today? There's not a table open.' She replied, 'I don't know, but I am pretty sure all these people at the other tables actually know each other as oppose to being rudely intruded upon.' Ah, nephew, the tone in her voice made me winky twitch." He sighs in a reminiscent state.

"Winky, Uncle, really?" I laugh at him.

"What? That's what we called it when you was little," he defends himself.

I hold my hands stretched out, "All grown up now," I announce.

"You're still a feckin' brat," he reminds me. I shuffle my hand at him to continue his story . . . God willing (I definitely don't need reports on his "winky"). "Right! So, I says to her, 'Now, I just saw this as a good opportunity to introduce me as a new part of your morning routine since you've been a part of mine for the last week.' She asked me what I was talking about. I explained to her that I find her very attractive, that her beauty intrigues me, so I make sure to arrive at the same time as her to see her." He shrugs.

"And this is the precise moment she dialed 911, right?" I ask half joking, half serious.

"No. Not at all," he says quickly. I stare at him, waiting for the next part of their conversation. "That was the precise moment she informed me about the mace she carries, and I should bugger off," he finally adds.

"What did you say?" I widen my eyes and try to keep my laughter at bay.

"I told her that was no way to speak to her future husband." He shrugs. *What's with the shrugging?*

"And?"

"She told me she was a lesbian. I spit me coffee everywhere; nearly choked meself blind."

"What? How did you not know she was gay? You're off your game, aren't ya, Unc?" Laughter has been officially released.

"Oh, she isn't!" he states with irritation.

"Why do you say that?" I inquire. I'm completely intrigued by this story. You have to understand that my uncle *never* has to chase a woman.

"Because she could barely spit it out!" he yells. He's a bit hostile . . . a bit unlike my uncle.

"Well, what did you do or say?"

"I leaned up and into her space, and I said, 'Are you sure about that, love?' She said yes so I said, 'I think you just haven't met the right player from my team. That is . . . until now.' And I kissed the corner of her mouth."

"You're my hero," I inform him, shocked at the size of his balls.

"Shut it."

"What happened after that?"

"She left. She seemed flustered. I can't wait to see her tomorrow." He smiles like the Cheshire cat.

"What if she doesn't show up?" I lean back into my chair.

"Oh, she'll show up." He winks.

"Did you get her name?"

"No." He wipes his face with his hands. "Listen, you almost ready there, boy?"

"Yes. Let me just add this up, and I'll be ready. Did you drive?" I ask before looking back down at the deposits I should've had figured out twenty minutes ago.

"Nah. Julie ubered me. She told me you called and asked for me to come down here to help."

"Oh, good. Thanks for doing that for me; we were swamped." I never called Julie to ask her to send him here—clever girl. She's had a tough day. "On second thought, I'm going to do this tomorrow at home." I put everything back into the deposit bag with the slips. I need to get home to my girl.

"Brilliant idea!" He slaps his knees before getting up. I get up as well and suddenly remember something he had said.

"Future husband?" I question him.

"I said it without any thought; it must be true." He shrugs . . . *again.*

"Aren't you out of sorts for you know . . . you?" This is odd.

"I can't stop thinking about her," he says as if he's in disbelief as well.

"Let's go, shall we?" I hold my hand out to lead the way. *Very odd behavior, indeed.* I'm half sure my godfather is possessed.

Chapter Eleven

Cynthia

Planets and Stars Align . . .

"Shannon!" I yell as I barge into the house.

"She's on the sun porch," Jack informs me like he couldn't care less that I *just* barged into his house.

"Thanks, Jack! Hey, congrats on the Patriots winning last night!" I add without looking back.

"The Red Sox won! You still suck at sports, Cyn!" he yells after me. I think he may have stated that I was an embarrassment to all other New Englanders and something about my lost soul. I yelled back at him that it was an honest mistake and that he shouldn't let his balls get deflated over it. I probably shouldn't have said that, but I'm not exactly sure why. . .

So touchy . . .

"Shannon!" I almost scream when I find her.

"What?" She jumps.

"I met someone!" I almost screech. "He's from the Mother Land!"

I add.

"Oh, you mean from 'Who-the-fuck-says-that-anymore planet?'" She looks up from watering her plants.

"I hate you. You need to help me," I plead.

"Usually, if *one* needs help, they don't start out by saying *I hate you.*" She smiles.

"Please?" I beg, sitting down on the wrought iron chair next to her.

"Is this the good-looking guy you see every morning at the coffee shop?" she asks with a gleam in her eye.

"It's a café," I correct her.

"Oh—fu-fu-pfbbsts!" She blows raspberries at me as she takes the seat across from me.

"It was crowded, and he sat at my table." I ignore her.

"I orchestrated that." She bites back her smile and winks at me.

"Oh, shut up!" I roll my eyes.

"I did!" She raises her voice. "I know people, goddamn it!"

"We *know* the same people," I remind her.

"I've managed to squeeze a few extra in in the past thirty years," she digs. *Ouch.*

"Okay. Well, do you want to hear what happened?" I move along. She says yes, and I quickly fill her in.

"Wow."

"I know, right? What do I do?" I ask frantically.

"Jump on his lucky charms! Taste the rainbow!" She smacks my knee.

"What? Shannon, please, this is not about getting laid!" I'm pissed! I need *real* help here. I haven't been with anyone since . . . well . . . well, that's just none of your damn business!

"Cyn, at our age—it's definitely about getting laid; we may croak tomorrow." She verbally slaps me.

"You're four months older than me." It's all I've got.

"Fuck you."

"What do I do?" I ask her seriously.

"Start giving your vagina pep talks. It's been a long time for her; she may not know a dick when she sees it."

"Can you stop, please?" I plead through my laughter.

Suddenly, Shannon takes on a serious look. "Cyn, our brains think we're in our twenties, but the reality is—we're not. Life is short, sweetheart; I don't have to tell you that. Don't push things—people—away for any cockeyed reason you come up with. Let things happen. Whatever the end result is, who cares? The point is: you put yourself out there. We don't know how much longer we have left on this Earth. Isn't it better to know your last few days were filled joyously?" Her eyes fill up. *Well, shit.* She's right. I can only say this because I know her days could possibly be numbered; nobody thinks about this stuff more than she does. I'd be really stupid not to take her advice. She may have MS, but I could get hit by a bus tomorrow. Also, I'm in my mid-sixties—shhh! I didn't tell you that!

"I think you need to get laid, Shannon." I try to distract her.

"Oh my God—No! Jack's been like a jackrabbit lately!" She's almost panicky.

"Oh . . ." I mean, what else do you say that? *I'm jealous* just doesn't seem right.

"He's got the libido of a twenty-year-old." Oh God, please stop with the overshare. "I don't refuse him no matter how I feel because . . ." Her chin begins to quiver.

"This must be why he got so bent out of shape when I told him not to let his balls get deflated." I try to distract her. She slowly starts with a giggle that turns into a complete belly laugh. This makes me happy.

"Poor bastard worships Tom like God specifically picked him out for the Patriots." She continues to laugh.

"I don't know what the hell you're talking about, but I'll just go with the flow." I laugh along.

"It's sports," she states as if to give me a legit reason to not knowing what the hell is going on. Pretty legit, though—I haven't a clue.

My thoughts randomly shift to my appointment with Maddie in an hour. "Shannon?" I ask as I fidget with my purse straps rather than looking at her.

"What?"

"Do you have any regrets? I mean, huge regrets . . . ones nobody knows about?"

"We all have regrets, Cyn."

"Yes, I know that. I'm talking about deep regrets that haunt you," I say desperately, willing her to say yes.

"When CiCi suddenly dropped out of college and dumped Drew, she was so different. I knew something had happened, but I didn't want to pry. I thought she would eventually come to me about it or that it was something silly and she would be back to herself again. I was wrong. Whatever happened changed her. I know it must've been traumatizing." Her chin quivers. "Somebody hurt my baby and I never knew how or why. I live with that regret every day. I should've dug. I should've known what happened so that I could help her. I wasn't there to protect her." She lets out a slight sob.

"She's okay now." I jump up to be by her side. "Kyle has seen to that. She's happy, Shannon," I encourage.

"Thank God for Kyle." She smiles up at me and pats my arm as I hug her. "He broke whatever nasty curse had taken her over."

"He sure did. And maybe that's all that should matter anymore," I offer. She simply nods in agreement.

"I'm okay." She pats my arm again to let her go. "Sit back down now and tell me yours."

"My what?" I ask as I reseat myself.

"Your biggest regret. That is . . . besides being at odds with Julie," she adds.

"I've been a terrible mother. That is my only regret."

"You're a goddamn liar. So typical." She chuckles.

"What? What do you mean?"

"Lying 101: try not to look to the left when you are lying; it blows your cover." She shuffles an accusatory finger at me. *I'm not lying.* Although, I am omitting something that brings my motherly douchebaggery to a whole other level. *Motherly douchebaggery . . .?* Shannon is really starting to rub off on me.

"I'm not lying," I finally say. "Though, I guess my other regret is never finding—or allowing myself *to* find—the greatest love of my life."

"I believe you find her every time you look in a mirror." Shannon winks.

"That is true . . ." I trail off into a sigh then laugh.

"You're not dead." She reaches across the table for my hand.

"Are you sure? My life has felt like hell for over thirty years." I blink away my tears.

"Well, you are a hot mess. However, you are not in *actual* Hell. You're in the hell that you created. The good thing about this type of hell is that you have the power to climb out of it, which you are. Stay focused on that, Cyn. The past is the past. There's nothing you can do to change it. Don't spend the present and your future focusing on unchangeable shit, goddamn it. Put that energy into making things right, going forward." She squeezes my hand for emphasis.

"I am, Shannon, I'm trying," I plead.

"I know you are. I don't want you to lose focus on that. When do you see Maddie next?"

"In twenty minutes, actually. I need to leave. We're discussing regrets today," I share.

"Ah," she sighs knowingly. Her lips curve into a soft smile. "I'm proud of you."

"What?" I'm barely audible, shaking her compliment away.

"I am. You should be too. With every new aspect you work on, it's like you're chipping away at this façade that's been in place for so long. The more you chip away, the more the real you is coming to the surface. I've always loved *that* chick."

"Why do you have to make everything so emotional?" I brush her off, a little angry. She does. She always finds some way to make me cry. It's pissing me off.

"I'd encourage you to keep chipping away to lose the side of bitch, but that's always been there . . . *lurking,*" she quips.

"It takes one to know one," I reply coolly.

"It obviously took a time machine to find that comeback." She tries to hold back her laugh.

"Fuck you. Is that better?" I ask.

"Now that's one that stands the test of time." She smiles. "Cyn?"

"What?" I huff.

"Do you want me to go with you today?"

"No. I . . . thank you for offering. That means a lot to me. I may take you up on it in the future. Right now, I need to get through some of these things on my own before I can handle the pressure of revealing things to others. I haven't told Maddie everything as it is. This is very hard." I look everywhere but at her.

"You don't have to do this alone. I think understanding that may be the biggest obstacle of all for you. I respect your decision, though." She takes in a deep breath then exhales. "Cyn, there is a reason why after all these years, I can sit here and easily pick up our friendship like it was never dropped." She glances over to the threshold of the kitchen and waves someone away. I look over my shoulder to find Jack putting his hands up like he's sorry to disturb us before walking back out.

"What's the reason, Shannon?" Because I still question this every day.

"Because it was *never* dropped. Not on my end, at least. I knew you were going through something that you had to work out on your own, so I gave you space. I knew you'd come around. I didn't know it would take you thirty-fucking-years, but then again, you *were* always a bit slow." She shrugs slightly. I pick up one of her pill bottles on the table and toss it at her head, but she blocks it, chuckling. I give in to a small giggle.

"I love you." I re-grasp her hand and squeeze.

"And I love you." She squeezes back. "There are some people placed in our lives that are meant to be there forever, no matter in what capacity. Think about it; we have remained in each other's lives regardless as to what has happened over the years, because of our girls. They've been the glue keeping us together until we could start to do it for ourselves again," she tries to explain.

"You are the most impatient person I know, yet, you've had the patience of a saint with me. I don't know how you haven't written me off." I shake my head in disbelief, thinking about all the awful things I've said and done.

"I'm not patient with you; I'm on a lot of medication," she admits casually.

"That would hold up in court," I surmise.

"Just keeping it real. I may have followed through with a choke hold or two if I didn't have these puppies to make me forget why I should hate you."

I stare at her. Shannon has never been one to hold back. I've always liked and disliked that about her. But sometimes she'll say something that I don't know how to bounce back from even though I know she didn't say it to really hurt me. An admission in jest means she's just as uncomfortable saying it as I am hearing it, I think. I need to discuss this with Maddie. "Maddie! Shit!" I practically yell, the panic setting in as I shoot out of my chair.

"Here," Shannon quickly starts turning her pill bottles before finding the one she's looking for and picking it up, "give her some of these; that'll help."

"I'm blaming you," I announce, pushing the strap of my purse up onto my shoulder.

"How's this my fault?" She widens her eyes in disbelief.

"Because you take a few pills and get all philosophical! Damn it! Of all people to be late for!" I groan.

"Remember—you are the elder! Don't let her treat you like a child for being five minutes late."

"I don't even like to remind *myself* that I am an elder. I'm not giving *anyone* that ammunition! Bye!" I quickly hug her and kiss her cheek before turning on my heels.

Sprinting in heels is one of my many talents. Catching an elevator at the precise moment I desperately need it, is not. I don't know what is more absurd right now: my blood pressure going through the roof because I'm ten minutes late to meet with Maddie or the fact that I am pushing the elevator button continuously like that will make the fucking relic move any faster. Wow, I've been cursing a lot lately. *Also Shannon's fault.*

"Shit! Shit! Shit!" I hear someone else running down the hall. I turn to find Maddie, just as flustered as I am, trying to straighten herself out as she gets closer.

"There you are! I was just about to leave," I announce.

She looks up at me as she approaches. "Cynthia! I'm so sorry. I didn't mean to keep you waiting!" Panic is all over her face. *She is human after all!*

"This is very unprofessional, Maddie." I try not to smile.

"I know you are not about to lecture me on ethics, Cynthia." She eyes me as if she's ready to square off with me.

"Certainly not. Especially since I arrived at this elevator in the same fashion you did." I let my smile peek through.

"Huh?" She tilts her head.

"I'm late, too, Maddie," I clear the air. "Although, you look as if you may have had a better, more *delightful* reason to be late." I raise an eyebrow.

She bites back her smile, but she can't hold her cheeks back from blushing. *I'm so jealous.* She clears her throat a little. "I have no one after you, so let's just say we telepathically agreed to push your appointment back by ten minutes."

"Whatever helps you to sleep at night," I say as we walk into the elevator. "Say, is there a phobia dedicated to being late?"

"Allegrophobia," she simply states as she presses the button for her floor.

"That sounds like you have a fear of taking Allegra."

"Yeah, a lot of the names for phobias don't make sense."

"I bet."

"Did you work on your homework?" She changes our conversational direction.

"Some of it. A lot of it was difficult," I admit, my voice quiet like I'm ashamed. That would probably be because I am.

"Okay. It's not a race. It's much healthier to work on the things we are ready to work on. If you force yourself to work on something you are not ready to deal with, it could set you back so far, you could possibly erase all the steps you took forward." She holds her hand out for me to go ahead of her as the doors open.

"I still feel bad, all the same, because I know what a burden this puts on you."

"It does," she says as she walks beside me, "but seeing how consistent you have been makes the load lighter. There's a lot to work through, Cynthia. It's not something that can be resolved in a matter of weeks." She opens the door to the offices, letting me go ahead of her. We both keep our silence as we head down to her personal office. Once inside, I head over to the designated confessional seat. That's how it makes me feel, anyhow. "Well, anything new this week?" she asks as she grabs her pad and pen from her desk before coming over to the chair across from me.

"Um . . ." I hesitate. No. I don't think I'll tell her about the guy from the coffee shop.

"Um?" Maddie tilts her head. "You never *um*—spill it, sister!" she demands as she crosses her right leg over her left. I quickly ramble about what Shannon said and how it made me feel. "We'll come back to that." She makes a little note on her pad. "Now, what was the 'um' for? You wouldn't do that and hesitate if you were only going to tell me about Shannon."

"It's nothing. If it becomes something, then I will tell you about it. Let's move on." I push her along. Though, now I have to talk about regrets, and besides what she knows already, I don't want to share that stuff either. "Maddie," I say quickly.

"Yes?"

"I don't think I'm going to be very good at sharing secrets this week. I realize that I'm hindering progress here, but I'm not ready for certain things as you said before. Can we work on the other stuff?" I pull at the hem of my skirt, shifting in my chair. I'm so fidgety today.

She watches me for a moment. Slowly, a small side smile comes into view. "Sure. Let's look at the list of people you want to make amends with and see how things are going there."

"Still the same people left." I save her from going through her notes.

"Oh. Okay. Any thoughts on when you may approach CiCi or Blake?"

"No."

"Okay. Have you worked more on your project for Julie?"

"No."

"Have you written in your journal?"

"Yes. Yes, I have done that." We both breathe a sigh of relief.

"I'm glad. And did anything you wrote this week stir up some feelings or thoughts you had pushed back?"

"Yes." My eyes fill up. "I'm not ready to share that yet."

"A regret?" she asks as she leans to her left to grab a few tissues for me.

"Yes." I shake my head as I grab the tissues from her.

"That's good, Cynthia." She smiles. "Even though you may not feel ready to divulge this regret to me, you are ready to start working on working through it, otherwise, you wouldn't have written it down. You put it out there in the universe. That's good. Real good." She nods her head in agreement with herself.

"How's Julie?" It's been so long since I've talked to her . . .

"She seems her usual self. My mom and I just had lunch with her the other day."

"Your mom has always been good to her. I'm glad she has her." I truly am.

"She has you too; she just doesn't know it."

"She will, though. And she'll know that I *want* to be there."

"She loves you, Cynthia," Maddie simply states. I shake my head vigorously opposing. She holds up her hand to stop me. "She does."

"I haven't been what she needs. That's just the light of hope in her, wanting and waiting for me to be." I feel my throat practically close up as I try to fight off the emotions.

"Good thing she has that," she says as she scribbles down something.

"Maddie?"

"What?" She looks up at me.

"Why did you say that that way?"

"We'd be wasting a lot of time if she didn't." She hits me with the truth. "We don't know how long that window is going to last, though. I'm glad you're working on this."

"Me too," I agree. "What's next?" I ask quickly.

"Nothing. That is, nothing until you've worked through the last few things we mentioned."

"Can't we jump around to things I'm comfortable with until I'm comfortable with the things I haven't been comfortable with?" I plead.

"No." She gives me a stern look.

"Why?" I practically gasp. I mean, this is horrific! I can't deal with stuff I'm not ready to deal with.

"Because you will continue to push things off that you are not comfortable with until you are *comfortable*, and that could lead to an indefinite timetable as you will find other things to come before. There are big issues to get resolved; you *need* to resolve them . . . not defer them like a college loan. They have to be paid up right away," she reprimands me in the most polite way.

"But you *just said* that it was healthier to work on things I was ready to work on!" I practically yell.

"Avoiding things that are uncomfortable is not the same thing." She maintains a stoic expression.

"That doesn't make any sense! I'm only avoiding things I'm not ready to deal with," I remind her.

"Have you written them down?" she asks.

"No."

"Then you are just plain avoiding them. It's not the same thing." She shifts her left leg over her right.

"What's the next step?" I give in.

"To work through what you are *not* telling me."

"What's that?"

"I don't know. You haven't told me, yet." She gives me a condescending smile.

"I've told you everything." I shuffle in my seat.

"And I'm really six feet tall."

"I can't." I almost cry.

"Write it down in your journal," she suggests. I nod my head. "I think we should wrap it up for today."

"I agree."

"Are we good for next week?" She asks as she grabs her planner.

"Yes." I get up.

"I thought you might be ready to go," she smiles softly, "but there is another thirty minutes left to your session if you want to stay."

"No thanks," I say quickly. "I have nothing left to share, only things to think about." And with that, I walk out of her office.

Chapter Twelve

Julie

Pass the medi-fucking-cation, please.

HE KNOWS.

Of course, he won't tell me he knows, not with words. How do I know he knows, you ask? Because it's just about 3am and he's handed me a cup of maple walnut ice cream with freshly cooked and chopped up bacon, which I have wasted no time to enjoy thoroughly. While I'm busy enjoying the taste of this salty-sweet goodness—I know you are not sitting there judging me about—he is enjoying the taste of me. I don't know which is distracting me more. And I honestly don't know which will give me the bigger orgasm.

Go ahead and put a point on the scoreboard for the Brit.

There's biting involved now for Christ's sake!

"It's a good thing I don't lack confidence, love." Blake chuckles as he leaves a trail of kisses up my stomach. I watch him as I suck the last bit of ice cream off my spoon before placing it on the nightstand. "Any other bloke may be put off by the fact that you continued with your ice cream while they pleased you. They may have even questioned the cause of your guttural groan, but not I." He pulls my left nipple into his mouth. The man has a talent for suction; the kind that causes your eyes to immediately roll to the back of your head. "You see, I know your motto very well," he says upon release.

"Bacon makes everything better . . ." I trail off, anticipating a duplicate assault on my right nipple.

"Indeed," he states before pulling my right nipple in, and my toes curl.

And then . . . I remember.

"Stop!" I try to push him off. With the sound of a "pop," he obliges. He brings his face up so that we are nose to nose. "Blake," my voice trembles.

"Shh." I feel the soft breeze from his shush on my lips just before he covers them. His kiss is soft—delicate—as if he were afraid he'd break me. He pulls away reluctantly and stares into my eyes. I can actually feel my eyes concentrating on his. I am almost hypnotized by the sound of our breaths.

He knows. He *definitely* knows.

Blake slowly slides his hand down my right side till it hooks under my knee. He lifts my leg, encircling it around his backside, situating himself better. And, he waits as he continues to stare into my eyes and match every breath that I take. With a slight nod of my head, my neck arches back upon his intrusion, and I feel whole.

Safe.

Right.

"It's going to be alright," he assures me as I am overcome with emotions. My fingers thread through his hair and grasp harshly as I slam my mouth against his in an effort to control myself. His tongue caresses mine urgently, his hips keeping pace.

I just want to escape.

This happens to other people, not me.

I'm so mad.

Why me?

On first warning of impending explosion of all kinds of wonderful, I tear my mouth away from his. His hand grasps my left hip, yanking it up at a higher angle to guarantee delivery. I open my mouth and belt out a note like I'm channeling the lead singer of a big-haired rock band in the 80s.

Move over, Steven Tyler.

The Brit is pulling oxygen through his teeth like he always does when he's trying to last longer but can't. I clench around him, sucking him into my glory hole.

Inner head tilt—glory hole?

Whatever . . . you bitches know what I mean.

"Christ, love!" he practically yells.

"C'mon, baby," I egg him on. He whips my left leg up and onto his shoulder as he pushes deeper, climbing to the place he wants to be. His lips part. His brow furrows, and his eyes close dramatically as I feel a rush of warmth. He hits me just right, and I'm lost with him. My toes curl unapologetically.

He collapses on top of me.

Lifting his head, he stares into my eyes again.

"I'm not going anywhere. I'm here—no matter what. I love you. We go through everything together. Do you understand me? I will *never* want anything more than *you*." As the words fall from his lips, they get lost in the air. I'm too busy hearing it all in the way he is looking at me.

"It could be nothing," I finally say.

"Let's hope for that but know that we can handle the worst." He pushes a few strands of hair out of my face.

"I was going to tell you . . ." I trail off.

"We can't always operate on *Julie time*," he answers. He's right. Who knows when I would've actually told him.

"I'm sorry." Guilt is suddenly weighing heavy on my chest.

"For what?" He looks at me curiously.

"I should've told you first. I should've come to you first. I . . . I was scared—upset. I'm still not sure how to process all of this."

"You did what was right for you at the moment. I'm okay with that. I understand, truly I do. However, there's not much to process, from my understanding, right now. You just need to slow down that 'doom and gloom' brain of yours until you know the actual results." He taps my nose for emphasis.

"You're right."

"Look at that!" He smiles. "See, you can do anything . . . manage through anything! Look at the way you just freely admitted that I was right."

"Shut up," I giggle.

"I love you." He kisses me.

"I love you, too."

"We can do this—we can handle anything thrown our way."

"Promise?" I'm still unsure.

"Cross my heart and testicles." He winks.

"Testicles? That's serious business!" I widen my eyes.

"You know I'm legit for sure now." Another kiss.

"Legitimately insane," I agree.

"Fair enough," he says just before he pulls out of me and pushes off to my side.

Suddenly, I think of Uncle Rupert. "Please tell me your godfather drank enough to knock him out," I plead.

"I'm sure we gave him a bit of inspiration tonight." He smiles mischievously.

"Ugh!" I groan.

"Just teasing, love. I'm sure he's off dreaming about the coffee shop lady."

"I hope so." I let out a big breath.

"Shh, go to sleep now. Tomorrow is a new day, and it looks promising."

"Why's that?" I look at him curiously as he reaches for the lamp to turn the light off.

"You're in my life—every day is promising." He turns the switch.

"If I weren't on the receiving end of all that cheesiness, I'd be barfing."

"Good thing you are. Let's count our blessings," he encircles me, "goodnight, love." He kisses my head. "I love you."

"Goodnight. I love you, too." I snuggle in closer and shut my eyes.

Apparently, *Titty-Torture Chambers* don't really pack them in around here (ahem), and I was able to be squeezed in (seriously, the puns are just endless . . .) today. I feel like I'm in the middle of an *SNL* skit. You see, I'm 5'10. The chick who's getting ready to smash my girls is shorter than Maddie, who's five-foot-nothing. She just turned to say something to me as she was adjusting the height of the machine and I was all *nipple in her face*. "My boyfriend uses them as microphones too," I joke, making things more awkward.

"Huh?"

"Never mind." I shake my head, silently agreeing with her that we should just pretend it didn't happen rather than acknowledging it. "I don't know the etiquette for this." *What?*

"The etiquette for what?" She stares at me. I stare back, willing for something somewhat logical to come out of my mouth.

.

.

.

"Right, let's just carry on then." I just sounded like Blake. Speaking of, where the fuck is he? If nothing else, he could at least be interpreting me for this chick!

"Julie, it's okay to be nervous." She smiles as she rubs my back while guiding me forward. "There's nothing to be worried about. These machines aren't like they used to be years ago; just pressure— no pain," she continues as she gets my right girl on the plate.

This bitch is a motherfucking, lying whore.

"Jules?" Blake calls out as he walks through the front door. "In here." I look back down at my Kindle.

"Hey," he sighs as if he's out of breath.

"Hey." I swipe to the next page.

"Did you get my messages?"

"Yep."

"I'm sorry, love. You know I meant to be there." He slowly heads my way.

"Duty called." I power my Kindle off and stand up.

"Are you going somewhere?" He eyes me up and down.

"Out with the girls."

"Where? Is it ladies only?" he asks as he gently takes my left hand into his.

"No, all the guys are going."

"You weren't going to invite me?" His head jerks back slightly, a hint of hurt in his voice.

"I didn't think you'd be able to go." I take in a deep breath before matching his gaze.

Suddenly, his eyes widen, pushing whatever feelings he was just having away. "Give me five—ten minutes—tops! I took the rest of the evening off." He kisses my cheek.

"You were supposed to have the *whole* day off," I remind him.

"I know. I'm sorry. I'll make it up to you. Five, okay? Don't leave without me." He squeezes my hand before letting go and jogging out of the room then up the stairs.

My intentions were to stay mad at him for a bit, but then he came in here with his wild, wavy, dark hair pushed back by a bandana, scruffy, in-between-shaves beard, tank top, and jeans that hang low on his waist. Dare we mention the accent? I think not. Besides, I did listen to his messages, so I know he's truly upset that he wasn't there. I know how hard things are for him right now at work. He doesn't need me to add any grief on; he's doing the best he can. And I appreciate it—everything. I'm just gonna stick my "pissed off" card in my back pocket, for now.

"Ready, love?" he asks as he comes down the stairs quickly.

"That was extremely quick! You sure you got all the funk off?" I ask incredulously.

"Amazing how quick a shower can be when you don't shave your legs." He winks as I make my way over to him.

I lean in for a whiff. I shrug, "You'll do."

"Fantastic! Now, where are we off to?" He grabs my hand, leading me to the door.

"Boston. It's Amateur night at Beantown Comedy Club." I grab my purse before he pulls me out the door.

"Are you . . .?" His mouth hangs open, letting the rest of his question finish silently.

"Knocking something off my bucket list? Yes."

"Oh, for fuck's sake, Julie, don't talk like that!" He let's go of my hand aggressively before locking the door.

"I'm not being morbid, Blake; it's just a saying. It's something that's been on there for a while. You know that."

"I just don't like the talk of it, not right now. Sorry." He takes in a breath like he's trying to calm himself. "Let's go, love. I can't wait to see you up there!"

"Are you nervous?" Maddie asks once we're settled at our table, drinks from the bar in hand.

"Does the Pope shit in the woods?"

"Not usually," Kyle joins in, "but I'm sure the bears wouldn't be offended if he did . . . you know, unless they were Catholic." He smirks.

"Why would a bear claim a religion?" I ask.

"Not sure. It could be the same reason why the Pope would shit in the woods."

"I think I've over-trained you, Sir Smirks-A-Lot," CiCi quips.

"Same here, beautiful." He smiles at her then looks back to all of us. "I caught her organizing our canned soups in alphabetical order the other day."

"That was just me keeping the spice in our love life alive," she says before finishing off her margarita.

"Can you guys speak up? We can't hear you down here," Charley yells down at us. It is a pretty big table with the ten of us, and it's as loud as all fuck in here.

"They are talking about religion, nature, and spices." Trent fills her in. Ava checks her phone for the millionth time. Her dad and Rosie are watching the twins tonight. I don't know why she's so worried.

"I'm going to take that phone away from you in a minute." I nudge her as she is sitting beside me.

"Sorry." She puts it on the table. "Both of them are teething," she states as this should be explanation enough.

"They'll survive. We all have teeth—it happens. Why don't you concentrate on your original baby tonight?" I offer my advice.

"What the fuck is that supposed to mean?" she snaps. The whole table hones in on her, as she is smack dab in the middle.

"It means just what I said. Why are you so damn testy lately?" Okay, probably not the best time to be calling her out on her shit, but when is there ever the best time?

"Maybe I should just go home, then? I wouldn't want to ruin your big night." She huffs, grabbing her phone.

"Sit down!" Trent grabs her arm as she goes to stand.

"I want to leave."

"No. Sit down," he reiterates. She complies . . . not too happy about it, I might add.

Just as I open my mouth to say something, one of the employees comes to our table, asking for me. "I'm her." I give him my full attention.

"Will you follow me, please?" He smiles.

"Sure," I say quickly before looking around. "Wish me luck," I beg.

"You'll do wonderful, darling." Blake beams at me before leaning in to kiss me.

"Thanks." And with that, I follow the dude backstage. I'm met by a group of people that, I'm sure, are the other amateurs for tonight.

Shit just got real.

I'm pretty sure we can dub this as my "mid-life crisis" episode. No, becoming a famous comedienne is not my *dream*, but I'm pretty funny (I laugh at all my jokes; that's how I know) and always thought it would be good of me to share my humor with the world for, you know—like a minute.

"Attention!" the dude yells. We all give it to him (that's what she said . . . shh! Pay attention!). "You will all get a number. This number is associated with your name so no need to defend your ego. I call your number—they say your name on stage. You only have three minutes for your set. Please say it with me! *Three minutes!*" we all yell with him. "It is okay to run under; you will be cut off if you run over. Does everyone understand?" he asks. We all announce that we do. "Okay. Tonight, is round one. If the audience and the judges push you into round two, we will let you know tonight, so please stick around. Round two will be next week. Any questions?" he asks.

"What's your favorite sexual position?" It really couldn't be helped.

"I will not be one of the judges," he answers straight-faced.

"What's theirs?" I ask quickly. Everyone laughs. Well, except for the dude I asked.

"You can't sleep your way to the top, lady." Dude seems a little perturbed.

"Oh, I'm on top every night—just ask my boyfriend." I wink.

"Okay, everyone, come over here and pick your number." He picks up a jar, ignoring my comment. Where is this guy's humor? "When you've picked your number, head over to Beth and she will put your name next to your number. Thank you, and good luck tonight!"

I follow the line of comedic geniuses, pulling my number out. I'm five. *Mentally too, sometimes.*

Number four is finishing up her set. She did the typical boy-friend-not-committing shit. She gets off the stage and walks by me, mouthing "good luck." Yeah, and after her set, all I can think is: *Bye, Felicia!* I know what you are thinking, but her name really is Felicia. Kinda makes it funnier, doesn't it?

Shhh! They're calling my name!

Stop panicking! I got this!

Yes, I know I'm the one panicking! *Shut up!*

Love you bitches, too.

Okay, bye!

I walk onto the stage like I've done this a hundred times. I have, really—at Mick & Marley's. Guess that might not count here, though. I channel my inner Rita Rudner because she is my comedi-enne hero . . . next to Joan, of course!

Let's all just take a moment to pay homage to Joan, please . . .

I grab the mic and give the crowd a stare down that may be deemed epic, you know . . . in my mind. I walk purposefully across the stage, honing in on as many people as I can. Secretly, I know who I'm searching for—it's habit. As quickly as I think of her, I push her out of my mind. I've made the audience wait long enough. And, I can't find the guest judge I planned my set around, damn it! Oh well . . .

"I know what you're all wondering as you stare up at me," I lead in. "You're sitting there, taking in my presence, and wondering—as most would—*what is this chick's favorite Dolph Lundgren movie?* I'm right, aren't I?" I ask over the sea of a few skeptical chuckles. Well, except for the table of ten—sans me—in the back (they're laughing obnoxiously, as they should). I stare at the crowd for a few more seconds before taking in a deep breath, making them wait.

.

.

.

"He-Man."

.

.

.

"I'm not even lying . . .

"So, go ahead and throw that into your blackmail jar. Although, I should warn you that if you use it, you run the risk of me clapping my hands together in a *boom* sort of fashion before shouting *He-Man!* every time I have an idea of how to get out of a sticky situation. That *could* make for a long day—my days are full of sticky situations. So, who'd be *winning*? Not Emilio Estevez's brother, what's-his-name. Nope, (I poke myself with my thumb) this girl.

"Anyways, back to the movie. It was *awful!* I mean, what were they thinking?

"Cha," I put my fist into the air, then bring it down, "Ching!

"I think the only reason I loved that movie was because I had a slight crush on the cartoon version. How could I not? The guy was ripped. He *totally* owned the mankini. He won all of his battles.

"He was kind, loving, and selfless. Most importantly—we *rocked* the same haircut back then, so . . . hashtag: *twinsies!*

"I think my best friend had a crush too . . . she still calls upon *the Power of Grayskull* when she's needing that extra something to help her get through."

I pause.

"Wow . . . that would've been a really cool name to give an upper," I trail off as if in thought. The crowd roars. My nerves finally die down a bit. "How do you make it through the day, Julie?" I ask as if playing someone else asking me.

Pops fake pill.

"By the Power of Grayskull," I answer.

"Sorry, Mattel." I give my most sympathetic look. "I'll shut up now before they throw *He-Man's* hair helmet at me.

"That's where you went wrong with that movie, though, Dolph, you didn't wear the hair, man—*epic fail!*

"Goodnight, everyone!" I yell into the mic. The crowd cheers, boosting the confidence I didn't know I kept around these shady parts.

I did it.

Holy fuck!

I make my way back to the table. There's no point in waiting backstage to see if I've moved to the next round; this was a one-time deal. Besides, I see the faces of my friends—my family—I've won.

"You're a natural, love!" Blake beams.

"Why are you acting so surprised—you know the carpet matches the curtains." I brush him off, causing a roar of laughter from him.

He pulls me into his lap, "I love you, you crazy, *amazing* lady." He paints kisses all over my face till I give in and give him a proper face-sucking.

"You killed it!!" CiCi screams, forcefully pulling Blake and me apart, then hugging me. "I'm so proud of you!" her voice shakes.

"I don't know. It would've been funnier if Dolph had made it tonight," I mention. He was supposed to be a guest judge, but he's not here. Something better probably came up, like another Sylvester Stallone—*old dudes still got it*—movie. I'm not judging; good for them!

"He is here! He was laughing his ass off." She pulls out of the hug.

"I didn't see him."

"He saw you! He's probably in the bathroom pumping his baby batter out to rhythmic cries of your name," she states, sure of herself.

"You're disgusting." I laugh because the visual just popped into my head.

"They all had He-Man's hair helmet," she adds.

"Shut the fuck up!" I go into hysterics. Even Blake is laughing now. He wasn't at first. You know, the whole thought of another man whacking off to the idea of me . . .

Out of my peripheral vision, I see Ava and Trent going at it. Not the way they used to go at it. I stop laughing, giving them my full focus. I can't hear a thing they are saying to each other; they're all teeth and anger. Suddenly, Ava picks up her drink and jerks it just right so that all the liquid hits Trent in the face. She jumps up, aggressively slides her purse strap up onto her shoulder, and turns to leave. The girls and I stare at each other in disbelief, our asses momentarily glued to our seats. Kyle quickly tosses a napkin to Trent. "Maddie, please—go after her," Trent begs, his voice laced with desperation. The look he gives her—defeated or like his puppy died—matches the sound of his voice. I've never seen Trent so beside himself when it comes to Ava. I have seen him in his darkest hour; don't get me wrong. But, Ava was standing with him then, not against him. I don't know what is going on with my friend, but my heart is breaking for both of them. Maddie's the first one to unglue herself from her seat to run after Ava. We all follow suit. I should say that I *try to follow suit*, but the Brit has grabbed my arm, jerking me back.

"Don't go," he pleads. There is a look of alarm in his eyes that I have never seen.

"What? Why?" I ask impatiently as I glance over my shoulders at my friends.

"I need you to sit this one out." He pulls a little harder on my arm.

"No—I will not!" I yell (mostly because it's loud in here, but I am irritated).

"Please, love." The expression on his face is haunting . . . as if I would cut off his oxygen by leaving.

"It's going to be okay," I assure him and use my free hand to remove his grasp from me before taking off after my friends. *Wow, Maddie's got a busy night ahead of her. I'm calling dibs as soon as I get out there. You know . . . so everyone knows I'm next after Ava.*

I step outside, the chilly air smacking me in the face. I look around and see the girls up the block to my right. Just as I'm about to book it down the street (fucking bitches; I have my five-inch heels on), some dude grabs my attention with an awkward "Hi." I look his way. He seems nervous.

"Fuck off, fellow ginger," I say before running after my friends. *Let's not discuss what running looks like in these puppies, please. We'll save that laugh for later.*

I finally catch up to them, and Ava is full-on sobbing. No, I don't know what the fuck she is saying, but I can see the hormones flying out of her from every angle. I'm no doctor, but if I were, I'd give her the diagnosis: *need-to-stop-refusing-the-dick-itis.* I'm sure Maddie is telling her this right now.

"It's not me!" Ava screams at her. "I don't need medi-fucking-cation!"

For all of you that don't have prescribing best friends—that's a

step up from regular medication.
Strong shit.
I love medi-fucking-cation.
Also, you mostly can't get it from the pharmacy.
You get it from the Pharmastreet.
I have a great Pharmastreet . . .
Shut the fuck up—I'm trying to hear Ava and Maddie!
Get your own Pharmastreet . . .

"I don't love him anymore! I can't stand the sight of him!" Ava barks.

Suddenly, I hear a strange noise behind me, like a kick to the gut. I turn to find the Boy-Wonder Posse. Trent is center stage, and the kick to his gut is all over his face. He looks as if the wind has been knocked out of him and he wants to cry. I lock eyes with my Brit. He stares at me, worry covering his face. I tilt my head. I'm not sure of what is going through his mind, but I can see this is all freaking him out. I just don't know why.

I look back over at Ava. She's looking straight at Trent. "I want a divorce," she states. I hear the wind fully expel from his lungs. I turn to the sound. Trent stands there, staring at Ava, his jaw twitching. He finally takes in a deep breath, turns on his heels, and walks away. The guys follow him. Blake turns to look at me again, his eyes sad. He shakes his head before facing forward and following the guys.

"You better come up with a good excuse!" I demand from Ava as I turn back to her.

"Ava, I think we should sit down and have a really good talk before you make impulsive decisions," Maddie counters.

"What is wrong with you?" CiCi yells.

"Ava?" Charley adds.

"I want to go home," is all Ava says as she crosses and rubs her arms.

There's only one thing that is clear tonight:
The Earth is off its axis.

Chapter Thirteen

Blake

It's all about the snacks.

I KNEW THIS WAS COMING.

Trent has let on enough for us all to know that there was trouble in paradise. He believes she's suffering from post-partum depression. That—combined with the loss they experienced this past year—I think it's safe to say it is no big surprise to anyone that they are having trouble. People can only take so much, right?

This is why I didn't want Julie to get caught up in this. Silly, I know. But, she's already very skittish when it comes to marriage and children. I certainly don't need her to witness, first-hand, the downside or the bad results of marriage. I know I'm being selfish; our friends are going through something God-awful. But I can't help it. I want to spend the rest of my life with Julie, and I can't help but think that this may have set back any progress I've made on that front. If Ava and Trent can't make it, who can?

"Are you okay?" she asks. I find it amazing that she even knows

I'm awake as she is turned away from me.

"Yes." *No.* "How did you know I was awake?" I inquire as I move her hair over a bit to place a soft kiss on her neck.

"I could hear you thinking. You breathe differently," she clarifies.

"Sorry. Did I wake you?" My right hand slides for a reach-around.

"No."

"What were *you* thinking about?" I continue to plant more kisses on her neck as I fill my hand with her.

"I was hoping you would molest me as soon as you woke up," she replies as she crooks her neck to look back at me. "Dreams really do come true, don't they?" she adds with a smile before kissing me.

"Indeed, they do," I answer between her slow, sweet assault. My hand travels down her torso, diving—casually, of course—underneath the band of her pajama shorts.

BANG! BANG! BANG!

"Wake up, you lazy arses! I've left you alone, and now it is noon!" Unc yells through the door.

"You are the biggest cock-block on the planet," I retort. "You know, in some countries, this could possibly get you shot!"

"Yes, we can have shots! It's five o'clock somewhere, mate!" That's his polite way of telling me to fuck off and get up. In my defense, I was trying to get the fuck off!

"That lady better fucking give it up to him soon or I'm going to follow him to that coffee shop and rip her hair out," Julie pledges.

"Let's not get carried away, love; you'd never get up that early on your own for that sort of conquest." I tickle her side, causing her to laugh and elbow me. With another quick kiss in, I slide backwards out of bed and grab her hands to drag her along.

"Okay, okay!" Her yell, laced with humor. As soon as we're nose to nose, I wrap her in my arms and let my hands slide down to the curve at the bottom of her lovely arse. *God, she's sexy in just my dress shirt.* Her eyes have a bit of an olive shade like they always do when she wakes. Her thick, straight, long, classic red hair falls just right. Perfect lips curve upward at my obvious attention to her gorgeous details. I palm her face, letting my thumbs trace over said lips before I collect them again. "Blake . . ." she trails with concern as she pulls away.

"Nothing's wrong, darling, I'm just letting my eyes love on you." I smile and quickly kiss her before moving to the side and yanking her forward at the same time. "Chop, Chop!" I bark as I slap her arse to get into the bathroom. She looks over her shoulder—mouth open—in shock, speechless. I raise my brows teasingly. She rolls her eyes and bites back her smile before turning to head into the bathroom. I throw on trousers and make my way downstairs.

"'Bout time," greets Uncle Rupert, looking up from his paper. *Isn't he a gem?*

"What's your problem, old man?" I ask as I make my way to the coffee pot.

"I have several. Which would you like to hear about?" He ruffles the paper before folding it long ways, then again.

"Pick your favorite," I offer, turning with a cup in hand. I bring it up to my lips and pull in a long sip of *liquid from the gods* (that's what Julie calls it).

"Just chosoe a door."

"How many are there?" I play along.

"Let's keep it to three. Which do you choose?"

"I'll take door number three, Unc, since I'm sure number one is that you haven't gotten laid or even gotten a date with your lady friend. Number two is probably something opposite of catastrophic just to downplay number one," I surmise.

"You overthink shit." He pushes back from the table and crosses his leg in a *period* manner, as if that action was a statement in itself.

"No, I just know you. Door number three," I insist.

"Your father will be here in a few days." He jerks his head back and his nose crunches up like he smells something bad.

"He's your best friend, you should be ecstatic about this," I remind him.

"Ha!" That was a condescending *ha*.

"What, you two fallen out?" First I've heard of this.

"He hates how close we are. It's no surprise that time magically appears for him to see you when he knows I'm here visiting." He taps the table as if to assert his theory.

"Well, let's take in the silver lining: if it weren't for you, I'd never see my dad." I shrug. I love my dad. My dad loves me. We're just not *mates* like we used to be. I know that it's not me; it's *definitely* him.

"It's wrong! Drives me bloody fucking mad that he does this."

"What's he up to these days?" I move on from his comment. There's no need to throw my feelings in the ring; what's the point?

"Still selling commercial real estate. But he's been dabbling in holiday homes as well as corporate digs. Been bringing in a fine penny or two on those sales lately." He grabs the next section of the paper and cracks it open.

"Did he ask about me?" I ask casually, bringing my cup up for another sip.

"Asked how the business was going," he answers without looking up.

"Bet he was disappointed to hear I haven't gone belly-up."

"Actually, he seemed very happy to hear how wonderful things were going—professionally and personally."

"Rubbish!" I spit out as if there were a bad taste in my mouth.

"Can't get anything by you." Unc looks up and gives me a small, sad-looking smile.

"Whatever! He'll never be happy unless I'm miserable with him. He's mad that I'm not hung up on my parents' divorce like he is. Why should I be? All they did was argue! Honestly, it's not like it happened when I was a kid!" I make my way over to the table and grab a seat.

"Eh, he was blindsided. It bothers him that you didn't take his side." He shrugs his shoulders as if to attempt in making a case for my father.

"Oh, please! Everyone saw it coming—for years! His blindness was his own fault. And, I didn't take any sides. They're both still my parents no matter what they are or aren't to each other anymore. For fuck's sake, this is ridiculous. I mean, who's the parent here?" I throw my hands up, "I don't want to discuss this anymore; it's like beating a dead horse."

"Fine. Let's move on to door number one, which you were wrong about. I'd like to gloat for a moment." His lips curve up Cheshire cat-like.

"No way! You took the ole cannon out for a spin?" I tease.

"No. I took her out on a date, though. Funny thing is," he pauses as he closes this section of newspaper and lays it down, "we went to the comedy club, as well—her idea."

"The same one we were at?" I jerk my head back. What are the odds of that?

"Yeah. We got to see Julie do her set. My lady friend laughed herself into tears over it." He crosses his arms over his chest as he leans back into the chair, a far off, distant yet happy, look comes over his face.

"Really? Julie would love to hear that. Even better, why don't you invite her for dinner one night, and she can tell Julie herself. Are these fresh?" I ask as I lift the lid to the box on the table. There are a few Danishes and scones inside.

"Yeah, bought them this morning while waiting for her. She never showed up. She sort of got weird on me after Julie's set," he offers as I grab a blueberry scone and take a hearty bite.

"Wha?" I ask—mouth full.

"I don't know. One minute she was cracking up and gushing about Julie. Once I mentioned that Julie was my Godson's girl-friend, she shut down. I don't really understand it. I thought we had turned a corner. I mean, she accepted the date without any hesitation after I sat down at her table without asking, again. She was different, like she was ready to be open about things. Very odd behavior . . ." he trails off.

"That is odd, Unc. Do you have her full name? Maybe you can look her up and see if you can bump into her outside of the coffee shop." Great, I'm giving my godfather tips on how to stalk a woman.

"I can do that?" He perks up.

"I wouldn't overdo it, but why not?"

"I only know her first name," he bites into his Danish. "It's Cynthia," he adds quickly.

Of course it is . . .

Really? Does the planet have to be this fecking small?

"On second thought, maybe you should just stay clear of her," I say quickly.

"Why?" His brows pull together. He sets his Danish down and grabs a napkin to wipe his mouth.

"She just seems like a lot of work. You don't want to have to work so hard and then deal with a dose of crazy as well. It's too much." I look everywhere but straight at him.

"I see it more as a challenge than lots of work. I like challenges."

"Unc, I'm going to ask you, as a favor to me, to stay away from this woman. I think I know who she is, and it's best for you not to be involved with her—*trust me!* And, for all that is holy, please do not talk to Julie about her anymore, and *definitely* do not mention her name." I can't help but sort of explode at him. I don't need anything else thrown at Julie.

"Can I ask you why?" He remains calm . . . or at least he's trying to remain calm.

"I just told you why."

"The fuck you did!" he raises his voice.

"Please, just trust me," I plead.

We sit, staring at each other for several minutes before he un-crosses his legs and stands up. "I'm going for a walk," he announces and then proceeds to do so. I prop my elbows onto the table and face plant into my hands. Hearing my phone buzz off for a text message, I pick my head up and reach into my pocket to retrieve it.

Mitch: Trent is staying with us.

Me: This is insane.

Mitch: Yeah, he's in bad shape.

Me: Why don't you all stop at the bar tonight?

Mitch: I don't think a public pow-wow is a good idea, man.

Me: Let me know where to meet you guys. I'll try to get out early.

Mitch: Let's go to Kyle's. He has the best snacks.

Me: Seriously, mate? The best snacks?

Mitch: Yeah—they don't disappear like they do in my house.

Me: Ah . . . gotcha! Text me if you disperse early. It's Saturday night.

Mitch: Ok. Catch ya later!

"Hey, where's Uncle Drill Sergeant?" Julie asks from behind me.

"He went for a walk." I glance over my shoulder at her. "Did you have a nice shower?" I ask before she leans down to kiss me.

"Yes. I love that new showerhead," she says before planting another kiss on me.

"So that's why you took so long. Replaced by a showerhead . . ." I trail off with a big sigh.

"Oh stop!" She swats my shoulder before getting a cuppa.

"Have you heard from any of the girls yet?" I pop the last of my scone into my mouth.

"I haven't checked my phone." She sits on my right and opens the box of goodies. "Ugh, I was hoping for crumb cake. Oh well . . ." She shrugs and grabs a Danish.

"Trent is at Mitch and Charlotte's. Mitch says he's a mess, poor bloke. I'm going to try to get out at a decent time tonight and head over to Kyle's." I get her up to speed.

"No fair! Why do you guys get to meet at their house? Can't you go to Maddie's?"

"What? Why is that not fair?" I sit back.

"They have the best snacks! We're women; there's going to be a lot of crying and screaming at our intervention. The snacks are essential for us!" She's dead on serious, people. *What the fuck is it with these guys and their snacks?*

"I think you and Mitch may be on the same cycle." I laugh. She remains expressionless. "Darling, have the ladies congregate here. You can go buy whatever snacks you want, and there are no children here like at Charley's," I add.

"What do you call Uncle Rupert?" She throws her hands out wildly, giving me "crazy eyes."

"You make a good point." I nod in agreement. "Go to Maddie's and have her send Hunter to Rosie's for the night."

"I guess. I'll text Jay to have Vic feed us," she says thoughtfully.

"If I know Charlotte, she's already cooking up a storm." Charlotte is about a month out from opening her new restaurant. She's been a nervous wreck about it. So much so, that the opening has been postponed three times while she's tortured Jay to change things. That poor bastard is learning quickly not to take his friends on as clients. It doesn't matter that he's learned this lesson, the GEGs will never let him abide by this new rule he swears he's sticking to after this. I know this for a fact because Julie has been emailing him every time she sees something new she likes for our remodel. I should say *her* remodel. That's a sore subject with me right now, so we'll just stay off it for a moment.

"Oh, you're right! Besides, Jay and Vic are still away on vacation." She grabs her purse which is currently hanging on the other kitchen chair. My guess is, she's digging for her phone. My other guess is that it is dead. This happens *at least* three to four times a week. "Shit," she sighs, confirming my suspicion. I open my mouth to say something but her hand goes up. "Don't fucking say a word," she says with a bit of irritation.

"No point to it anyway," I concede, and pass her my phone because I know she's going to ask for it next. She gives me a condescending little smile before grabbing it aggressively. She puts my passcode in (*yeah, ask me if I know hers* . . .) and begins texting frantically. I think I may need to go for a walk as well. You see, it takes *a lot* of patience to be with Julie. I've just reminded myself of several things—things I haven't talked to anyone about—that I push back in line to deal with later. I do this because I love her. I don't want to lose her over little things that will probably fix themselves over time.

Well, that's what I keep telling myself.

Chapter Fourteen

Cynthia

It's A Small World After All . . .

KARMA REALLY IS A FUCKING BITCH.

It's becoming clearer and clearer to me that I'm just meant to walk this world alone. I just want to throw in the towel on everything. I'm obviously not worthy to have any sort of normal in my life. I know this is my fault, but—*goddamn it*—do my hands have to be nailed to the cross? Have I been that bad of a person? *I don't even have anyone to turn to about this.* No, I can't talk to Maddie.

This is what I get. This is what I get for being excited about something . . . about the possibility of *something*.

His fucking godfather?

As soon as he reveals who I am, he will be talked out of the idea of me. He'll hear all the bad things. I feel like Regina in *Once Upon a Time*. She's trying so hard to be good, but everyone still thinks of her as the evil queen. If you haven't seen that show, you could do the Netflix and catch up. I love it. Julie recommended it to me. I mean, she recommended it to her followers on the blog.

I could call Shannon. But honestly, I feel weird doing that. Yes, we talk every day. I'm still amazed as to how quickly we were able to step back into our friendship as if thirty years hadn't been lost. But, I feel like most of the time I'm asking her for advice. There's a lot of take on my end and not enough give. I'm trying to not be that way anymore. Then again, Shannon makes it difficult because she's such a mother hen (that's my nice way of calling her a nosy bitch).

I don't know what to do. I *really* like him. That scares the shit out of me, you know. I go for all the wrong guys. He's probably a psychopath or drug addict or something. You should've seen how he started out our date! He picked me up. As soon as I answered the door, he pulled me to him and kissed me—tongue and all! Then, he said, "I'm at an age in my life where I'd rather start off with a promising 'hello' kiss than worrying about a 'goodnight' kiss for the entire date." I just stood there dumbfounded. Who does that? Who behaves like this not even five minutes into a date? Apparently, I didn't mind this in the heat of the moment because my tongue danced with his like it had a damn mind of its own! *I feel like such a hussy.* Does anybody say that anymore—hussy?

I never did get to kiss him goodnight. I'll never kiss him again. It's just too close to home. Things are complicated enough. Agreed? Oh, why am I asking you? You're one of those people who believe in "happily ever after," aren't you? Or, "happily fucked-up ever after" as Julie likes to call certain characters in the books she reads.

Wasn't she funny last night? You know, I remember her having a crush on He-Man. I remember thinking what a strange child she was. I mean, who has a crush on a cartoon character? I can't tell you how relieved I was when that phase passed. I think she moved onto the actor who played *The Karate Kid*. He was a cute kid; I approved. She moved on again, of course. Kirk Cameron. Let's just remember him the way he was before his ignorance shined so brightly. I overheard CiCi say once that Jesus was up in heaven, flipping Kirk off for being such a douchebag. The visual alone was perfection. But, I'll give him this: he's passionate about his beliefs. It's good to be passionate, as long as it doesn't hurt others. So, there's that.

And then, she fell in love with the *New Kids on the Block.* Thank Jesus! I knew it wouldn't be just a phase. You know how? She made fun of those guys so bad but would hurt anyone else who did it. I remember getting a call from the principal in middle school. Apparently, Julie kicked a boy in his balls because he said Joe sucks Donnie's—ahem. Apparently, she kicked him so hard, he cried, and his parents had to pick him up from school. And, *apparently*, that boy never spoke ill of the *New Kids* in front of Julie again.

That's the moment I had thought I was doing everything right. I thought I had taught her well. I thought she'd never rely on a man for happiness. I patted myself on the back.

Fucking idiot.

I was so blind.

In my defense, when you spend years with a man who traumatizes you, you can't really help but feel that all men are just like him. I didn't want her to suffer the consequences of the same mistakes I made. You have no idea the lengths I went through to protect my . . . never mind. What's the point in rambling on? It's not going to fix the past. I just need to stay focused on the here and now. I'm certainly not going to allow myself to get sidetracked by a man. I don't care how devilishly handsome, witty, or charming he is. And the accent? It does *nothing* for me.

Yes, I *will* keep telling myself that!

I snatch my keys up off the counter as well as my purse. It's two hours past my usual arrival at the café, surely, he isn't there waiting for me.

"You're late!" Jessica beams at me.

"Had errands this morning," I explain as cool as I can. *Can she tell I'm lying?*

"It never ends, does it?" she asks as she begins to make my usual. I'd like to say I'm one of those fancy drinks that make the barista look like an artist at work, but I only like the tea here. Plain, boring old tea. Well, it's got a dash of cream in it. I know, I'm such a rebel. "Oh, shoot! I almost forgot!" She brings my attention back to her. "There's a note here for you, and I think Eric and I will be ready to start looking next month!" She hands me my tea then quickly heads over to the register. She picks up an envelope and waves it at me. *That's odd!* It's probably a potential client. "He's pretty cute . . ." she trails off in a dreamy state. *Oh—not a client.* Also, yes, I realize that we're in the era of emails and texts; the probability of a client sending me a physical note is pretty much slim to none. But, I'm from a time when that was the norm, so I forget.

I grab the note from her. "Have you gotten pre-approved yet? It really will save a lot of time and aggravation." I ignore her excitement over the note and go right into realtor mode. I am the best around here, if you're looking. It's how I keep Julie's trust fund funded. *Shh—she doesn't know that.*

"We did! I can't believe we're going to buy our very first home! I'm so excited, I could cry!" And then, she does.

"It is a very happy occasion and exciting!" I widen my eyes to share in her joy. "Send me an email of what you are thinking you may like. I will start working on a portfolio of options." The reason why I'm such a successful realtor is because I *actually* do the work. I can't tell you how many clients have come to me, complaining that they did all the footwork for their last realtor. It's terrible! But, with the internet as a helper, it's becoming more and more the norm.

"Already working on our list! I'll send it to you as soon as it's mostly done! See you later!" she ends our exchange as another customer walks up.

I take in a deep breath and head to my table. *I wonder what he said,* I ask myself as I stare at the envelope. Slowly, I open it.

Dear Cyn,

I'm not quite sure what happened. I thought we were having fun. You seemed very stressed out when I informed you that my godson was with that girl on the stage. Is she somebody to you? Is my godson? I've been wracking my brain, love. I can't seem to come up with any answers.

All I can think of is how much I enjoyed spending time with you. I absolutely DID NOT enjoy the kiss before our date. It was awful (awfully good—I cannot tell a lie.).

Look, if it has anything to do with the kids, just stop. If they have a reason to have an issue with us, they need to sort it out! It's no skin off my back!

I'm not one to chase . . . yet, here I am. Please don't prove me to be an old fool. Talk to me. Let us work this out.

I hope that my assumptions aren't completely off. Just talk to me, please. If you're not interested in me, I can respect that and leave you alone. But, talk to me. Tell me what you are thinking.

Love,

Rupert

Insightful, isn't he? Still, this letter was sweet, and—old school. *I think he already has my number.* But, I don't have his. His actual number, I mean. What do I do? Do I leave a response here with Jessica? That seems so . . . so . . . *Sleepless in Seattle* or something. Maybe an earlier romantic movie, but I'm trying not to *date* myself too much. It is sort of a romantic thing to do, though, right—leave messages for each other in a café? It's something Audrey Hepburn would do in one of her movies. I've always idolized that woman and have hoped to have an "Audrey" moment in my life. I guess this is it!

Dear Rupert,

I do apologize for my behavior, and it has absolutely <u>nothing</u> to *do with you. I was having a wonderful time despite that dreadful kiss in the beginning. Honestly, if you ever do that to me again, it will not be soon enough!*

The truth of the matter is: Julie is my daughter. That's why I dragged you to that comedy club. I knew she was going to perform. I try to catch anything that she does. I am very proud of her. Of course, she wouldn't know this because I've spent more time on telling her what to improve instead of singing her praises. I'm ashamed of this. I'm ashamed of a lot of my past behavior. To answer you: no, I don't have a problem with the kids. They have a problem with me. Rightfully so.

Since I met Blake, I've belittled him. I've tried to talk Julie out of a relationship with him. I didn't want her to end up like me. I was so blinded by worry that I didn't see Blake for the guy he is, just the monster I created in my head. For that, I am truly sorry.

I think I've said enough. I do enjoy your company, Rupert, but perhaps it would be best if we don't see each other again. Things are already complicated, and I don't want you dragged into the middle of it. I've been working very hard on myself so that I can work on my relationship with my daughter. She is, by far, my biggest focus . . . the most important to me.

I genuinely don't believe I have anything to offer you at this time. Thank you for understanding.

Fondly,

Cynthia

I reread it. *Maybe I should edit the kiss part out.* No. I will not second guess myself. I fold the letter and seal it into the envelope Jessica so graciously offered me. "Will you give this to him tomorrow?" I ask as I extend my right hand out, offering her the envelope.

"This is so romantic," she gushes as she grabs it from me.

"Yeah, well, don't get yourself all dreamy-eyed. I don't believe things will go on much further than that envelope," I assure her. "See you tomorrow, dear." And with that, I turn on my heel and walk out of my "Audrey" moment. Whether it leads to the beginning of something or the end of it, I don't know.

For now, I have clients to meet for several showings in Bedford. I've been working with this couple for six months now. There's no sense of urgency in their purchase, obviously. The husband is looking to upgrade to a more party-friendly home. He made partner at his firm over a year ago and so desperately feels the need to keep up with "The Joneses." The wife is dragging her feet simply because she loves the home they are in. She's really not interested in what everybody else has or does. They are equally the cause of hindrance in finding anything. Today, I think, will be the lucky day! I found a gorgeous house on a pond. There is also an outdoor kitchen and dining area—covered, of course. The patios and decks are spacious and well-maintained. The inside has everything they've been looking for as well as plenty of space and character to bring parties indoors, if need be. And, it's way under their budget!

Just as I wave one final time to the Winters, "Big Girls Don't Cry" starts playing on my phone; Shannon's ringtone. *Great! Maybe she'll be up for a celebratory dinner—my treat!* "Hey, Shannon! I just sold one hell of a house, and I'm treating you to dinner!" is how I answer her call.

"Help—I've fallen and can't get up," she says.

"Ha-ha, very funny. Press your Life Alert button, dear." I humor her.

"You are my button. I'm serious. I've really fallen. And I really can't get up." She starts laughing hysterically. "I'm going to stop dying my hair, goddamn it."

"You fell because you were dying your hair?" I get into my car and start the engine.

"No! But if I'm going to be like those goddamn old ladies in that commercial, I might as well look the part. Owwww," she groans.

"Where's Jack?" I ask as I make my way onto the main road.

"He went out with a friend. I didn't want to call him, or he'd never leave me be again. How far away are you?"

"I'm in Bedford." It'll take me a half an hour to get to her.

"Well, shit. Glad I don't have to pee or anything."

"Did you break something?"

"Probably the goddamn floor."

"Shannon! Are you hurt?" She can be utterly frustrating.

"No, no. I'm just too weak to pull myself up," she says seriously this time.

"Okay, well I'm on my way. Do you want to stay on the phone with me?"

"That may be better than a half-hour session of self-loathing. Hold on," she grunts, "let me see if I can drag myself over to the wall to rest my back."

"Okay," I agree as I turn onto the highway. I hope the traffic isn't too bad yet. You never know, though. It seems no one works anymore with the amount of traffic I see at all times of the day. After some more grunting on her end, she finally says hello like the wind has been knocked out of her lungs. "Are you okay?"

"Yeah," she sighs as if it's nothing. This is followed up by a whole lot of silence and then crying.

"Shannon?" I frown on the inside. Botox won't allow it on the outside, not for—at least—another week or two.

"I'm sorry, Cyn," she cries. "I'm just so fed up with this shit! Why does this have to happen to me? I can't keep going through this," she sobs. My heart breaks. Life really isn't fair.

"You go ahead and cry, Shan," I encourage her. "This disease sucks, and it's okay to have a pity party for yourself every once in a while."

"Ugh, don't call it a disease! Makes it sound like I caught something from one of the ten sailors I screwed the other night." She complains.

"You slept with ten sailors?" Christ, she's high.

"It was Saturday. I'm always promiscuous on Saturdays, remember?"

"No."

"Well, it's Thursday, and that's always been your gullible day. Good job sticking to routine!"

"I'm going to stick my finger up and honk my horn as I pass your house, if you keep being an asshole to me," I threaten . . . jokingly, of course.

"No need to announce your IQ to everyone, Cyn," she jabs back.

"According to you, you've got a bunch of dumbasses for neighbors. They'll probably think it's a greeting."

"You're right. Fucking dumbasses . . ." she trails off.

"Okay, I'm about ten minutes away. The traffic isn't too bad.

"Tell me about the house you just sold."

I give her every detail to make the next ten minutes go by more quickly. I especially vent about how trying this couple has been. "In the end, it was worth it! I'm getting a beautiful commission!"

"I can just imagine. I should've gone into real estate goddamn it," she huffs.

"You wouldn't make a dime!" I laugh. "You'd be too quick to tell people what you think of them."

"I guess you're right. I wish people didn't get on my nerves."

"And, yet, you went on to create five more for the world."

"Consider it my contribution to balancing out the world. Not everyone can be a dumbass. We need some smartasses out there, too."

"Well, we both contributed greatly in that department! Hey, I'm pulling into your driveway now," I inform her.

"The spare key is under the fake dog shit," she says nonchalantly like everyone does this.

"Jesus! How will I know if it's fake dog shit I'm picking up?" I ask, panic lacing my voice. That would be just my luck!

"Cyn?"

"Yeah?"

"Stop being so pretty." This is her nice way of calling me an idiot. "Do I have a dog?"

"Oh . . . no. Right!" I groan lightly, more to myself. "Okay, I'm hanging up," I say as soon as I get to the door and see the pile of very convincing dog shit next to the bush. Only the O'Briens . . .

I crouch down and let my facial muscles (that aren't temporarily paralyzed) express my disgust in touching the decoy. After retrieving the key, I unlock the door and make my way into the living room. "Marco!" I yell.

"Polo!" she yells back from the kitchen.

I hasten my pace to find her with her back up against the wall, near the kitchen dinette. I take a moment to get jealous of her thick, always-falls-perfectly, dark brown hair. She likes to keep it in a short, wavy bob, which is perfect for her round face.

"Don't just stand there, soaking in my beauty; help me up, goddamn it!" She throws her hands out at me in frustration.

"Conceited much?" I laugh and shuffle behind her as she scoots. I bend my knees and get my arms under her armpits. "Okay, on the count of three. One . . . two . . . three!" I go to lift her, but I can't seem to budge her. "Good, God—what the hell have you been eating?" I ask as I strain to lift her.

"Cyn?"

I stop and gasp for breath. "What?"

"The size of my ass may have changed, but you are still a complete bitch."

"Well, we can't all redefine ourselves. Can you try to get on your knees? This way you can hold on to me while you bring a foot out to get up," I instruct.

"I can't get my legs to do anything." She softly begins to cry.

"Okay, okay, let's try again." I count to three, again but my feet slip, causing me to come crashing down behind her. Within a few seconds, we are both laughing hysterically. "Ugh, when the hell did we get so old?" I ask as our laughter dies down.

"We can't call any of the boys," Shannon says quickly. I understand why.

"I have an idea!" I say as quick as it comes to me. I reach up to the table and grab my purse.

"I don't know if I like the sound of that."

"Shh! I'm calling a client of mine. I sold him a house several weeks ago. He's a firefighter. I'll see if he's available to come and help us," I say quickly before Chad picks up. Just as I start to think it's going to voicemail, he answers. I swiftly tell him what's happened. He's on duty but can come by as there is no emergency going on at the moment and Shannon's house is only minutes away from the department. "He's on his way," I inform her when I hang up. We both take in a big sigh of relief and just wait it out.

Chapter Fifteen

Julie

Apps, Paps, and Snacks . . .

I PULL UP TO CICI AND KYLE'S. WE DECIDED IT WAS BEST TO RIDE together so we could have our pre-show rant before the main event. If you are one who belongs to a freakishly large group of best friends, who've been together since before most of you got your first period or kiss—like us—then you probably understand the "pre-show" rant. For those of you who don't, let me explain. We're talking about five (six, including Jay when he's not on vacation somewhere exotic, scaring off the natives with his need to wear *Speedos*) personalities that, though have enough in common to remain solid friends, are still very different. There is *nothing* we wouldn't say behind each other's backs that we wouldn't or haven't said to each other's face. The pre-show is to let off steam about the things we cannot change about each other. We all do it. We all know we do it. And, without ever saying it—we respect it. Because, if there were no pre-show, there probably would've been a lot of explosions over little things that may have ended friendships in our circle. So, yeah . . . we talk about each other behind our backs. Let someone else out of our circle try it though, and we'll knife a bitch. Know what I'm sayin'? It's different—we're family. It's therapeutic. None of us feel crazy if at least one other feels the exact same way about something.

I have only one more thing to say about this: if you are a part of a large group of friends and you are adamantly disagreeing with me as if you guys don't have any sort of pre-show rant, you're a fucking liar, and you should be ashamed of yourself. Own that shit. Otherwise, your friends will keep discussing your denial issues behind your back. You'll thank me later—trust me.

All right, here she comes. Don't ask me why she's crouching down like she's on some sort of secret mission. She opens the door and quickly jumps in. "Okay go!" she huffs as she grabs her belt. "Go, Julie!" she yells.

"What the fuck is your problem, and what's in that bag?" I eye her lap as I hit reverse.

"The snacks."

"We're going to have snacks at Maddie's." I shoot her a strange look.

"Maddie is serving fruit and veggies. Isn't that awesome?"

"Yeah, but your sister is cooking; we'll gain ten pounds just from the smells alone." I wave her off.

"I'm not fucking around. A shit ton of estrogen plus emotional topics, minus chocolate equals a recipe for disaster." She reaches into her bag and pulls out a Kit Kat bar, wasting no time to tear into that bad boy. Breaking it into two blocks of two, she hands me my half.

"Did you bring Mounds for Ava?" I ask.

"Mounds, Dove Chocolate, and Nutella. She'll come to her senses about Trent. I don't care if we have to force feed her chocolate all night."

"Do you think we will bring her to her senses? I've never seen her go to this extreme before." I quickly glance her way.

"I don't know. It all depends on if she's willing to see that her hormones are off," she answers nonchalantly.

"Do you think it's just that? Maybe it is something deeper, and we're just looking at what seems to be a simple answer." I take the next left.

"She's been pumping hormones into her system for years trying to get pregnant. She finally succeeds. During her pregnancy, she loses Hope, and then almost dies at the hands of Declan's ex." She throws her hands out. "She's had one crazy thing happen after another. Now that her body is trying to regulate, her brain is going haywire. We've just gotta keep her grounded before she makes the biggest mistake of her life."

"I hope we don't make things worse." I let out a big sigh as I drive past Ava's house. It's the house she grew up in. She and Trent took it off her father's hands shortly after the babies were born. Her mother, Ivy, passed away in the kitchen approximately ten years ago. It was a brain aneurism. Losing Ivy hit us all hard. Obviously, Ava has never fully recovered from this loss. I can understand that. I've never fully recovered from the loss of my father even though it's been just about thirty years for me.

Another left turn and I'm on Maddie's street. I drive up a ways and pull up to the front of her house. "You're talking about us—of course we'll make things worse. But, we always manage to make it better after fucking it all to hell." CiCi gives me a side smile and a little nudge. "C'mon, let's go lighten up this situation with our witty, yet, completely inappropriate comments."

"Yes, I'm sure they are struggling right now without that." I laugh and climb out of the car.

We head up to the door and can already hear arguing. *Shit.* This is probably going to end before it really begins. Ava doesn't like confrontation at all. If it gets hot in the kitchen, she walks out, and yoga poses the shit out of her frustrations. I call it her "Zen You!" phase of arguing.

Ceese opens the door and waves me ahead of her. "Chicken shit," I mutter to her as I walk in.

"Am not! I just don't have enough sugar in my system to keep my mouth shut."

"When the hell has sugar ever kept your mouth shut?" I give her an eye roll.

"Just go with it." She pushes me forward. We make our way down to Maddie's kitchen.

"I didn't come here to get ganged up on!" Ava yells.

"We're having a gang bang? Why am I always the last one to find this shit out?" CiCi asks, breaking the intensity in the room.

"Who am I scissoring this time? I need to know in case there's a height challenge," I add.

"You're like an Amazon woman—there's always a height challenge with you," Charley throws out there.

"You didn't mind it the last time, whore." I waggle my eyebrows at her and blow her a kiss.

"Best, non-existent fifteen minutes of my life . . ." she trails off in a dreamy state.

"Sometimes fake sex is the best sex. Well, it can keep your arrest record shorter," Jay quips.

"What the fuck are you doing here?" CiCi asks.

"Don't ask," he groans.

"You got voted off the island because of your Speedos, didn't you?" I ask as I walk up to him for a hug.

"You're just jealous."

"Yes, Jay, you're right. I often daydream about wearing Speedos, all the while, commanding the respect I feel I should deserve for doing so. So jealous, dude . . ."

He ignores my comment but mouths "what the fuck?" when I pull back from the hug. I mouth back, "No fucking clue."

"Okay, who's ready to have a food baby?" Charley asks.

"I'm ready!" Maddie makes her way over to her to see what she's plating.

"I think I'm just going to call a cab. I'm not really up for this tonight," Ava announces.

"Ava, I think it's best you stay." Maddie looks up to give her attention.

"No." She shakes her head.

"Don't make us tie you down, because you know we will," CiCi threatens.

"I don't want to do this. I know what this is." She grabs her purse.

"It's a girls' night with dinner and drinking," I state.

"Get a fucking plate, Ava," CiCi snaps.

"Maybe you should all be worrying about the stick up Ceese's ass instead of me!" She throws her purse back onto the . . . what the fuck is that thing called? Chef's rack? Butler? Anyone give a shit? Because I don't.

"Only stick up my ass is the one I welcome there. Hey . . . maybe that's what you need," CiCi fires back in a condescending fashion.

"I highly recommend it!" Jay offers.

"Fuck you both!" She huffs before going for a plate.

"Eat another Kit Kat." I whack Ceese's arm.

"I'm going right to the hard stuff." She makes her way over to the wine glasses.

"Ava, we're here for moral support. If you don't want to discuss things, we don't have to," Maddie offers in a calm, yet assertive tone.

"I just don't want to be ganged up on. I don't want everyone announcing to me their solution for what *they* think is my problem. That is all." She holds her dish out to Charley, "Only a quarter of the amount you want to give me, please." She raises one eyebrow up pointedly at her. When Charley cooks, she will pile that shit on your plate like you are some undiscovered man-beast.

"I know, I know . . ." She holds her spatula up in defense before she slices a square she pre-cut into a smaller piece.

"What the fuck is that?" I ask in astonishment. I can easily tell you it looks like I'll be five pounds heavier by the end of this night.

"A scalloped potato casserole I concocted. It's the first time I've ever made it," she informs me as she piles the usual sized heap onto my plate. I thank her with my impression of Chewbacca. *Yes, one of my many hidden talents.* "You guys have to let me know if you think this should make the menu."

"Don't you have the menus printed up already?" Maddie inquires.

"Well, this could be good for a special or something." She shrugs.

"Just like you—special or something." Jay smiles at her then turns to us and rolls his eyes dramatically. I know she's been driving him nutso with this shit.

"You just made my vagina quiver for you, you sweet talker." She coos at him.

"Please. I'm trying to eat here." He gives her a disgusted look. These two always say the most obscene shit to each other. So much so that Mitch thought they were legit screwing behind his back. He didn't know Jay was gay or that this and buying each other the most ridiculous items for birthdays and holidays was their "thing."

"There's plenty of meat in there, so you'll love it." She winks.

"Especially with all the *cheesy* goodness—your signature touch." He kisses the air at her.

Jackasses . . .

We all finally sit around Maddie's kitchen table. Awkward silence is live, yo. You all know we can't do the awkward silence.

Fuck, I guess it's my turn.

"Ava," I turn to her, "because I love you and want to support you, I will go first," I announce.

"What? Go first at what?" she asks, obviously confused.

"First, I'm really upset that you didn't wear your leather pants. I mean . . . if you wanted to distract us from what is going on, that would've been your best bet," I complain. "Second, my doctor found a lump in my breasticle. I got my tits smashed the other day and am waiting for the results while I mindlessly search for the perfect red lipstick like that chick from the movie I made you all watch because none of you would read the *fucking* book," I say quickly before shoving a pile of potatoey goodness into my mouth. *Shit, I think my period is coming. This tastes way too good.*

"What?" CiCi gasps after five millenniums pass by. I look over at her and am slightly shocked that her eyes are filled up. I glance around at everyone else who all are pretty much reacting the same way.

"I don't know anything yet," I say quietly then turn back to Ava. "But, this here," I point out to her, "is exactly why it's the best place to lay out all of your feelings . . . your fears. Because we are all loved here. We are all family. No matter how much we get on each other's nerves or how ridiculous we act, this is the foundation of our friendship: the love and support. There are things in life that we think we can deal with on our own, Ava, but we're wrong; we can't. We need that support no matter how much we fight it . . . no matter how stubborn we become." I take in a deep breath. "That's all I want to say to you about anything you are clearly going through and don't want help with."

"Do you want help?" she asks me slowly.

"I'm scared," I admit, my voice cracking.

"Okay." She grabs my hand as she is sitting next to me. "I'm going to pick you up at ten tomorrow, and we're going to get you the right shade of black lipstick, because fuck you, cancer, and you're not a follower." She squeezes.

"It's a date," I say through the tears I didn't think I invited to this party. I was all ready for Ava's instead.

"I'll wear my leather pants," she agrees.

"Your ass looks ah-mazing in them."

"I know." She smiles and winks. We laugh.

"You're not allowed to have cancer," CiCi announces, bringing our attention to her. "You're not allowed to have cancer because Caroline has cancer. She already has it, so you're not allowed to have it!" she yells. "She's my twin; I don't even fucking like her, but I love her because she's my sister. But *you are my* best friend—I love you for legit reasons. You're not allowed. You can't have it! My sister has it," she states matter-of-factly. "Quota met—you're not allowed to have it too. Don't be a selfish, greedy bitch; pass that shit on to someone we don't know." Her face is fighting what her eyes, so full of tears, are revealing. "You can't have it!" she yells.

"Okay . . . I just won't have cancer," I agree. "I'll contract an STD instead." I shrug like "no big deal."

"Yeah . . . do that." She nods in agreement.

"Done." I smile and reach for her hand.

"You know . . . it's not like you haven't imagined you had them before," she adds.

"Exactly." I squeeze her hand.

"Caroline has cancer?" Charley bellows through. "What?" she cries.

"Stage 3 cervical," Maddie answers.

"What? Why do you know before me?" Charley yells.

"I'm sorry," Maddie cries. "Preston told me. He's been helping her through this."

"I fucking hate her. I *fucking* hate our sisters!" Charley screams in a crying fashion.

There are five O'Brien sisters. Caroline is CiCi's twin, though you'd never know it. Caroline, Colleen, and Caitlyn moved away years ago, leaving the care of Shannon and Jack up to Charley and CiCi. CiCi and Charley have always been the closest (obviously), but it's always been a mystery as to why the other girls have stayed away. I mean, they were raised by the same awesome parents; it makes no sense. I know that Ceese and Charley have been irritated by this. Not so much that they are the ones taking care of Shannon and Jack, but that their sisters only bother with them to tell them when they think they are doing something wrong.

Caroline has always been the love of Preston's life. He's Maddie's brother. Hell, he's a brother to us all. Well, the brother during the teenage years that does everything he can to drive you mad. Yup, Preston's never grown out of that phase. Anyhow, about six or so months ago, Caroline got back into contact with him. I guess this is why. I know he was hopeful that she was getting ready to leave Lucky Charms, or Seamus, as most call him. Preston is actually one of the most sought-after OB/GYNs in southern New Hampshire. She was connecting with him for medical help. *Selfish bitch.* I wonder if she's ever or will ever realize she's the reason that man hasn't married anyone. She's still "the one" for him. *Romantic dumbass.*

"Well," Charley turns her focus back to CiCi, "how did you know about Caroline's cancer?"

"The twin thing . . . I felt it," she states.

"Really?" Charley furrows her brows.

"Yeah. My phone was on vibrate; the bitch wouldn't stop calling me."

We all sit here, staring at CiCi as she continues to eat. She looks up, probably noticing the silence. "Oh my God, you dipshits, she called me to go and get checked out because we're twins. Believe me, there is no other connection between us besides AT&T, or whoever offers me the best deal once a year."

"Wait! When the fuck did she call you?" I ask.

"Last week," she mumbles.

"Last week? She's known for how long?" Now I'm the one who's yelling.

"Well, you know Caroline—doesn't shy away from a competition to save her life . . . or mine, for that matter."

"That fucking bitch! That selfish, two-faced fucking bitch. She's lucky she's not here!" My hands ball up into fists.

"She's flying in tomorrow," Maddie offers.

"Maddie, are you looking to have Julie thrown in jail?" Jay asks.

"Ha! She won't be alone!" Ava adds. I look over at her, and her face is beet red with a look of disgust to add to it.

"Ceese?" Charley gets her attention. "Are you up to date on everything? I am."

"Yes, Mr. Belvedere sees to that." She gives her a little smile.

"That's two of our sisters down. We better call Caitlyn."

"Are you guys going to tell your parents?" Maddie jumps in again. They both shrug as if they are unsure. Honestly, I don't know if Shannon could handle this news. Suddenly, I hear a random gaspy sob from Ava. We all give her our attention.

"Sorry. It's just . . . you ever suddenly realize something that you already knew but you just re-realized it?"

Oh, fuck, here we go . . .

"Every time I go out in the world thinking I can 'people.'" CiCi does air quotation marks. We all laugh. CiCi doesn't *people* very well, and I'm right behind her.

"Yeah, that must be very difficult for you. I praise you for believing in yourself, though. Never give up, Ceese. There may be someone out there one day that you can tolerate immediately." Ava gives her usual sarcastic encouragement. She cracks me up because she's so damn sincere about it.

"Kyle's family pretty much filled my quota at the moment. Maybe next year," Ceese replies.

"On that note," Ava turns to Maddie, "give me the name of someone you trust. That's all I will say about this."

"You got it."

"The right stuff!" the rest of us yell. Well, except for Jay. He's shaking his head like he knew that was coming.

Chapter Sixteen

Blake

It's all in the Cards

JONATHAN HAS BEEN A GODSEND! THIS KID HUSTLES LIKE HIS ARSE is on fire. He's been here almost a week and is already re-training Willow! If I could get three more "Jonathans" in here, I'd be solid!

Uncle Rupe is closing shop for me tonight so that I can meet up with the guys. Jonathan's staying too . . . to keep an eye on Uncle Rupe . . . and the Scotch—*ahem*. Yeah, poor old man; he's had a rough go of things. Hasn't been to the coffee shop in a few days. At least me Da will have someone to mope around with when he gets here (if he ever gets here.). *There's another one for ya!*

"Alright then, Unc, I'm off!" I yell down the bar. He quickly glances my way and waves me off, returning his attention back to a patron. My eyes search for Jonathan, and when I see him, I give him a nod to let him know I'm leaving. He gives me a thumb's up. It's sort of funny nowadays to see a human give you a direct thumb's up, not an emoji one. I like it. I give him one back.

Okay, that felt awkward.
Like I was supposed to pop a Mentos before I did it but forgot.
Probably best to leave that as Jonathan's "thing."
Right-O!
On my way out the pub, I pull out my cell to text Mitch.
Me: Everyone there?
Mitch: Everyone but Fancy Arse.
Me: How are you surviving, mate?
Mitch: Terribly. Dec is too Americanized for me to pick on him, and I've got nothing new to bust on Kyle about. Please hurry; I need someone to bully.
Me: You know that term has a whole different meaning in England. Who's the fancy arse now?
Mitch: No, it doesn't!
Me: I'm afraid so, mate.
Mitch: What does it mean?
Me: I think you know. Wink at you in 10!

I'd send him a couple of emojis blowing a kiss, but I think that'd be overdoing it. My guess is that Mitch is too busy Googling whether "I need someone to bully" has a different meaning in England. Ahh . . . it does a heart good to feck with him!

I knock and open the door to walk in anyway. I can hear their voices coming from the kitchen. Man, this house makes me feel like after I take my shoes off, I need to bathe my feet before walking in. It's not normal. I'm impressed, but it's still not normal. They don't even have a maid. This is all Kyle. I guess we all do have our *thing.* This would be why CiCi calls him Mr. Belvedere, rightfully so. Of course, I wasn't in the States at that time. I had no idea it was a TV show in the 80s.

Moving along, I make my way into the kitchen, my nostrils greeted by the glorious smells of pizza, wings, Chinese, etc. "Vic! When did you two get back?" I ask, surprised to see him. I thought he and Jay were supposed to be on holiday for at least another week.

"Jay made us fly back," he answers before sucking whatever sauce it is on his thumb. The five of us just stare at him blankly. "Wha?" He furrows his brow.

"Jay?" Mitch ask with as much confusion as we are all probably feeling.

"I was annoying him. I kept worrying about the restaurant. I have newer staff, so I couldn't shake the feeling of doom. I wasn't very much fun." He shakes his head, looking a bit aggravated with himself.

"You know you are never going to live this down, right?" Trent slaps him on the shoulder as he makes his way towards me. "Hey, man." He fist bumps me before going in for a hug. It's hard seeing him like this.

"I know. I'll make it up to him in a few months," Vic answers Trent as he pulls back from me.

"Can we bring our plates over to the table, please?" Kyle begs.

"If we go over to the table, there's a lesser chance of us dropping shit all over the place," Mitch pops a little drumstick in his mouth then pulls it out cleaned to the bone, "you'll have nothing to clean up, man; we wouldn't do that to you. We care about you too much," he adds. We all laugh but make our way to the table just the same.

I make my plate up as everyone else settles into the happy quiet that happens when you're chowing down on food you don't eat on a regular basis. The fact that my pub's got me running ragged is my only saving grace, otherwise, I'd be living off the food there and be a certifiable fat arse. We can't all have Julie's metabolism. I swear, I don't know where that girl puts it all. I, too, settle into my mountain of nonsense.

"When you're ready to come up for air, mate, we're all ears," Declan states. I look up from my trough (yes, that's what it looks like, fit for a prize pig) to see that he's speaking to Trent. Trent nods but continues to eat his feelings. I know I shouldn't *assume* he's doing that. I mean, it's not like I'm in his head. But, he's being so aggressive about it, how can I *not* assume?

Suddenly, he throws down his fork in the same passionate nature he was just shoveling food into his mouth. "It's like she's a completely different woman! I don't know how to reach her!" he says angrily.

"Maddie says, and I think we can all agree with her, that Ava may be suffering from Post-Partum Depression," Dec offers.

"No. See," Trent shakes his head adamantly, "she's as happy as a lark with the babies. It's not for show, either; she's just as happy with them when no one's looking. I think it's something deeper. I'm just not sure what it is. Then again, maybe that's just me being in denial." He gets a little choked up. "I'm beginning to think that maybe what she's been saying to me is truly how she feels about me. Maybe she doesn't love me anymore."

We collectively oppose this idea in a verbal chaos that becomes incoherent. The gist is: NO FUCKING WAY!

"No, listen to me!" He puts his hand up. "I've really been thinking about this. Look at everything we've been through. Not just the past year—the past ten years: IVF, foster children, adoptions that fell through, the loss of Hope, and finally the birth of the twins. Look, none of that was easy, guys! Most of it was a downright nightmare. Sometimes I'm in awe that we made it through all of that. But that got me to thinking . . ." he trails off, taking in a deep breath before continuing, "Our focus, for *so long*, was to start a family. It kept us chugging along. Then, one day, we finally had one. It wasn't long after the twins arrived that she started changing towards me. I think that maybe she fell so in love with the idea of her own family that she fell out of love with me but was so focused on succeeding at becoming a mom that she didn't realize any of this until after the twins came. She just woke up one day, looked at me and thought, 'shit, I don't even like this guy anymore.' Now that she has what she always dreamt about and prayed for, she doesn't need me anymore. She has no problem walking away." He finishes, his eyes full of tears. It's not the first time I've seen my friend like this. He's not lying—they've been through the ringer.

"Trent, I feel for you, man. I can see how you could come to this conclusion, but, you're forgetting one thing." Kyle reaches for one of the Chinese food containers.

"What's that?" Trent and I both ask.

"This is Ava we're talking about. She's the most sentimental out of all the girls. It's what the girls love and hate about her most. She always brings up memories that half of them have forgotten about, and they are so vivid when she retells them. We've all seen her in action; she gets emotional—in a good way—about them." He shoves a bite in before proceeding, "My point is: Ava never forgets to remember. It makes her love for the people she cares about that much stronger. We could all take a page out of her book, to be honest. It's so easy to get swept up in the day-to-day stuff that we forget to stop and remember."

"Kyle's hitting the nail on the head, man. It's got to be something else," Mitch adds.

"I'll mention all of this to Maddie, see what she thinks," Dec says before downing the rest of his beer.

"Why don't you start texting her random memories about you two," I suggest.

"Hey! Now that's a great idea!" Vic practically jumps. "That just might get me out of the doghouse, as well!"

"Don't be doing that, otherwise, she'll think he stole the idea off you!" Mitch looks at Vic like he's the dumbest person in the world.

"Eh, in all fairness, Vic is not known for his romantic side,"

Trent says with a little apprehension.

"Not a drop in me. I'm not even sure how I've managed to keep a guy like Jay. Still, I won't steal any of your thunder. Until, you know . . . your storm has passed." He pushes at Trent's right shoulder.

"Alright, well, I'll try anything." Trent shrugs.

"Okay, anyone else need spousal advice?" Dec asks.

"What, are you making a list for Maddie?" Vic asks.

"She's capable of making her own lists. Pretty sure you'll be on it after Jay talks her ear off tonight." He picks his empty bottle back up and tilts it in a salute to Vic. We all laugh in agreement. Jay is anything but reserved with his feelings. I'm sure we'll *all* know how Jay feels before the day is through tomorrow.

"Well? How about it? Everyone else okay?" Mitch looks around the table.

"Yes and no," I say just as everyone else finishes nodding.

"What's the matter?" Trent's the first to ask.

"It's little stuff, but it's becoming a collection that I'm afraid will bust out," I admit. I'm rather shocked at myself, really. I had no intentions of talking about Julie and me at all tonight.

"What is it, man?" Mitch asks, his voice laced with concern. I'm not used to this Mitch.

"They found a lump in Julie's breast. She went for a mammogram the day of her comedy thing. We should hear back on Monday," I inform them while staring down at my food like it is the most fascinating thing I've ever seen.

"Why the hell is it taking so long?" Kyle asks.

"I'm not sure. I think the office is shut down for a vacation, but I still can't understand why she has to wait. I mean, can't the radiologist call her?" I finally look up. I'm quite angry about all of this. Vacation is the only response Julie has been able to get about it.

"How's Julie doing with all this?" Dec asks.

"I don't know. One minute she seems nervous as hell—angry,

really. Then I wake up on a day like today, and she's staring down at me with a bald conehead on, like *Saturday Night Live,* because she wants to make sure I can handle it all, should she have cancer."

"Did you ask her to take you to her leader?" Trent says through his laughter. I'm sure the visual is strong for him.

"Dude . . . she is *the* leader." I laugh.

"Admitting you have a problem is the first step." Dec smiles.

"Thanks, Mr. Maddie." I flip him off.

"Has she told the girls?" Kyle chimes in.

"Did you get a report?" I look at him like he's the dumbest person in the world.

"Right," he states. I'm guessing he realizes that was a stupid question. The girls tell us everything. No, really—don't roll your eyes—they do. We didn't believe it, either. Honestly, we all wish they didn't tell us. "Well, maybe she'll tell them tonight." He shrugs.

"I don't know. All I know is that I want this to pass. I'm hoping it's a false alarm. We have so many other things to work through, and God help me for saying this: Cancer will be just the distraction for her to push off our other problems." No, I can't believe I just said that, either.

"What problems?" Trent asks.

"She doesn't want to have kids." I push at my left forefinger with my right. "She wants me to live at her house but not claim to live there because I only 'sleep over.' This leads into not wanting my input on any remodeling for *her* house." I push down on my third finger. "There's more, but those are the ones that piss me off the most," I inform them.

"Wow. That's kind of annoying, dude," Mitch states.

"Just a bit!" I agree passionately. Not a second goes by and I'm already feeling guilty for complaining about her.

"Look, man," Kyle jumps in, "I think I can probably relate to you the most in this situation. The only thing I can tell you is to ride it out—stake your claim, of course—but, ride it out. If Julie is anything like CiCi, and we know she is, she's already accepted things in her heart, but her brain won't give up any power it thinks it has. Also, CiCi said she didn't want to have kids, either." He leaves it at that and throws back the rest of his beer.

"What changed her mind?" I ask.

"Nothing." He shrugs. "It's bullshit. She's not on anything, and I don't use any protection. She doesn't say a word about it. Oh, she'll yell at me the day she sees two lines on a stick, but I'll just remind her how those two lines got there." He smirks like the Cheshire cat.

"Jay wants to adopt," Vic announces.

"It's so tough, man," Trent says.

"I'm . . . well, we're not even married." Vic shakes his head in a manner that could easily be understood that he is *not* on board with this idea.

"That doesn't stop anyone these days," Mitch says.

"Eh . . ." Vic trails off, getting visibly uncomfortable as he is seemingly avoiding everyone's eyes.

"Have you told Jay that you don't want to have kids?" Dec asks in an accusatory tone. None of us like being lied to but Dec makes it an art out of getting pissed off right away if he thinks someone's being shady. After what he's been through, it's understandable.

"It's not that I *don't* want to have kids. It's that I'd have to explain who the other parent is to my family." Vic lowers his head like he's examining his food.

"What does that mean?" Dec lightens up slightly in his tone.

"Ugh!" Vic groans, dropping his fork forcefully. "It *means*: I haven't come out to my family! Yet another argument Jay and I keep having. Look, can we get the spotlight off of me now?" He looks up at us, his eyes pleading.

"You need to tell them." Dec points a finger at him. Vic nods. "Okay, well, let's turn the focus elsewhere, then." Dec then looks to Kyle. "How's the wedding coming along?"

"Getting CiCi to pick what flowers she wants so I can make

sure they go with our color scheme is like pulling teeth. Every flower I suggest is the wrong one. I made her a binder of every flower that comes in suitable colors, and I don't even think she's looked at it! She hasn't settled on a flower girl dress for Brooklyn. Don't even get me started on the food!" Kyle gets flustered. We are just sitting here, staring at him like he's an alien.

"I've got a solution for you." Mitch is the first to break the awkward silence.

"What's that?"

"Forget CiCi and marry Jay; this shit would've been sorted months ago." He laughs. We join in.

"Shut up," he says to Mitch just as Vic passes something over to him. "What's this?" he asks Vic.

"My Gay Card; it's all yours, man." We all roar now. I'm clutching my stomach. It's been a while since I've laughed this hard.

"You guys are assholes." He waves us off like he's pissed but there is a smirk making its way through.

"Just go to Charlotte, Kyle. She'll help you with everything." Mitch slaps him on the shoulder.

"For once, I think you may have a good idea there." He nods in agreement.

Slowly but surely, our conversations change course to more familiar waters: sports, movies, music, and business. I've got a great group of friends. It's odd to think that I've only known them for a couple of years, yet, I've been through a lifetime of shit with them already. I'm pretty sure the feeling is mutual.

"Blake?" Kyle breaks me out of my thoughts, grabbing the plate in front of me.

"What?" I get up to help him clear.

"Is Julie talking to her mom again?"

"No. She hasn't had contact with her or seen her since that day in the hospital with Hope." I furrow my brows at him. "Why?"

"She's been hanging around with Shannon. It seems they've

patched things up," Mitch says as he places the case of poker chips down on the table.

"Patched things up?" What the hell is he talking about? Shannon only tolerates Cynthia . . . like the rest of us.

"Oh, you don't know?" Kyle jerks his head back.

"Know what?"

"Shannon and Cynthia used to be best friends," Mitch answers for Kyle.

"Get out of here—no way! I've been around these girls longer than any of you, and I have never heard that," Trent argues as he passes around the pipe tobacco. We all pull out our pipes (go ahead and say it—*that's what he said*. Better now? Good.) and start filling them. This is something we started several months ago for whenever we have a poker night. We tried the cigar thing, but all of us got flak from the girls because we stunk, and so did Maddie's house. It was three poker nights after that that Mitch gave us all a box. We each received a pipe. I immediately cracked an appreciative smile. Mitch and I had a lengthy conversation about our grandfathers, what stand-up guys they were, and how they both smoked pipes. We reminisced about the comforting smells of vanilla and cherry that would waft from those pipes. Turns out, the other guys had similar memories whether it was a grandfather, uncle—what have you. There were no complaints from the girls, either. Now, it's tradition.

"It's true, man," Kyle takes a seat and grabs the cards Dec has dealt. "She seems to be changing her ways altogether," he adds.

"What do you mean?" I ask.

"I mean, I think this cutting her out of her life has finally worked. I think a switch has been flipped in Cynthia . . . a good one. What are we playing?" He brings his attention back to Dec.

"Follow the Queen," Dec calls out as he picks up his own cards.

"Which one? We've got three in the room." Mitch laughs.

"Feck off!" I throw a Twix at him, hitting his forehead.

"Stop." Kyle grabs the Twix. "So, you guys haven't heard from her?"

"No. Not Julie."

"You?"

"No. I think my uncle is sweet on her. He's been seeing a mystery woman, and all arrows are pointing to her. She got weird the other night on him."

"Cynthia-weird or normal person-weird?" Trent asks.

"Normal person. She dragged him to the comedy club for Julie's thing. As soon as Uncle Rupe mentioned his Godson was dating her, she got weird and ended their date. He hasn't seen or heard from her since. I told him he's better off for it. But, truth is, he's really down in the dumps. I've never seen him like this."

"Something's up. I wonder if there is something medically wrong with her." Kyle changes out two cards and puffs on his pipe.

"How did you guys find out that she and Shannon used to be friends?" I ask.

"Happy told us. He said it's as if thirty years haven't passed at all. Shannon's spirits have been up even though she's not doing too well with her MS. She's happy to have her old friend back." Mitch throws a ridiculous amount of chips on the pile. This can only mean one thing: Mitch has a shit hand. The boys and I all give each other a knowing smirk. We all bet accordingly.

"So, is her behavior isolated or has she been a *changed* woman for a while?" I inquire. I'm finding it hard to believe that this leopard has changed her spots.

"From what Dad says, she's been very consistent for a few months now," Mitch offers.

"Do you think she will be approaching Julie soon? I feel like I should prepare her and yet, I feel like I should just let things happen," I admit as I fold.

"Well, we all know that we're damned if we do and damned if we don't with these girls. I'm not sure what the right answer is,"

Mitch says as he lays his cards down with a smile. "Read 'em and weep, boys!" *Well, I'll be damned!*

"Why don't you give Maddie a call?" Dec suggests.

"Eh, I know she gets bogged down by everyone coming to her, mate. I'd hate to ask her."

"I'll mention it to her and see what she says." He gives me a knowing smile. He's had to take Maddie on a lot of sabbaticals this past year. She's been burdened with things beyond the usual.

"I wish these girls came with a manual," Trent states as he blows out smoke.

"You mean a survival guide?" Kyle gives me an exasperated look.

"Maybe a memoir to leave behind for the grandkids," Declan adds in.

"Eh . . . c'mon. In the grand scheme of things, you all know how lucky we are. They're good women. Crazy as fuck, but good women nonetheless." Mitch shuffles, a slight smile taking over his lips, and I know he's thinking of Charley.

You know what?

He's as right as rain.

Chapter Seventeen

Cynthia

Control Freak

I MAKE MY BED EVERY MORNING. MY HOUSE IS SPOTLESS. YOU won't find a gray hair on my head. My nails are always polished. I'm winning the war on wrinkles. My clothes scream success. I hold my head up high to project what I want others to think.

These are the things I can control.

My daughter wants nothing to do with me. My best friend is suffering from Multiple Sclerosis with no remission in sight. My dad is trapped somewhere in the devastatingly painful world of Alzheimer's, only to escape and come back for a moment here and there. I have made choices that I can't take back. Things that have affected my life negatively in so many ways, I can't share the half of it. I have pushed away the possibility of a happy ending because I don't feel that I deserve it, though the selfish side of me believes I do.

These are the things I don't have control over.

I'm sure there's more to the list of things I can't control, but it's depressing so I'd rather not acknowledge it. I bring my pen up to my mouth and bite on it as I stare up at the ceiling, trying to come up with more that I am possibly comfortable with. Maddie will be out here for me at any moment. She's not going to be too happy with me; I haven't talked to Blake or CiCi. The opportunity just hasn't presented itself. *Bullshit* is what she will call that. I may have to tell her about Rupert. That will at least cover my reasoning behind not speaking to Blake yet.

"Cynthia?" Maddie calls. I look up to find her at the entrance of the hall leading down to her office, a slight smile on her face. I return it and get up to follow her.

"I've worked on the list of things I can and cannot control as you suggested a few months back," I mention as we enter her office and I grab my seat.

"Good!" she states enthusiastically. I'm sure she's glad I've offered something for her to work with. "However, I'd like to discuss something else." She seats herself across me.

"Oh? What's that?" I pull at the hem of my skirt, avoiding her eyes.

"Rupert Donnelly."

"I have nothing to say." I look up at her indignantly.

"This is a pure example of the cons you will face having me as your therapist, Cynthia. I mentioned this to you in the beginning. I'm going to know or find out about things you may not necessarily want to share with me." She stares me down. She's got moxie; I'll give her that.

"Okay," I concede. "What do you want to know?"

"Everything."

"How did you find out?"

"My fiancé is close friends with Blake. Need I say more?" She raises an eyebrow.

"No. Does Julie know?" I ask quickly.

"No."

"Are you sure?" I plead.

"Yes. Blake didn't want to mention it with all she's going through right now."

"Going through? What do you mean?" My anxiety goes through the roof. My heart is beating so fast that I think it will explode out of my chest. Maddie's expression falls, she pales and looks everywhere but at me. "Maddie?" I grab her fidgeting hands. "What is it?"

"I'm not at liberty to say," she just about trips over her words.

"Oh no you don't! This is a con for you as well! Tell me what's going on with my daughter, now!" I almost yell. Maddie becomes more visibly upset, tears welling up in her eyes. "Maddie," I softly plea, reaching for and squeezing her hands.

"They found a lump in her right breast. She's waiting for the results." She takes in a shaky breath.

I nod slowly, barely able to see Maddie through my tears. I give her hands one final squeeze before letting go to retrieve my list. I tear it off the small pad and hand it to her. "Here. Do me a favor?" I ask. "Add what you told me to the list of things I can't control. I need to go. My daughter needs me," I state as I stand up.

"She can't know that I told you!" Maddie says in a panic.

"Watch out, Maddie, I seem to be rubbing my narcissistic ways off on you." I pull my purse strap up my arm onto to my shoulder.

"That's not fair, Cynthia," she says through her teeth.

"Not much in life is, but I will try to conceal who told me." I pat her shoulder before making my way out of the office.

My feet move swiftly, my mind focused on one thing and one thing only—Julie. I will no longer stand in the shadows. She may not like it but, quite frankly, I don't give a fuck. I throw my purse into the passenger seat as I jump into the driver's side. I throw my sunglasses on and press the button to bring my car's hybrid engine to the quiet hum that always has me wondering if I've actually started it. Not today, though. I put the gear in reverse and check my surroundings before pulling out like a bat out of Hell.

Ugh! I hate this car!

I press the ignition button again, my foot firmly on the brake.

I put it in reverse.

It does nothing.

I take several deep breaths then give it my undivided attention.

I coast out of my spot like a ninety-year-old with cataracts.

I hate this car.

Pulling myself together, I let my renewed focus fuel my urgency in getting to Julie's. I may have run a few lights. I may have flipped a few people off. I don't care. All I care about is getting to her. The torture of traffic is nothing compared to the random flashbacks of Julie growing up, playing on loop in my brain like a movie. *She was the most amazing and beautiful baby.* When she was a toddler, she used to smash my face between her little hands and rest her nose against mine. *"I love you, Mama!"*

She did.

She truly loved me.

That was enough.

That's all that mattered.

Why couldn't I see that?

I finally pull up to Julie's house and get out of my car as quickly as possible. Her car is in the driveway, so I know she's home. I run up the walkway and bang on the door. I hit the doorbell a few times just to add to the urgency. The door swings open and a confused, yet pissed off, Blake stares down at me. "What the bloody hell is wrong with you?" he barks.

"Where's Julie?" I ask frantically.

"She's on an interview. What's the matter?" He opens the screen door.

"Don't lie to me, Blake, her car is right there!" I point out the obvious.

"Right, and my car isn't because that's the one she's taken! What's got you off your rocker?"

"Is she okay?" I start to cry.

"What are you talking about?"

"The results! Did she get them?" I yell just as Rupert walks up behind him.

"Cyn?" He steps onto the stoop, his face full of concern.

"Did she?" I ask Blake again, ignoring his godfather.

"Yes," he says almost breathless. "Everything is fine, Cynthia. It was benign."

"Oh, thank God," I cry then begin to sob uncontrollably. Rupert catches me as I almost go down. It's like thirty years of grief is finally making its appearance.

Put this on my list of things I can't control.

"Darling, come inside." He holds me tight and kisses the top of my head. "Put the kettle on, son," he instructs Blake as he leads me into the house.

"I shouldn't stay." I shake my head. "She wouldn't want me here," I add.

"It's okay, Cynthia," Blake assures me.

"I'm sorry, Blake," I blurt out. "I've been lousy to you for no good reason. You're very good to Julie . . . for Julie. I shouldn't have treated you the way that I did," I say as we make it into the kitchen.

"Why did you?" he asks out of curiosity's sake, I'm sure.

"For my own selfish reasons and fears." I grab a Kleenex out of my purse. "I didn't want her to end up anywhere close to the situation I found myself in. But, I'm learning that she is not me. Thank God, right?" I offer a little chuckle as I try to pull myself together.

"Don't say stuff like that, love." Rupe takes my free hand.

"I'm surprised you're even talking to me. You haven't replied to my letter," I say as quietly as I can.

"I didn't know there was one. I haven't gone back. Doesn't seem right without you there." He gives me a slight smile.

"Look, I don't mean to be a third wheel here, but if we could finish our conversation first, I'll be more than happy to leave you two lovebirds alone." Blake pulls up a chair, not a hint of a smile on his face to go along with that statement. *What was I expecting?*

"I'm sorry. What else did you need to know?" I give my full attention to him.

"I need to know what you meant by 'you didn't want her to end up in the same situation as you,' why the hell you've been acting so strangely to everyone, and why the hell you are being so pleasant to me now?" he yells.

"Aye, Blake!" Rupert yells back at him.

"No, Unc!" he rebuts. "What is she playing at . . . being nice to everyone out of the blue? What is your end game, lady?" He brings his focus back to me.

"The person you know is not who I used to be, Blake," I confess. "I've made so many mistakes. I'm trying to correct them. As we can see from your own outburst, it's not going to happen overnight." I reach forward and grasp his hand. "I promise . . . this is the real me, not the lady you've learned to hate. I'm . . . I've done everything wrong, Blake. I've realized that now. I'm trying to change things: the way I behave, everyone's perception of me, and what I thought was the right thing to do," I confess.

"All she's ever wanted was a mum she could call when things in life seemed a bit off or really fantastic. She wanted nothing else from you; she never has." He walks away from us.

"I know. Blake, believe me—I know now." I cry. "I am trying. I want to be the mom she needs. I'm trying," I plea.

"Right. I'll let you two get on then," he states quickly before storming out the door. I look at Rupert to find an impressed grin on his face.

"I don't understand the expression on your face," I admit.

"He's giving you a second chance, love." He brings his grin toward me.

"How do you know?" I'm so confused.

"He didn't kick you out. He left you with me after warning me to stay away from you." He grasps both of my hands in his. "He believes your intentions, love." Without any notice, he covers my lips with his. I welcome them . . . graciously. "I have no interest in the *Cat and Mouse* game, Cynthia," he declares after pulling away.

"Okay," is all I can muster.

"You will be the center of my universe," he announces.

"Okay," I agree.

"It's settled then?" he asks.

"Okay." I take in a deep breath.

"Love, you'll need to learn some more words to keep my attention. Not many, but a few more would suffice," he teases.

"Okay." I smile and boldly leap forward to connect our lips again. He gives me a groan of approval. *That's all I need . . .*

He begins to pull away but gives me another quick peck, "C'mon, let's get out of here."

"Oh, I . . . um." I hesitate.

"We're going to drive somewhere and go for a walk or have a cuppa. If we stay here, Julie will see your car. Emotionally, I think you've had enough today. Let's save the reunion with your daughter for another day." *He's a wise man—that's definitely a plus!*

"I agree." I smile and stand up with him.

"You didn't think I was going to let you have your way with me, did you? That would be very forward of you, Cyn; we've only known each other a short while. I'm not that sort of bloke." He's so straight-faced, I can't tell if he's teasing me or not, so I just stare at him. After a few seconds, his eyes crinkle in the corner as a slight smirk appears. He gives me a wink. "Let's go, love." He tugs me to go ahead of him and smacks my butt, making me gasp. I look over my shoulder at him in shock. "That was just as satisfying as I thought it would be, thank you." He flashes me his brilliant smile. I don't know what to say, so I just look forward and make my way down the hall leading to the door.

We make it outside just as the skies open up. I hold my purse over my head and make a mad dash to my car, grabbing the door handle as quickly as possible to get in. Rupert and I jump into our seats and slam the doors in a synchronized fashion. We look over at each other at the same time. "We look like a couple of drowned rats!" I declare as he lets out a hearty laugh.

"And, yet, you still manage to take my breath away with your beauty." He leans over and kisses me.

"Oh stop," I say and turn to start the ignition. The universe is good to me; my car starts right up. "We'll go to my place to dry off. I'll make you dinner."

"You're still not getting into my pants, love."

"But I said I would make you dinner," I tease back with a smile as I put the car in reverse and turn my wipers up to the max.

"I guess we'll just have to see how well you cook." His left hand pats my right leg and he leaves it there the entire drive to my house.

Within ten minutes, we're racing into my house. We are both now completely soaked to the bone. "I can offer you a robe while I put your things in the dryer," I offer as I pull off my shoes. I look up when I realize he hasn't moved nor answered me, and I find his eyes glued to my chest. I wore a white blouse today. "Do you like what you see?" *Oh my God, did I really just ask him that? This is all Shannon's fault!*

"I'm very glad that we are not out in public because I'd be very upset with you."

"Why?" I look down then immediately bring my arms across my chest. "Oh," is all I can manage to say about not wearing a bra that is padded.

"Let's not wear that one again, aye?" He palms my face. Bringing it forward, he plants a prolonged kiss on my forehead. "Alright, darling, go and get yourself into some dry clothes and bring me back that robe. I think I'll take you up on that offer."

"Okay. I'll be right back."

Rupert has been here for several hours and is now back into his regular clothes as we are cozied up on the couch with a glass of wine in our hands. Dinner was superb, if I do say so myself. I haven't made Stuffed Chicken Florentine in years. It's nice having someone to cook for. It's quite chilly tonight, so we decided to get a fire going in the fireplace. "Hmm . . ." I sigh, cuddling into him more, "this is so nice."

"Very," he agrees. "Okay, love, let's start from the beginning.

"What do you mean?" I crank my neck to look up at him.

"I've been looking around the place since we got here. Everything I see says there were happy memories here. What gives? Why doesn't Julie want anything to do with you?"

"Oh, Rupert, please. We're having such a nice evening. Can we just leave it at that? I don't feel like spoiling it by describing to you what an awful mother I've been." I lean forward to sit up, removing myself from the comfort of his arms.

"I want to help you." He sits up as well.

"By prying?"

"I just want to know what the story is. Perhaps it's not as bad as everyone thinks it is."

"Did you ever tell a little lie to save face, but then finding yourself having to add another lie to back the first one up, and then another till you're in the middle of a snowball effect?" I turn to him.

"Once, and it's one that I will take to my grave," he admits.

"Well, I thought that too. Some lies get so big, though, you have to finally give up and begin unraveling the web you've woven. That's what I've been doing the past several months." I take another sip of my wine.

He reaches toward my face and pushes my hair behind my right ear. "And how far have you got?" he asks.

"I really don't know. Maddie calls the shots."

"Who's Maddie?"

"Oh goodness! Please don't tell anyone I said that," I plead.

"Wait . . . have you been seeing Julie's friend Maddie?"

"Yes. She's the only one who can help me . . . that I feel comfortable enough with." I stand up, suddenly feeling extremely nervous. "I think I've said enough. I should probably get you home now." I start to pace. Why am I pacing? I don't pace.

"Sit your lovely arse down." He grabs my hand mid-pace and drags me back to the sofa. "Stop panicking. I'm not going to say anything, love. Remember—it's them against us." He smacks my leg then squeezes it. "Now settle back down with me and tell me how all of this started." He scoots back again and waits for me with open arms. I feel like we're breaking some sort of rule by being so familiar with each other. Is this the norm nowadays? "Why are you hesitating? It was fine a few minutes ago."

"Don't you think it's a little odd for us to behave so familiarly with each other?"

"Are you analyzing things to get out of explaining your story?" he replies with a question. I wonder if he was in politics.

"No. I just don't know what the protocol is for this." I inch closer to him.

"The protocol, in any given situation, is to do what you feel comfortable doing when you feel comfortable doing it. There's nothing else to it, so stop trying to build some sort of moral case against a simple snuggle and chat on the sofa." He waves me back— impatiently, I may add.

"Okay, okay," I concede and skootch back into his arms that wrap around me like a cocoon. "I don't know where to begin."

"Start with the person who made you feel like you had to lie," he suggests.

"That would be me."

"Yes, but why?"

"Everyone warned me that David was the scum of the Earth, but I felt they were all wrong because I knew him best," I start.

"Was he your first love?"

"No. That was Allan." I feel myself get choked up. I haven't said Allan's name in years. The memory of him almost seems like it was a dream I once had, that he didn't really exist.

"What happened with Allan that made you end up with David?"

"He died in combat—Vietnam." I can feel my eyes fill up.

"I'm so sorry." He squeezes me to him.

"Me too. I would've had a much different life than I do now . . . a much better life," I add.

"Eh . . . you don't know that, love. You can only assume. If Allan had come home, he may have suffered terribly with PTSD or any other number of issues. Your assumption is based on the Allan you knew before he went off to war."

"You're right, I suppose." I take a few moments to collect myself. Allan always made me feel like I was worth everything in the world to him. All of my friends swooned over the way he treated me. My dad adored him. That alone made him gold because I worshipped my dad. "It's just . . . when I lost Allan, I lost everything. No one else treated me the way he did or looked at me the way he did. I was no longer this amazing catch. I wasn't much of anything anymore."

"Why do you say that?" he asks as his hands glide up and down my arms slowly before encircling me in them.

"I don't know. I guess it's just how I felt." I close my eyes and try to collect myself as all those old feelings swarm through my heart and mind. I suppose they are not so old; they've just resurfaced with Rupert's entrance into my life. "How else are you supposed to feel when the love of your life is gone? He wasn't just *gone* as in I could possibly fix it; it was final. There was nothing I could do. I wasn't naïve, you know. He was going off to war. Deep down inside, I knew there was a chance that our goodbyes would be our last, but you're not the one that that stuff is supposed to happen to. It happens to *other* people. I wasn't going to lose him. And, he was so brave, strong, smart, and a bonafide good person; surely God would keep him down here to keep balance in the universe, right?" I pause, taking in a deep, shaky breath. Rupert places a long, comforting kiss on the side of my head. "I can't blame those thoughts on youth, either; we all feel somewhat immortal no matter what age we are, right?" I turn my neck to get confirmation from him.

"I agree. I'm very sorry that you had to experience a loss like that, especially at such a young age." He squeezes me to him. "When did the arsehole in question come along?"

"A year or so later. I got involved with him on a bet." I cringe. Honestly, one of the most stupid things I've ever done in my life. But being stupid brought me Julie. Sometimes a something wonderful can come out of a something stupid.

"A bet?" Rupert sounds confused, rightfully so.

"Yes. I had a coworker friend that irritated the piss out of me. She kept getting on me about dating."

"Did she know about Allan?"

"Yes, but like I said, it had been over a year. I was getting asked out on dates—I just wasn't going. Well, she got on my damn nerves so much that I took her up on her bet: the next guy to ask me out— that I thought was attractive—I had to say yes. David was very attractive. If only I knew how ugly he was on the inside."

"Obviously you fell for him," Rupert leads.

"Yes. He had a wonderful way of making me feel like I was the luckiest girl in the world to have his attention." I shake my head in fury. "It's amazing how talented people can be. They find someone who is down for any number of particular reasons and they feed on it; they slowly destroy them as they build them up. I never in my life believed that I would fall for that sort of behavior, become a victim of brainwashing. But, there I was." I hold my hands out in disbelief as I try to shake the tears away. "Slowly, the isolation began."

"What do you mean?" He squeezes me to him again.

"He started putting thoughts in my head about my friends, especially Shannon. You see, Shannon already had two girls by then, and I would often help her out. He helped me come to the conclusion that it was the only reason why she kept me around—to be her babysitter."

"Did you really feel that way?"

"No. Not until he started pointing things out to me. Things like never having time for just me." I take in a deep breath. "It wasn't until later that I realized he manipulated the whole thing."

"How so?"

"She would set aside time for me, but then we somehow always had a function or something we were already committed to that he would swear up and down that he'd already told me about. Because it was hard for her to get free time, she could never reschedule. She could only be kid-free when others offered to help her out, but he made me think she did it on purpose . . . that she always picked the dates she knew I would otherwise be occupied. And, I fell for it. I was so young and naïve." I push my angry tears away.

"What happened after you got married?" he asks as he grabs my right hand and brings it back towards his lips, leaving a prolonged kiss on the back of it.

"I got pregnant with Julie. I was so excited, despite the way he was now treating me." I lean forward out of his grasp. "I don't want to talk about this anymore. I've said more than enough." I get up.

"Don't do that," he states with a sigh.

"Don't do what?" I snap.

"Don't stop because it's becoming uncomfortable. You need to work through this, Cynthia. It's troubling you. There's no sense in keeping things bottled up anymore."

"Oh! I should tell you everything, then? Dangle all of my weaknesses in front of you? As if I haven't already learned my lesson!" I shoot.

"I'm not David," he simply states.

"But you are a stranger! How would I know you aren't just like him? You haven't told me anything about yourself! Why should I trust you?" I point an accusing finger at him.

"What does your heart tell you?" he asks patiently. "I am an open book, love, all you have to do is ask."

"Why are you not married?" I don't waste a moment.

"I have only fallen in love once before; she was my best friend's girl. Obviously, I didn't pursue."

"Did he know?"

"No one has ever known, except you." He runs his hand through his hair, seemingly frustrated.

"Why me?" I almost gasp.

"It seems only right since you are sharing very difficult things with me."

"Are you Blake's father?" I ask without a second thought.

"No. I am only his godfather. I never consummated my love for his mother."

"So, it is his mother you are speaking of."

"Yes."

"She's the reason you never married? Have you been married?" I'm really not sure.

"Yes, she's the reason . . . up until now. No, I have never been married." He stands up and approaches me. "That was a long time ago, Cyn."

"Do you still love her?" I ask. It couldn't be helped, as you know.

"I still love the woman I used to love. I don't know her anymore." He gives me the sincerest look I have ever seen.

"So . . . what now?" My heart races. I've never felt so all over the map. This may be too much for me, what with the talk of David, and now this. This is very . . . well, this sort of thing doesn't occur in my life. I'm not sure how to respond to any of it.

"Now, there's you. I'm bloody smitten with ya." His hand reaches for my cheek.

"I don't understand why. None of this makes sense." I walk away before his hand lands.

"Love never makes sense—until it just does," he says.

"Love?" I question. "We don't even know each other." I turn away. This isn't right. I'm vulnerable, and he's sweet-talking his way in. I . . . this isn't right. I turn back to him swiftly. "I need you to leave."

"What? No. We need to talk about this!" He tries to stand his ground.

"You need to leave." I'm adamant. I'm not going to allow this to happen to me again!

"Cynthia, don't shut me out. You're scared; I understand. I don't want to rush you into anything, but I'm not David! I haven't got some masterminded plan to execute. Honestly! Please, don't shut me out," he pleads.

"This is too much for me." I'm completely honest. "I don't share like this, certainly not with strangers. I've said more than I have ever been willing to say, and I'm done. I need you to leave. I need to process things. This is overwhelming," I mention again.

"Cyn, you have spent the better part of your life, I gather, not letting things out of the bag. Of course this is overwhelming! It doesn't have to be. It can be very *freeing*. You just need to push through. You need to put your side of the story out in the universe. I'm just a prop. You need to put it out there for your own ears. You need to be able to forgive yourself . . . to understand yourself. I don't know the half you've been through, but it's not about me—it's about you. You need to be able to forgive yourself for whatever it is you think you need to be forgiven for. You are your first step, love. Not Shannon, Blake, or Julie! It's you! You need to forgive you!" The passion in his voice is so powerful, so compelling.

"I haven't had sex in years!" I scream at him. *What the hell was that? I've lost my damn mind.*

After a moment, he sputters, "That was so random!" He raises his voice, sounding exasperated. "Are you reaching or is this a real concern of yours? I honestly have no problem showing you how the pedals work, but if you're just throwing this out to distract me from the real problem, all I can say is: well done, lady! I can't think straight now!" He paces, hands gripping at his hair. I can't seem to restrain the giggle that erupts from my throat. He stops and stares at me, and I try to collect myself. "You're going to drive me—literally—mad!"

"I'm sorry," I offer.

"You're not!" he accuses, causing another giggle to erupt.

"David? Where is he?" he asks.

"Roasting marshmallows in Hell," I answer.

"So, he's dead," he confirms.

"Unless I'm in the middle of a *Days of Our Lives* episode, then yes."

"Cheeky thing." He winks.

"I don't know what that means."

"In this instance—smartass."

"Oh."

"How did he die?" he inquires.

"He gambled. He messed with the wrong people. He became a poster child for what happens when you mess with the wrong people." I shrug.

"The version you gave Julie?"

"Died a hero," I answer quickly. "Wait! How did you know I gave her a different scenario?"

"She doesn't hate him. Though, I suspect she should." He raises

167

an eyebrow.

"I didn't want her to be embarrassed." I lower my eyes to the carpet.

"That's enough for tonight," he says as he approaches me. I stand cemented to the ground. He lifts my chin with his forefinger. "We can cuddle and talk about present things. We can proceed to make out like a couple of teenagers. Or we can do both and let it lead to me showing you how the pedals work?" He lets his smile hit his eyes. *He's so handsome.*

"Cuddle." I'm barely audible because all I can think about is how much I would love to peddle right now.

Chapter Eighteen

Julie

Titspiring

WHY IS IT THAT WE DON'T THINK ABOUT JOINING THE BANDWAGON for something until it finally hits home for us? My ta-tas have been cleared. I should be so happy to move on with my unaffected life, but I can't. Two days ago, I was picturing myself as the older version of Jenny Stanzowitz. She was a girl that went to high school with us. Had mosquito bites for tits, poor thing. Now, my C's are staying, but I still feel like I should join the cause. I'll start by really sending my Yoplait lids in. They go pink every October. Ten cents for every lid goes to Breast Cancer research and whatnot. I save them; I never send them. I'm going to send them this time! Danny Wood, a member from New Kids on the Block, has an organization in honor of his mom Betty, whom he lost to breast cancer. I'm going to be more active there. My agenda is growing by the minute.

There's just as much relief as there is guilt for being cleared. Why was I spared? I feel unworthy. Is that weird? I feel weird about it. Maybe it's normal to feel weird? Or . . . you could be weird for feeling normal, right? I mean, what the fuck is "normal" anyway?

I pull out my phone.

Me: I'm having a cigarette-worthy moment.

Ava: You don't smoke.

CiCi: But kudos to you for rubbing one out anyways!

Maddie: Test results?

Charley: It's going to be okay. Where are you?

CiCi: Shit! Julie?

Ava: Let's go shopping.

CiCi: Julie?

Charley: Yes, let's go shopping! I need a new strap-on.

Me: Cancer does not want tickets to this circus.

Me: Congrats on keeping the love life spiced up, Charley!

Charley: What? Wait! OMG! Hahahaha! STRAPLESS!!! Fucking autocorrect!

Ava: Likely story, Charley. Remember, I like the realistic ones. ;)

Charley: Yeah, yeah—veins and shit.

Me: CiCi, I'm okay.

CiCi: I hate you.

Me: Are you crying?

CiCi: Yes, you fucking bitch! Don't ever scare me like that again!

Maddie: Don't cry out loud. Just keep it inside; learn how to text your feelings . . .

Jay: Fly gay and proud . . .

Charley: The token piece speaks . . .

Jay: An anthem beckoned me . . .

Me: Shopping?

CiCi: What are we buying?

Jay: Not class . . . it's so overrated and so "last year" anyhow!

Me: I don't know.

Maddie: What's the matter?

Me: Survivor's guilt.

Charley: Uhh, I don't think you can really claim that.

Me: I am a survivor! Don't take that shit away from me.

Ava: Okay, but that's a big statement. It's not really comparable to women who've really survived breast cancer.

Me: I'm a ginger girl in a not-so-friendly ginger world.

Jay: Ginger is SOOOO in this year.

Me: So, I have to survive THAT complex now!

Maddie: You're reaching, Jules.

Me: You're killing me, smalls.

Jay: Can we just meet up for dinner at Vic's?

CiCi: Is he going to make us pay for freeloading again?

Jay: You were the only one who got the shits, and it was the flu.

CiCi: He gave me the Man-flu!

Jay: Next time, put your balls away, and you won't get the Man-flu.

CiCi: I would, but then I'd lose your attention.

Charley: Can you 2 shut up? Are we meeting at Vic's?

Maddie: 7?

Ava: Working on a babysitter as we speak.

CiCi: We're not speaking; we're texting.

Me: Thank you, Captain Obvious.

Charley: There's only one captain around these parts . . .

Maddie: 👌

Me: Love you too, biatch. See you assholes at 7!

"Julie, come and have lunch, dear; it's ready."

Oh, did I forget to mention that I've been at Judith's most of the day, waiting for my results? The reason should be self-explanatory to you by now. I did, however, manage to attend the interview at Merrimack College. It's for an English Internship. I was all ready to nail it, but then . . . my interviewer was a woman. I'm just not into scissoring no matter how many times I joke about it with my friends.

"I don't think I'm going to get that internship," is how I respond.

"I'm sure they would be complete idiots not to give that to you."

She waves me on toward the kitchen. Yes, there is no eating in the living room at Mrs. St. Claire's house! "Is Blake able to take the day off?" she asks.

"Why—you want to get rid of me?" I sit at the table. "Tuna Salad?"

"Yes." She smiles.

"Yes, you want to get rid of me?" I act hurt as I lift half of the overstuffed croissant to take a bite.

"No, silly! It's Tuna." She shakes her head at me.

"I didn't ask him. There's really no need."

"Are you going to call your mother?" She's acting nonchalant, waving her napkin out to open and put on her lap, keeping her eyes everywhere but on me.

"I have no reason to," I say after clearing my throat.

"I just thought . . ." she hesitates.

"That a near-death experience would change my mind?" I finish for her. I let a light laugh out through my nose and shake my head. "She'd probably tell me that I didn't try hard enough."

"To get cancer?" Judith knits her brows together.

"She's an asshole, remember?" I roll my eyes then fix them back onto my sandwich. "I don't want to talk about it anymore."

"Yes, I know," she states quietly then begins to eat as well. And suddenly, it's awkwardly quiet in here. Judith has never made me feel guilty before, but she just has. I feel guilty about not calling my mom. It's that perpetual five-year-old in me, always looking out in the crowd for her.

"She abandoned me when I was five. It was only for a few months, but when you're five—it feels like forever and a day." I don't know why I even just thought about that or why it fell out of my mouth.

"You've never told me that. Where did you go? Who were you with?" Her right hand reaches across the table and lays on my left forearm.

"My grandmother; the one I didn't like. Ugh, I was so miserable. I wish she had sent me off to Nana's." I smile at the thought of my dad's mom. She was squishy and warm. Always smelled of Jean Nate. Of course, I didn't know what that scent was until I was older and smelled it in a store. I bought some that day even though CiCi teased me about smelling like an old lady. She wouldn't have said that if I had told her it was to keep the memory of one alive. She can be a prick, but she's a sensitive one.

"Nana?" she inquires and tilts her head slightly . . . just like Maddie. I can't help but smile at this.

"My dad's mom," I offer before taking another bite.

"Is she gone, dear?"

"I don't know. I haven't seen her or even heard about her since my dad passed away. I stopped asking a long time ago." I grab my glass of iced tea and take a long swallow (psst . . . that's what she said).

"What was her name?"

"Nana," I reiterate.

"Her real name." She laughs lightly at me.

"Edie. Well, Edythe. I don't remember her last name because it was different from mine. I just remember people calling her Edie." I shrug.

"Was she a young grandma or an old one?" she asks as she gets up and walks over to her junk drawer—the overly-organized junk drawer.

"I was little; anyone over the age of forty back then was an old lady. What are you jotting down, detective?" Her odd behavior is slightly amusing.

"I've been poking around on Ancestry.com. I want to see if I can dig up any info for you." She glances over her shoulder.

"Knock yourself out." I shrug. "I don't know that I have any more information to give you."

"This is a good start!" she states enthusiastically and heads back over. She sits, giving me one of her beaming smiles.

I carry on with my story about staying with Grandmommy Dearest. How she tried to "mold me into a proper young lady." Epic fail on her part, huh? As soon as I get to the memory of my first dance recital, how I stood on stage forever, peering out . . . straining to see my mother in the audience, I feel it all well up inside of me again. The feeling of abandonment. Feeling like I wasn't good enough. I had wished that my dad would show up, too. But, it was mostly Mom that I longed for. How could she leave me there? Didn't she love me? Was I not pretty or smart enough? Didn't I make her happy at all? That's too many questions for a five-year-old to ponder, especially when she's got her whole life ahead of her to ponder it.

"What did she say when she finally came home?" She collects my empty plate and puts it under hers.

"That she missed me. She had business." I play with the napkin, making little creases. "I always felt that was a lie."

"Why is that?"

"She cried all the time when she first got home. I think it's because Grandmother made her come home to me, and she didn't want to be there. She didn't want me. Maybe she felt stuck. She's never done or said anything to me to ever give me a different impression. She was very different after that trip, though. I was different," I add.

"How so?" She grabs my hands and squeezes them.

"I felt alone." I can feel my chin quiver.

"Where was your dad?"

"In and out. He had a lot of business trips." I let go of her hands and sweep mine through my hair to pull it up into a ponytail. "I wish he didn't travel so much; I could've spent more time with him. It's because of him that I'm comfortable. He left me a nice trust fund, as you know. He died saving a lady's life. You knew that, right?" I squint, trying to remember if I've ever told her.

"No, I didn't know that." She seems surprised.

"He jumped in front of a guy with a gun who had it directed at a woman that stupidly parked far away from the store, all for burning off the calories. The guy was trying to rob her. I don't know much more about it." And suddenly, I wonder why. It must have made the paper. My mother must have that article. It *must* say that in his obituary. "My mother never really talks about it," I add. "That's enough about that." I shake it off. "You know what? I think I'm gonna go pop in on Blake." I reach for the plates that she stacked up.

"I think that's a great idea. Leave these," she swats my hand, "I've got them."

"You sure?" I ask.

"Yes; go on—shoo!" She smiles.

"I knew you were trying to get rid of me," I say with a wink as I stand up.

"I'm not even going to dignify that with a reply. Do you want some tuna for home?" She stands up with me.

"If CiCi were here, she'd tell you that replying that you won't reply is an actual reply. No need for tuna; I'm going to have a fat sausage tonight." I wait to see if she catches on.

"I'm not going to dignify that one, either." She tries to stay serious but the tiny smile she's trying to hold back just keeps growing.

"I love you." I go around the table and go in for a hug. "Thanks for always being there for me." I squeeze.

"I love you, too . . . even without your filter," she says as I pull back from the hug and look at her. We stand here for a moment, looking into each other's eyes. *I am so thankful for her.* I pull her in for another quick hug, then abruptly let go and turn on my heel to leave. "Tell Maddie to call her mother!" she calls after me.

"She calls you at least twice a day, Ma!" I yell back as I make my way down the hall.

"It doesn't count when she does it in between clients so she doesn't have to stay on the phone long. I found a dress for her. I need to tell her about it and see if she wants me to pick it up," she continues, following me down the hall.

I turn to face her. "Did you take a picture of it?" I've told her to do this a million times. I've shown her how to send pics *a million times.*

"Yes, but it doesn't do it justice, so I want to tell her about it."

"And that would be why she only calls in between clients." I smirk. "You drive her crazy sometimes with your need to explain every detail."

"Well, it's who I am; she needs to get over it." She shrugs.

"I'll be sure to pass that on." I laugh and give her another kiss on the cheek. "Bye, Ma!" I say in an exaggerated manner as I turn to leave—again.

"Bye, dear. Give Blake our love!" She waves as I pick up my pace down her walkway.

You ever get a random weird feeling that you can't shake off?

I think it's just from all of the recent stress and anxiety, but today's conversation with Judith led me in directions I wasn't expecting to talk or—quite frankly—think about. And it's just . . . I don't know; I feel weird.

I hit the voice dial on my car, "Call Blake," I order.

"Calling Blake's Auto . . ."

"No, you dumb shit!" I yell, stopping the call. I press it again, "Call Bah-lake," I say it slowly.

"Calling Bass Lake Golf Course."

"Ugggh! You're mother's a whore!" I hit end.

At the red light, I physically dial the Brit's number. "Why can't I ever get my car to call you?" I ask as soon as he picks up.

"What did you say to it?" There's a little mirth in his voice that is quite suspicious.

"I asked it to call you. I said, 'Call Blake.'"

"Well, that's why then."

"What else would I say?" I'm getting a little frustrated.

"You should've asked to call The Peen in Your Ass," he simply states. Yes, he would simply state that because it would be the obvious selection (to him) to make—simply because he changes his name in my phone as often as the ringtone! It's obnoxious, but it really is the only stupid thing he does. Most of the time it cracks me up. Today? Not so much. I'm actually on the verge of tears. I'm taking deep breaths because I don't want to lash out at him. I'm trying to come to him for comfort. "Love?"

"Where are you?" I ask just as the skies open up and a torrential downpour happens, taking away my thunder.

"The pub. Are you okay?" he asks, his voice laced with concern.

"I'll be there in a few. I'm fine. I just need you," I admit.

"Okay, love. I'll be waiting. Wait!" he says quickly. "Is this an 'I need you' like a hold you in my arms and keep my mouth shut sort of need you or is it a keep my mouth shut as I drag you into a dark room, booty call sort of need you? I think it's only right I should be prepared; I don't want to fuck about, doing the wrong thing."

God, I love him . . .

"Be prepared for both . . . as you know," I advise.

"Right! I'll welcome you with a full salute and open arms. I'll let you decide."

"I love you." I feel like I can breathe a little easier. Just one little, simple dose of him on the phone even helps. How did I ever get so lucky?

"And I love you."

"See you in five." I hang up.

Chapter Nineteen

Blake

Spilling the Seed

"Jonathan, I'm heading into my office," I call down the bar to him.

"Okay, boss." He smiles. God love him; he's always happy!

"I'm expecting Julie at any moment. Can you please send her my way?" I ask.

"Sure thing!"

I hope it's a sure thing! I feel like a complete arse thinking like this, but Julie's been a bit off lately, and that has made its way into our bedroom. It's understandable, of course. I'm not a complete arsehole. It's just been hard (*really, really fecking hard!*) not being able to touch her the way I want to.

To be honest, part of me wishes she wasn't stopping by. I feel weird keeping her mother's visit from her. I'm not sure if that's the right thing to do. I don't know *what* to do about that. It's just one of those awkward situations where you're damned if you do and damned if you don't. *I hope she wants sex.* Yes, that would be much easier . . . more distracting. Right? I mean, what would you do? Would you tell her? I don't even know how Cynthia knew? I feel as if there are a can of worms that I want no part in helping to open. *However!* If I don't say anything, I'm royally screwed that way. So, what do I do? I think I'm going to plead with The Almighty to help me find a way to distract her long enough to come to the correct plan of action. That's all I can come up with at the mo'.

I make my way into my office and quickly clear most of the things off my desk in case, you know. Taking a seat, I log into my computer and start looking at the numbers. I am doing spectacularly well. I don't want to get too used to these additional profits, though; they're only there because we're understaffed. I am really hoping to change all of that soon. Kyle is still helping me. Although, Jonathan has been the best help anyone could give me.

I look up as I hear my door open. Julie closes it behind her and locks it. "Unzip your pants, Blake," she commands. I obey because . . .

Sex-explanatory, right, loves?
Let's carry on then.

She makes her way over to me and drops to her knees just as I've finished revealing myself for her. I should be embarrassed to admit that I'm already rock solid, but I'm rather proud and impressed with myself. Her smirk tells me she is too.

Gently, she takes hold of me in her hand. Her eyes slowly rise to look me in the face, and she holds her stare like an innocent schoolgirl (older . . . legal one, by the way! Don't be getting your panties in a knot, thinking me a perv!). I can barely control the rhythm of my breathing. I'm hypnotized. Her green eyes, commanding my submission.

Jesus, I wish she would stop reading those books to me!

Julie licks her lips slowly, soliciting a low growl from me. She brings her focus to the bomb that is ready to detonate in her hand.

I know how ridiculous that sounds, but that's what it feels like. I bite my bottom lip, anticipating her tongue, and she doesn't disappoint. My eyes roll into the back of my head as her tongue licks up the length of my cock. A few quick laps at my tip and my hips are already flying out of my seat. I exhale forcibly as she takes me in almost to the base. She gags slightly. Fuck if I didn't just get harder from that. I close my eyes, trying to keep my wits about me. Trying to not blow my load so quickly. It's not an easy feat; she's working me good, tearing down my defenses. Just as I'm about to lose my mind from the ball cupping and whatnot, she pulls away. I open my eyes in confusion and disbelief, only to find her standing up and sliding her panties down from under her skirt. She plants her arse onto my desk and spreads wide, waving me with her long, beautiful finger. The same finger that is now slowly sliding inside of her. She throws her head back as she adds a second one. I am sitting here dumbstruck . . . mesmerized, really. Watching her pleasure herself is almost more than I can bear.

I stand up, my hand working on my cock, prepping it. I pat her hand gently, letting her know it's my turn. Her eyes open and she stares at me with that stare that makes my cock twitch. She brings her fingers up to her mouth and slowly slips them in, sucking her taste off them. I lean in to kiss her, once she pulls her fingers out. "What do you want, Julie?" I ask breathlessly.

"Gentle tongue; hard fucking," she answers calmly without hesitation. That is her favorite combo. I give her another chaste kiss, then work my way down. I taste her. *Mmm.* I'm slow and methodical, driving her insane. I take my time and listen to the sounds that escape her throat. She *loves* when I drive her crazy with a slow tongue. It makes her so wild. So out of control. Once she starts begging "please" over and over again, I torture her for another five or so minutes. It's when she's on the line of giving up and wanting to cry from frustration that I slam into her. *She's just about there . . .*

"Blake!" she screams. *Oh, fuck!* I take in some deep breaths, trying to talk myself down from the ledge. "Oh, please," she begs again. I pull back and slam into her even harder. I let go and pray I can get her there before I lose any self-control. She throws her ankles onto my shoulders and cheers on my efforts. I work harder, pumping faster than I can ever remember. I cover her mouth as well because she's loud as fucking hell. I love it; don't get me wrong, but no one needs to hear what my lady sounds like in bed . . . er, on my desk.

Her legs start to shake, and I can feel her begin to milk me— *thank God!* I let out a sequence of harsh breaths as I build up to the point of losing all self-control. I break my hand away from her mouth to grasp both of her hips, pulling her up toward me to give me the perfect leverage. She slaps her own hands against her mouth to keep quiet. *Good girl.* I grit my teeth as my balls tighten. My pace quickens, encouraging my release.

And then it happens . . .

The most glorious feeling in the world.

"*Fuck!*" I yell. *That sounds so civil compared to the Neanderthal I must've just sounded like.* I take on a slow, deep pace as my seed spills inside of her.

Oh, for fuck's sake!

One last thrust and I collapse on top of her. "I beg of you; please don't read me any more passages from those books," I plead.

"What are you talking about?" she asks as her fingers play with my hair.

"I just had the actual thought that I was *spilling my seed* inside of you. Do you know how bloody ridiculous that sounds?" I half-heartedly complain. Julie giggles, and I raise my head to look into her eyes.

"Well, you did make my sex *very* moist."

"Were you waiting for that with bated breath?" I kiss her smile.

"I almost forgot to exhale," she offers, and we both laugh. Slowly, I climb off of her and make my way into my private bathroom. I grab the dump wipes (Kyle's name for them that we all deemed genius because it sounds more manly than flushable wipes), clean myself off, and then make my way back out to clean her. However, I stop dead in my tracks, mesmerized by the site of Julie having another go at herself. Her lips form a beautiful "O" shape as she reaches her climax. Her body visibly relaxes. "That was utterly beautiful, love," I say in sheer wonderment.

"It felt beautiful," she replies. I bite my smile back and make my way over to her. "What's that look for?" She leans up on her elbows as I part her legs.

"I just love you," I say as I begin to clean her up.

"Do you have nice memories of your parents?" Her voice is quiet and vulnerable. That gets my attention more than the odd and random question she just asked me.

"Do you mean with me or memories of them together?" I try to clarify.

"Them." She sits up when I finish.

"From when I was younger, yes. They seemed very happy. But, I also remember them arguing a lot. Well, it felt like it was a lot. Probably because I was a young chap. Kids don't like to hear their parents argue." I help her off the desk and grab her panties from where she chucked them. She rolls her eyes as I bring them up to my nose for a sniff. *It couldn't be helped.* "Why do you ask?" I offer them back to her.

"I don't have any nice memories. Nothing. Odd, right?"

"No, I don't think it is. You lost your father at a very young age; we don't remember every detail of our youth, especially the younger years." I pull my jeans up and buckle my belt.

"I have tons of memories from then; I don't have any of them together. . . in a nice way. They always seemed to be co-existing, not that I knew what that was when I was a kid."

"Why are you thinking about this?" I palm her face and wait for her eyes to meet mine.

"I don't know. Things just . . ." She shakes her head slightly like she's trying to figure out what she's feeling or trying to say. "Things I never really thought about before and memories I haven't visited in years surfaced today. It's making me feel strange—off."

"Well, you're very intuitive, love." I kiss her forehead gently.

"I am?" She pulls back slightly.

"Yes. Look at the first time we met," I offer.

"What about it?" Her brows knit together.

"Well, you knew from the moment that you saw me that I would be the love of your life. That's why you fought me off so much, remember?" I half smile.

"Oh yeah . . . it's all coming back to me now." She laughs. "You're right, though; I am intuitive because I also remember thinking you would probably be a dumbass. I nailed that shit."

"You certainly did," I humor her.

"I want to find my nana."

"I didn't know you had a nana that was missing."

"You don't know a lot of things about me."

"It's very intriguing." I lean in and sweep her lips.

"That's how I keep you coming back for more. Well, that and my super pussy, of course." She kisses me again, and I laugh against her lips. The first time I manned up and went to the store to buy Julie tampons, I had to call her to coach me through. The variations are enough to make you rip your hair out. She broke down the code for me like this:

Brand: Playtex (because I like to play with her pussy).

Super: Because she has a super pussy.

I have not fucked up the tampon order once! She's a genius, right?

"Well, now that you've gotten that out of your system, shall we have a cuddle?" I jerk my head in the direction of the couch. It's quite comfortable—I have spent many nights on it. She simply nods. I take her hands, guiding her over as I walk backwards. "Do you want to talk at all?" I ask as we get comfy on the couch; my back up against the arm, legs stretched out with her between them. I wrap my arms around her and squeeze her to me tightly for a moment.

"No," she breathes. "I just want to be held."

"As you wish." I kiss the top of her head.

"Do you think I should reach out to my mother?" she asks after lasting a whole two minutes of enduring silence.

"What does your heart tell you?" I rest my chin on her ginger locks, breathing in the lovely and familiar scent of her shampoo. My stomach begins to slowly knot itself at the mention of her mother. *Should I tell her?*

"My heart always tells me to reach out to her, but my mind is screaming at my heart to shut the fuck up, all the while, pointing out the scars my mother has left." She stops, turns her head and looks up at me, "I don't know what to do," she admits.

"Maybe it's best to wait, then," I suggest. "This is the longest you've gone without talking to her. I understand that it's just as hard as it is easy. But, perhaps this has been best."

"You think she'll finally come to her senses this time because I stood my ground so long?"

"No," I squeeze her to me again, "I think you will finally come to yours."

"Come to mine? What do you mean by that?" She sits up and turns towards me.

"I mean," I lean forward and reach to palm her right cheek, "that having this length of time apart from her may help you to realize that you cannot change her behavior, only your expectation of it. I think that the best way for you to have any sort of relationship with your mother is to accept that she will never be all that you imagine her to be as a mother. It's not in her. She only hurts you because you allow it by not accepting who she is." I wait for her to say something, but she remains quiet, drawing swirls on my knee with her finger. "What she's taught you is just as—if not more—important as anything Judith or any of the other moms have taught you. She's taught you how *not* to be. Because of that, you will always have people around you, who love you; you will never be alone." I stop as soon as her beautiful green eyes come up to meet mine. Tears are pooling, threatening to run down her cheeks.

Just as one slips down, "I don't want her to be alone," her voice cracks. "I shouldn't care. That's what pisses me off the most. At the end of the day, though, she's still my mom. I don't want her or anyone to feel as alone as she has always made me feel. It's awful." She pulls back to move my hand off her face and runs the back of her hand across her nose. I turn and reach over to the small bookshelf, I keep all my music on, and grab the box of tissues. I retrieve a few and hand them to her.

"I can understand all of that, Jules, but I also understand that you've just gone through an emotional rollercoaster which may be heightening your emotions on this matter. I truly believe you should give yourself a few days before you make this decision. Make sure it's what you really want and not what you think you should want."

"I'm sure you're right. This week has been tough. I feel relieved and guilty all at the same time," she confesses.

"Guilty?" I question.

"Yeah. I mean, of all the women on this planet, why do I get to be one of the lucky ones? What's so great about me? I feel awful for the other women who didn't get such great news today."

"Why not you? I could give you a list of what's so great about you that would keep us in this office for at least a week!" I challenge her. Of all the things to say!

"Don't be upset with me." She grabs my hands. "This week has just made me think a lot, not just about my mother but many things. I feel like I have no roots. I . . ." she trails off, bringing her attention to the floor instead of me. "I don't know what happened to my family. My mother and grandmother are all I know. I used to know and love more. I cherished my nana. I feel almost as if I was trained to forget about her. This all sounds so stupid coming out of my mouth." She shakes her head as if willing the thoughts away. "I just feel like I have no roots or family. I know I have the girls and their families, but I don't have my own. I want my own." She sniffles, letting go of my hands to bring the tissue back up to her nose.

"Let me be your family," I blurt.

"What?" She looks up at me.

"Build your own roots . . . with me. Let me be your family. Marry me, Julie." *Once a train starts, it's hard to stop it.*

"Blake."

"Wait! Just hear me out!" I beg. "You can't change the past, Julie. You can search for the people from it, but you may never find what you think you will. You know what you have in front of you. Build on that . . . bet on it . . . trust in it . . . in me. You can't fully have a future if you're always looking over your shoulder into the past. You can try to understand the past, forgive it, but you can never change it. The only thing you can change is your future, and that starts by making the right decisions in the present. I'm your present, Julie. I want to be your future. And, someday, I want to be part of your past—the happy memories. To have those happy memories of the past, we have to move on to our future. I can't imagine anyone but you to be a part of all my future past happy memories. Make this moment one of them, love; say you'll marry me." I finish, my heart nearly beating out of my chest.

This was not a planned event, just so you know.

And, I'm nearly shitting my trousers.

Romantic, aye?

She stares at me, making my anxiety climb up even higher on that mountain that anxiety creates. Finally, she lets out an aggressive breath and stands up. "I can't believe you just made this about you," she states. "I came here to lean on you, and you just tried to use my vulnerability to your advantage. I can't believe you. I can't believe you just did this." Her calmness should piss me off even more, but I think I'm already past my max.

"I didn't make this about me," I say through my teeth, trying to keep my anger at bay.

"Yes, you did! I'm surprised you didn't throw in the hundred kids you want to have! You have some nerve, Blake!" she yells as she grabs her purse. Because she's getting ready to run.

Anyone here shocked?

"For Christ's sake, Julie—just tell me you don't want to marry me! Spare us both the theatrics and just fucking say it!" I yell back at her. My chest is getting tighter by the minute, no doubt due to my heart shattering.

She stops in her tracks. She's visibly shaken; tears are streaming down her face, her breath is rapid, and her chin is trembling. "I don't want to lose you," she cries.

Have you ever had the feeling of your heart dropping?

Does it make you gasp, too?

I rush towards her, grasping her face in my hands, pulling her to me. "I'll take it," I announce before slamming my mouth against hers. She lets out one of those heart-dropping gasps, and we lose ourselves in our kiss.

See, the moment she admitted she didn't want to lose me, she admitted to me that I am the only one she can see in her future, as well. She's scared of formalities. It's going to take a while longer, but we are getting there—we really are.

"I have to go and meet the girls," she says as we finally detach our lips.

"Where will you be?" I give her another soft kiss and lean my forehead against hers.

"Vic's."

"Girls only?"

"Yes."

"Call me if you drink," I demand.

"I will be drinking."

"Call me when you need me to pick you up."

"I will."

"Can't they meet you here?" I really don't want her to leave.

"No. It will be too uncomfortable to talk about you behind your back," she says. I'd tell you she's joking, but we both know she isn't. I'm confident, though; if she tells them about my proposal, they will verbally kick her arse. I'm sure she won't mention it at all . . . sadly.

"I love you. Be safe, love." I give her another kiss.

"Love you, too. We just had unprotected sex; it's a little too late for the 'be safe' speech." She winks. I only reply with a smile before she walks out of my office.

Chapter Twenty

Julie

We're Only Human

I LOOK DOWN AT MY PURSE TO GET MY PHONE OUT AS I MAKE MY way out of Blake's office and into the bar. I'm running pretty late, and Maddie will have my ass for it.

Me: Sorry, I'm running late!

Maddie: Me too, actually!

CiCi: You both got cock-blocked, didn't you?

Ava: Me too!

Charley: Good for you, Ava!!!

Ava: Huh?

CiCi: Just hurry up! I can only gaze into my sister's eyes for so long.

Charley: Yes, please! It's like some weird Single Guy Convention here!

Me: Great! We'll bring our tits!

Ava: I'm still trying to find mine.

Maddie: Shut up; your tits look great! See you all in 10!

Just then, I walk right into someone who should've seen I was busy texting and moved out of my way. *The nerve of some people!* I look up. "Hi," he says nervously or, at least, he seems nervous.

"Yeah, I'm not available for D—all of the above; I've got a boy-friend, and I've got plenty of friends. I'm about to have a drink with them, which means, I have no time. This place is slamming, though. You should definitely hang around till you see the next whatever-it-is-you're-looking-for walk through that door. Good luck, and God's speed. Look out for pedestrians who text. Excuse me, please." I try to get around him.

"I saw you at the comedy club the other night. You were hyster-ical." Brave soul, talking to me like this. Didn't I just dismiss him? I need to have drinks with my girls and not share Blake's proposal with them.

"That was a one-time deal, and I don't give autographs. If you don't mind; I'm running late," I say with a bit more impatience. There's something oddly familiar about this guy. *Fellow Ginger!* "Dude, were you outside the club that night?" I ask.

"Yes!" Okay, a little too excited about that, he is.

"Are you stalking me?"

"No! I mean . . . no." His face has just gone fire-hydrant red.

"I need to go. I'm late," I reiterate.

"Sure. Uhh . . . great talking to you. I feel like we really con-nected." His statement is flat.

"Was that sarcasm?" I jerk my head back slightly.

"One-hundred percent." He shoves his hands into his jean pockets and moves out of my way.

"Impressive delivery," I remark.

"Glad you approve," he says as I walk away. I turn my head back toward him because I could almost swear he said my name after that statement, but he's already looking away. *Fucking weird.* At least I have something to offer the girls other than my tits-epic scare and Blake's plea for matrimony!

IT TAKES ME about ten minutes, but I finally reach Stavros (Vic's restaurant). I walk in, and the girls wave me down. My eyes scan the place from left to right as I make my way over to them. *What. In. The. Actual. Fuck?* I shit you not; this place is full of men in dark suits. Besides the GEGs, there are maybe five or six other women that I can easily see. It's like Alaska up in this bitch—*The odds are good, but the goods are odd.* That's the state's unofficial slogan because they have thirteen men for every woman. You know why? Because most women hate to be fucking cold; I know I do. All you ever see about Alaska is glaciers. It's beautiful. I'd like to visit someday. However, they should share with people whether it's ever friggin' warm there; they may get a few extra girls to even that shit out. *Just sayin'* . . .

"You guys weren't kidding!" I greet them as I arrive at the table, my eyes bulging wide-open for emphasis. "Did Vic tell you what the hell is going on?" I take a seat.

"Yeah, there's some sort of reunion going on, and his contact at the Sheraton has been directing them here instead of suggesting their own restaurant. I guess it's the guy's last *'fuck you'* to his boss," Charley updates me.

"Oh. So weird." I take another look around. "I wonder what kind of reunion it is." I unroll my napkin and place it on my lap.

"I'm guessing it's the sword-crossing alumni from an all-boys school." CiCi glances around, nodding slightly as if to agree with herself.

"Sounds legit." I shrug. "Where're the other asswhores? I can't believe I got here before they did." I open the menu.

"Maddie's in the bathroom, and Ava just walked in the door, wearing the same expression you had just a minute ago." Charley waves her cocktail in that direction. We all wave her down.

She hastily makes her way over to us and sits down abruptly. "Is it just me, or did you all feel like a big vagina on legs, walking over to the table? What the fudge is going on here?"

"Fudge?" CiCi looks at Ava like she smells something bad.

"I'm trying not to curse," she answers.

"This is the big kid table, babe; you can drop the f-bomb." I wink.

"Are we sure about that?" Maddie asks as she sits down.

"I'm surprised you made it back alive, shortstack." CiCi grabs her beer and takes a swig.

"Alive, but not unscathed. I had multiple offers of various, complex things." She bites her lip then giggles.

"Listen," CiCi gains our attention, "order whatever you want; I'm treating."

We all stare at her as she looks down at the menu.

Charley clears her throat. "You're treating?" she asks.

"Huh?" CiCi looks up at her.

"You're treating?" she asks again . . . apprehensively.

"Absolutely not." She shakes her head.

"Why would you offer to, then?" Charley is a glutton for punishment.

"I like to check from time to time." CiCi goes back to looking at her menu.

"Check what?" Charley, of course.

"To see if I'm over my 'cheap bitch' phase."

"Vic is not even going to charge us," Charley states with irritation. The rest of us girls just look at each other and silently laugh.

"That's true," Ceese looks up again, "So, order what you want. I'll take care of the bill tonight. Charley, you can take care of the tip."

"I'm sure she's heard that line a few times." I laugh.

"Fuck you," Charley mumbles toward CiCi.

"That's *fudge* you, please. Ava's cutting back on the big kid words; let's be respectful."

"Okay, let's get right to the point of this meeting, please." Maddie rounds the wagons.

"My tit is clear," I announce.

"Yes, we know. Why are you being a spaz about it?" CiCi asks.

"I just don't understand," I admit.

"You don't have cancer; what is there to not understand?" CiCi seems very irritated, like she wants to change the subject.

"Why me? Why do I deserve to live out my life with no worry?" I feel hostile. I'm sure I sound that way as well. "Where the fuck are our drinks?" I look around. Drinks will make this all go away, right?

"Guilt after a feeling of relief is normal, Julie. It's okay to feel like this," Maddie gives her professional opinion.

"I'd like to talk to my friend and not the professional, please," I snap.

"I am speaking as your friend," she states in a very perturbed manner.

"Whatever . . ." I trail off. I have nothing else to offer as a good response, so . . .

"There's no reason to feel like this. But, it's a great start to doing some good." Maddie offers me an encouraging smile.

"I know that, but I feel even stupider for it."

"That makes no sense." Ava puts her menu down to give me her undivided attention.

"Yeah, it does. I had a scare and now, all of the sudden, I'm gonna go all Joan of Arc for the cause? I'll look like a fraud," I answer truthfully.

"I don't think that's true." CiCi looks up again. "Sometimes we don't realize what our cause should be until it personally affects us. That's how most people get involved in the charities they are involved in. I donate to a lot of things I wouldn't have donated to before: MSAA, ASPCA, and BJKC." She shrugs.

"Wait," Maddie holds up her hand, "I know that MSAA is for Multiple Sclerosis and ASPCA is for animals, but what the hell is BJKC?"

"Yeah, what is that?" I add.

"Blow Jobs for Kyle Cooper," she answers. "I'd venture to say his *organ* thinks it's a very successful campaign." She waggles her eyebrows.

"You're such an asshole," I say through a laugh.

"True dat."

"Well, they say that charity begins in the home . . ." Maddie trails off.

"Yeah, *they* tend to say a lot of bullspit," Ava mentions with air quotes.

"Bullspit, huh?" CiCi asks. "Clever. I like that one."

"Why, thank you!" She smiles brightly.

"Where the hell is Jay?" I blurt having just realized he wasn't here.

"He had a last-minute emergency meeting with a client. Let's order. I'm hungry," Charley practically whines and starts waving the waiter down.

Just then, a few runners come to our table with food. "Moussaka?" the girl asks.

"That's me," CiCi says.

"Did you guys order our food ahead?" I ask.

"No," Charley answers, "but we order the same shit all the time; I'm sure Vic put it in, God Bless his soul . . ." She grabs hers.

Food is just about the only thing that will shut our mouths simultaneously. "So, the weirdest thing happened," I say after my fifth or so bite. What? I didn't say they all stay shut forever! "When I was leaving the pub to come here, I literally bumped into this guy."

"I bet you were texting. You always bump into people and things when you are walking and texting; how is this weird?" CiCi rolls her eyes.

"Shut up! Anyways, he tries to strike up a conversation with me and proceeds to tell me that he saw my act the other night."

"In Boston?" Maddie asks.

"No, at the Apollo—of course in Boston!" I can't believe I

caught that before CiCi did. "I asked him if he was stalking me."

"And?" Ava and Charley ask together.

"He said no. It was almost like he was appalled that I even asked that. But, that's so random. I mean, what are the chances?" I shake my head, feeling very eerie about this encounter. "So, if I go missing . . ." I joke, but not really.

"Did he creep you out?" Maddie asks.

"You mean him, in general?"

"Yeah."

"No. But I think that is freaking me out more. It's always the people you think are regular, couldn't-hurt-a-fly, Joes who end up being serial killers." An unexpected chill comes over me, making me shiver. The girls ask me to describe him, and so I do. We move on to other topics like Caroline's visit. Charley won't talk to Caroline. CiCi is swinging back and forth between pissed and on the verge of tears. Maddie, God love her, is coaching them both through as much as they will let her. "How's your mom doing with this?" I ask to try to change course someway.

"Pah! She hasn't told her! She's just here for an *undetermined* amount of time," Ceese informs us. "It's just as well. Our mother has enough on her plate. Though, I'm sure she'd appreciate having some of the focus off of her for once."

"Aren't your parents questioning what's going on? Did she bring the kids or is it just her?" Ava seems just as confused as I am by all this.

"Alone," Charley states disapprovingly.

"Have you all called Caitlyn and Colleen?" Maddie grabs her glass of wine and takes a sip.

"Yeah. They are fine. What's going on with you, Ava?" She changes the subject abruptly.

"Lists. Working through them. Staying focused. Staying positive. Focusing," she mentions again.

"Lists? What kind of lists? Mitch has an amazing list of different ways to referencing a guy whacking off; it's quite educational." She snorts.

"Not that kind of list." She smiles despite herself, I think. "No. I have my first appointment next week with a colleague of Maddie's. Until then, I'm trying to organize my feelings."

"Kyle can help you with that. He'll even make you pie charts and shit."

"I'm sure he would, but this is something I need to do for myself." She takes another bite of food and gives Charley "the look." I'm sure she didn't think any of us saw that, but I did. Charley's her number one, and she wants her to change the subject.

"Shit, Maddie, the holidays are coming again; did you guys get Dec's schedule yet?" Charley asks.

"Oh, we got that a month ago. Or, I should say that *I* got it a month ago. I'm sure he had it way before. I survived last season. I'm sure it will all work out." She waves her off unconvincingly.

"Oh my God! I forgot to tell you all; Bennett went into a bouncy house! He did the slides and all!" Charley practically cries with excitement.

"You're kidding me! When did he do that?" CiCi is right there with her. Bennett is a sensory kid. Two months ago, he'd cry if he even thought you were going to put him in a bouncy house.

"Yesterday. He got invited to a birthday party, so, of course we went. I didn't care that it was at a bouncy house place," she explains. Though, she doesn't have to; he's overlooked a lot by peers and other parents. It breaks Charley's heart more than it does her son's. "I didn't tell him where the party was. When we got there, his best friend, Molly, ran right up to him. She grabbed his hand and took him around, showing him everything. It was the sweetest, most endearing thing I've ever seen in my life. What an old, patient soul that girl has. She asked him if he would go in with her. He said, 'Okay!' just like that." She shrugs in disbelief. "I couldn't believe my eyes." She pulls out her phone. "Look at his face—pure joy." She shows us the pics. "That was such a great 'mom' moment. All the hard work, hours of therapy, struggling before I met Mitch because I put Bennett's needs first . . . it all paid off." She's full-on crying now. "I'm sorry," she tries to wipe the tears away, "it's just—when you're a mom, it's so easy to point out everything you think you are doing wrong. When what you've done is so right, it slaps you in the face—in a good way—it's overwhelming."

"Is that what it really feels like? I mean, being a mom . . . you really think you are doing it all wrong?" I ask because I've never heard anyone come out and actually say this. I've heard comments in jest, but you don't think they *really* feel that way.

"Oh, I fuck up on a daily basis," she states in a comically exacerbated way.

"But you're a great mom."

"Thanks, Jules, but that doesn't mean I don't make mistakes."

"But you have a great mom. That helps." I bring my focus back to my food.

"Wait!" Ceese yelps. "Is there a hostage situation going on in your uterus?"

"What?" I look up.

"Oh my God! Are you pregnant?" Charley screeches excitedly. I look around at all of them. These assholes are looking at me like I'm about to tell them the best news they've ever heard in their lives.

"No." I burst their bubble.

"Are you trying?" Maddie asks.

"No." I shovel a forkful of food in my mouth.

"You're gonna be a great mom," Ava throws out the final thought on this subject. I know it's final because I just gave CiCi "the look."

"Why don't we do a fundraiser concert through *Two Steps Forward*? We can split the proceeds between *MSAA* and *Remember Betty*," CiCi offers. *Two Steps Forward* is an organization that

Mitch and Charley started about a year ago. They haven't opened their doors yet as they have only recently found a location down in Boston. It's projected to officially open next spring or so. Right now, they have been working on getting the right people involved to help with all the services they want to offer. It's basically a one-stop shop for all needs. Getting help in any capacity for anything can be such an ordeal. They want to make it so that if you come to them for a service that they do not provide, they want to be able to tell you exactly where you can go for that service without having to jump through an obstacle course. They just want to be able to help people with whatever they are going through. They want to give hope without frustration. We're all signed up in some way or another to help out where we can. I'm excited about it. I'll be helping out with the education department, teaching GED classes and refresher courses to take college entrance exams for adults that have been out of school a long time.

"That's a great idea!" Charley grabs Ceese's arm. It really is. I know Mitch will be on board since his mother, too, had MS and ultimately died from breast cancer.

"Well, it looks like we have a new project on our hands," Maddie surmises and grabs her phone. "We should have a meeting asap to get a team in place. This could get really big."

"Agreed." Charley nods, then picks up her glass. "To the greatest women I know."

"To the GEGs!" we all yell and clink glasses.

I think we're all having a great "human" moment.

Note the flying of our capes.

Chapter Twenty-One

Cynthia

Keeping Company

It's been a week since my meltdown in front of Rupert. We've been solid since. No, I have not been pedaling. I'm old-fashioned. Also, I'm nervous. I don't exactly have anyone to talk to about this. Karma really is a bitch, I've discovered. If Julie and I had the kind of relationship we should've had, I could easily talk to her about this. I don't think she would cringe like other daughters would. She's really cool and laid back about stuff like this. I used to make her very aware of my displeasure with this personality trait of hers. Self-reflection really is a bitch. I'm aware now that I was jealous, not disgusted. It represents a freedom that I didn't allow myself.

I'm about to see Maddie. I just don't feel that we are at the point in our relationship where I can ask her how I should be groomed these days in the nether region. I have thought to ask Shannon because even if she doesn't keep up with the latest trend, she would know because of her girls, right? However, she's been distracted with Caroline's visit. It was very impromptu. She doesn't have her family with her, and she hasn't been forthcoming with why she is here or how long she will stay. She has been spending a lot of time with Preston, Maddie's brother. It's all been unnerving for Shannon. She even accused Jack of keeping information about her condition from her. I can understand why she would think that. Your daughter randomly shows up out of the blue with no end date for her visit in sight? It does look like she's there to be with Shannon for the end of her life. Charley and CiCi brought her to her senses, though. Poor Jack. He looked so tired yesterday when I popped in.

Ah . . . yesterday. Yesterday was a big day. That visit was monumental. What happened? Oh boy. Well, after I arrived, I went straight to the bathroom. I took a little longer than usual because I was contemplating the landscaping possibilities. I know—TMI. Sorry. I got moving once I heard yelling down the hall. When I made it down to the kitchen, Caroline was yelling at Shannon and Jack. Not scolding them, but yelling about what a shit job CiCi and Charley are doing with their care. That it doesn't take a rocket scientist to find good doctors. "I told them two years ago you needed to sell this house! You can't take care of yourselves, let along the burden of this old place! I don't know why you guys have them as your POAs. They don't know what they are doing!"

My blood was boiling. My friend just sat in her chair looking down like if she just stayed quiet, Caroline would eventually shut up. We all know that is not like Shannon at all. In all the catching up we've been doing, Shannon's told me about the feud with the girls. Colleen, Caitlyn, and Caroline are all bitter about Charley and CiCi having Power of Attorney over both parents in line, of course, after Jack for Shannon and vice versa. They gave Charley and CiCi dual control over everything. The other girls have no say in anything. And that's why it's a big deal. It's not because any of them have done anything to help in any situation.

"You two are getting to the point where you can't make big decisions anymore!"

"Now, you shut your damned mouth, you ignorant, selfish girl!" I yelled from behind her, making her jump and turn in my direction. "You watch how you talk to your parents! And you are going to stop treating them like they are invalids! They are still young and vibrant and *very fucking capable!* And as far as Charley and CiCi matter, none of you other girls can hold a candle to them. It's real easy barking orders from the other side of the country, or flexing your damn keyboard muscles as long as you're not the one here actually having to figure shit out! Who do you think helps them with the doctors, which, by the way, are *the* best on the East coast? Who do you think helps them with the repairs to this home—the very home you had the privilege of growing up in because of these two hard workers? Who do you think takes care of their medical bills when it surpasses their budget? And don't try to use Mitch or Kyle as a reason; these girls had been taking care of all this before those guys came along. Any time they called you girls for help, which was rare, you three always had an excuse as to why you couldn't assist. Everything else was more important than your own parents. What does it say about you three, when your sisters can turn to their three best friends quicker than you? My daughter, Maddie, and Ava have been more like daughters, in every way, to these people than any of you! Why is that? Why do you think it's okay to treat them like this? Do you know how lucky you are to be able to pick up the phone and have a coherent conversation with both of your parents? You are an ungrateful, spoiled . . ." I had my finger in her face. I wanted to punch her. I groaned in frustration instead. "You want to know why they've entrusted Charley and CiCi with their lives? How about because they're the ones who actually give a shit about the lives they have been entrusted with—without thought, without motive, and without an ounce of resentment! It's hard to believe that you are CiCi's twin; she definitely got all of the heart. And it shows in everything she does. It would do you a lot of good to be more like your twin and your younger sister. Otherwise, you're going to grow into an old, spiteful bitch." I looked back at my friends. Their jaws were hanging. Shannon had tears rolling down her cheeks. "I can't stay, Shannon. I may throttle her if I do. I love you. I'll call you later. Don't take any more shit from this one." I hugged her, turned on my heel, and walked out of the kitchen and right into CiCi. She stood there, eyes full of tears, staring at me. "And I meant every fucking word of it!" I asserted. "I am really proud of the woman you turned into," I said in a calmer fashion. "I need to leave now," I announced. She moved to the side, still speechless. "Give her hell, Ceese," I ordered as I headed on my way.

"I think you did a better job of that then I would've," she finally spoke just as I made it to the door. I looked back and gave her a small smile. She gave me one back. Is it odd that it felt like we hugged spiritually in that moment?

I'm sure Maddie knows of this exchange. If not, I'm more than happy to fill her in. I feel like things are really moving into place. Roads are being built. My heart feels brighter. My breaths feel deeper. I actually smiled at myself in the mirror this morning. And then I laughed, of course, because I felt so silly smiling at myself. It was a great laugh. And . . . it was so good to see me smile.

"Cynthia?" Maddie catches my attention.

With gusto, I jump up and sashay past her. "It's been a wonderful week!" I sing.

"I guess so," she says from behind me. I can hear the smile in her voice.

I make my way into her office and sit in the hot seat. "Have you talked to CiCi?" I ask straight away.

"Uh, not since Monday. She did text me to call her as soon as I get the chance. Why?"

"I think you are going to be very proud of me." I straighten a wrinkle out in my skirt.

"Do tell . . ." she trails off in a gossipy way. I give her the play by play. Maddie's facial expressions go from anger to excitement, like her team scored the winning point (I got a high-five during that expression), to a frowny sort of smile and eyes full of tears. "I would think that you are very much aware of what that meant to CiCi, overhearing you like that." She dabs under her eyes with her fingers. I grab a few tissues out of the box and hand them to her.

"I can't tell you how relieved I was to know she overheard. Usually people only overhear you when you are saying bad stuff about them," I say.

"That's very true. You should probably buy a lottery ticket on the way home." She laughs. I nod in agreement. "It always hurt her." Her tone changes.

"Huh?"

"The things you've said about her over the years, how you made her feel." Maddie pushes her hair behind her ears, looking down rather than at me. My heart slumps to the pit of my stomach.

"I always wanted Julie to be better than CiCi. I think, in my mind, if she were better, then I would have something to defend myself with. I'd have something to throw back at Shannon's 'I told you so.'" *I can't believe that just came out of my mouth.* I can't believe I just openly admitted to something I had never realized I was doing. I knew I always pushed Julie to be the best, to never settle—to only depend on herself. But, I always told myself it was because I didn't want her to be blindsided like me. I didn't want her to ever be in any type of situation that would resemble mine in the slightest. And yes, while that is all still somewhat true, it is not the real reason.

I made Julie my pawn.

A pawn . . . in some weird chess game where I was the only player.

"I wish I could disown myself," I announce.

"What do you mean by that?"

"I keep pulling these curtains away. You've *helped* me pull them away. But there are curtains that I didn't know existed, and man, when I pull away one of those . . ." I shake my head, "my *asshole light* shines brighter than I could ever have imagined. No wonder no one likes me. I don't even like me." I tear up.

"I like you." Maddie reaches forward and grabs my hand. "And every time one of your asshole curtains gets pulled away, I like you even more. Also, we need to change the topic or just stop mentioning your asshole having curtains." She starts to laugh, then goes into a full-on hysterical laughing fit, accompanied by snorting, of course. I join in, thanks to her visual. *Nutcase!* How can you not love this girl?

"Okay, that's enough now. I have to tell you about the rest of my week!" I slap her knee.

"Yes, please do. Julie didn't come banging on my door, so I assume you didn't tell her that you know." She dabs under her eye one final time.

"No. I did run right over there but was met with Blake. We had a somewhat of an awkward exchange at first because I was so worried. He told me the results. We had a small chat. I apologized for everything."

"What happened?"

"He left me alone with his godfather. Rupert did say that was a good response, otherwise, he would've booted me out." I grab my phone as it starts to vibrate and ping. I look down quickly before turning it off. It's a text from Rupert.

That was a good rub, love. Thank you!

I meant on the steaks, of course! ;)

Though, I give you free range to rub anything you'd like . . .

"What's that smile about?" Maddie inquires. I look up to find her head tilted as she studies me. I show her. "Wow, you guys are like all domesticated with each other. So, I take it things are getting serious?"

"He doesn't sleep over," I say quickly.

"People have sex during the day." I can see she's fighting hard not to smile, looking down at her notepad and chewing on her pen suddenly. Maddie never chews on her pen.

"We just spend our free time together during the day." I ignore her comment.

"Rubbing things?" She lets out a giggle.

"Very professional, Maddie," I try to scold her. *Try* would be the key word here.

"Sorry." She laughs a little more before pulling herself together. "How has it been to suddenly have this type of relationship in your life?"

"Wonderfully scary. I feel like I'm eighteen again. I've told you about how Allan always made me feel."

"Yes, I remember. I see that feeling this way is making you very anxious."

"Why would you say that?" I look back up from staring at my hands.

"Your fingers were doing some sort of weird Tango with each other, and your right leg was bouncing like you were getting your head scratched real good." She points out all of my dead giveaways.

"I'm worried that it's all a mirage," I divulge.

"Most likely, it's not, though."

"I know this. It's why I'm trying to accept it as a wonderful change in my life. I'm trying to not dwell in the doom and gloom of the negative what ifs."

"Good." She smiles wide. "You didn't hesitate with that answer at all. That's really good, Cynthia." She takes in a deep breath. "Gosh, I'm proud of you!"

"Oh. Oh . . . well." She shouldn't be proud of me. There is so much I haven't told her.

"What's that about?" And there's the head tilt—damn it.

"Maddie?"

"Yes?"

"I have a dilemma." I need to distract her from digging deeper. I'm not ready for that.

"What's that?" She straightens up.

"I have questions about things . . . you know . . . relationship things. I don't have Julie to ask, and I'm certainly not at an age where I could go to my mother—not that I ever would. It's just, I don't want you to feel uncomfortable with me asking you. It would make me uncomfortable to know that you are uncomfortable. I don't want you to say that you are not uncomfortable so that I feel comfortable. That would make it more uncomfortable for you to lie." I stop when she raises a hand for me to do so.

"I have to tell you that I'm really uncomfortable with the amount of times you just used uncomfortable and comfortable in your short explanation of which you've explained nothing. Is there an actual question here?"

"Eh, it's just that. . ." I trail off.

"It's an uncomfortable question?" She bites her smile back.

"Yes."

"Just Google it. If that doesn't help, come back to me. I can promise you that I've heard everything," she assures me.

"I'm your best friend's mother, though," I remind her.

"Shannon is also the mother of two of my best friends," she reminds me.

"Point taken." I nod.

"And so is the last minute of our time. Nice dodging of that bullet, by the way." She raises her eyebrow up at me.

"Learning all of my tricks, huh?" I get up.

"I've got your number, lady." She stands, as well. "This was a great session, so I won't hold it against you." And then she hugs me. I'm a little taken aback, but don't waste too much time giving in. It's one of the best hugs I've had in a long time. I let go and rush out before I burst into tears. I so want to hug Julie like that again.

I barely make it to my car before the dam breaks.

"Wher'ya off to, love?" He looks over his shoulder at me as I get up from the table.

"Well, since you won't let me help clean up anything from this delicious dinner you made us, I thought I'd go do a few things on the computer: pay my bills, check my email, and see if Julie's posted anything." *Look up what the new grooming trend is . . .*

"She hasn't posted anything today, so save yourself the trouble."

"How do you know that she hasn't?" I question.

He turns the faucet off and grabs a dish towel to dry his hands as he turns to face my direction. "I was trying to save you some grief tonight. I didn't want you to look and be disappointed by any-thing she may or may not say. I also didn't want you to be disap-pointed to find nothing there. I was just trying to be helpful, love." He gives me a half-smile.

"I'll look for myself, thank you," I snap slightly. Well, what was I supposed to do? He has no business looking into my business, right? I leave the kitchen and make my way into my office. I go right to Julie's blog. Her blog with a *new* post! A-ha! See? I look at the time stamp.

Oh.

It was published five minutes ago.

"What's the verdict; am I a dirty-rotten liar?" His voice grabs my attention. I look up and over my shoulder.

"No. She's posted, but only a few minutes ago. I'm sorry." I go to stand, but he holds his hands up.

"It's all right, love. Carry on with your business. I'll finish in the kitchen." He throws the towel over his shoulder.

Deciding not to dwell on the guilt, I read Julie's blog.

Red's Got the Beat

Confessions of a Blog Star

A few months back, I did something I never do—I read a book and didn't review it. I know a lot of people do this. Most people do this, actually. However, as I am a blogger and reading is my passion, this was very out of character for me. It wasn't because I didn't like the book; I adored it. The author reached into the depths of my soul. She held my heart in her hands, causing it pain, joy, and slight flutters of both at times. It wasn't a story that paralleled with my life, per se, but it hit home just the same. I tried to write the review, but I was so conflicted with everything I was going through, the feelings it brought up, that I just couldn't get the words down. So, I let it go. I forgot about the book without ever really forgetting about the book. I know, you're probably scratching your head over that one, huh? What I mean is that I pushed the book away every time it popped up in my head. I did this in order to push away the feelings it provoked from me. Feelings I did not want to court. Eventually, the book stopped haunting me as much.

Recent events in my life have brought the memory of that book back. I reread it last night. It evoked the same feelings. But, it was different this time, and I can't help but wonder if maybe it is because I am ready to examine the feelings that it brings up.

My boyfriend said something very profound to me the other night. He basically told me that I need to be the one who changes. I need to change my expectations of others when they have proven over and over again that they cannot meet them. I need to accept that people are who they are. He was right. And so was the book because that was, basically, the main message.

Just think about it. Think about how much time we all waste waiting for people to live up to our standards of how we think they should be. And if it's somebody you love—someone you have a certain connection with—look at all the good stuff you're pushing away with the bad.

Does she remember the good stuff?

I feel a spark of hope ignite inside of me as I read on. She's encouraging others to forgive and find a way to adjust their expectations. Maybe she's ready to or, at least, starting to think about talking to me again.

I wish she didn't use her blog to talk about these things. I understand that she's trying to help others who are going through what she is going through. However, she's sometimes vague, and I think she may soon start to lose followers. People don't like to hear or read about other people going on about themselves, especially on a public platform. It becomes obnoxious. The world isn't our diary. However, I guess I can understand that this may be one's way of "putting it out in the universe." I also am beginning to understand that this is not an opinion I should ever voice to her. I've always come off so judgmental. Mostly because I was.

Anyhow, this post is very encouraging. It's the cherry on my cake of a week!

Although . . .

I look over my shoulder to make sure I'm still alone, then quickly type in the latest trends on grooming down below. I click on the first article I see. Ah! This lady seems to have done quite a bit of research. And . . . she also seems to not have found a distinct answer. Apparently, it depends on age, location, and, ultimately, comfort.

"Love, why are you looking at women's genitalia?" Rupe asks from behind me, causing me to yelp and shut my laptop.

"I'm not looking *at* genitalia. I'm researching." I try not to project offensiveness.

"Researching?" he asks slowly.

"I—God, this is so embarrassing," I groan.

"Tell me." He squats in front of me, now that I'm completely facing him.

"I wanted to know what I should be doing down there." I can't believe I just admitted that to him! Why can I not lie around this man?

"Come again?"

I explain to him what I was looking for. This is not my finest hour, I should mention.

"Are you comfortable now? I mean . . . with your grooming situation?" He's so endearing, so delicate in the way he is asking.

"I'm not sure what you mean."

"Do you feel uncomfortable?"

"Down there? No." God, I can't even look at him.

I feel his forefinger push my chin up to look into his eyes. "If you are comfortable, then that's all that matters. My only preference is that you are just you. You never need to go out of your way to do something you *think* I would prefer. I just prefer you." He leans forward and plants a soft, lingering kiss on my lips. My heart leaps all over my chest like a fifteen-year-old girl getting a kiss from her crush. *How is it possible to feel this way at my age?*

"Now, finish up here," he starts once he pulls away, "I'm going to draw a bath for you. Get your pretty, little arse upstairs in five minutes, okay?"

"Okay," I agree before quickly wrapping my arms around his neck, pulling him to me for a long, very much needed, hug. "Thank you." I kiss his cheek and hug him again. He gets up, his eyes twinkling at me, and heads off to his duty.

He's drawing a bath for me . . .

Le sigh . . .

WALKING UP THE STAIRS, my nerves begin to ricochet all over the place. Questions have suddenly risen: is he taking the bath with me? Is he going to make love to me? Will I let him do either?

Yes.

What?

The answer is yes.

Oh God, you're right!

Yes, you are.

Amazing how agreeable one can be with themselves, right? Jesus! I feel like I need to call Shannon. That's that fifteen-year-old reaction though, right? Call your best friend to announce that you're about to get laid? Laid? Does anyone say that anymore? Oh God, I don't even have the right lingo to have sex this year! What is it called? Are we pounding it out, bumping uglies, boning, porking, getting it on, making love—no, it can't be that simple term.

"Any reason why you are hyperventilating, love?" Rupert pulls me out of my hysteria.

"What is this called?" Seriously? Can I please stop acting like this is my first visit to Earth?

"A bath," he answers. However, you can hear the trepidation in his tone.

"I mean for what's after."

"Eh . . . sleep?" he questions. His face is balled up in confusion. Dear God, I suck at this.

"Will you bathe with me?" I ask, grasping some bravery from somewhere.

"No."

"Why?"

"I didn't think you wanted me to. I didn't want to be presumptuous."

"I want you to bathe with me." I pull off my shirt.

"I will bathe with you," he states quickly. "Your breasts are lovely," he adds.

"I will take my bra off now," I announce.

"Your comfort always comes first." His eyes continue their admiration.

"Ready?" Why the hell am I asking him this?

"About five weeks ago, love." He licks his lips.

"Is the water hot?" I ask as I unveil. "I like it hot."

"Oh, it's going to be very hot, love."

I don't think he's talking about the water.

"Turn around," I command.

"What?" He's almost breathless.

"I want you to turn around, so I can finish getting undressed and get into the tub."

"I'm bathing with you," is his answer.

"Yes. Now, turn around." I raise my eyebrows up at him.

"Jay-sus!" he groans but turns just the same.

I quickly finish getting undressed and make my way into the tub. "Okay," I announce. He turns and stares at me. His eyes not leaving mine, he pulls his shirt off and slowly unzips his pants. He pulls them down along with his underwear, and I quickly turn my head.

"Why do you turn away?" he asks.

"Should I scoot forward?" I ask, avoiding his question.

"Yes."

I scoot forward and close my eyes shut tightly. My anxiety feels like it's getting ready to go through the roof. *I shouldn't be doing this. I'm a good girl. Good girls don't do this.* I feel the water shift as he steps in behind me and lowers himself. His legs stretch out on either side of me. Just as I'm about to oppose this whole operation, Rupert pulls me back to him. I relax against his chest, and my anxiety slowly becomes non-existent.

"I fell in love the moment my eyes laid upon you. I will bring you no harm. I only wish to love you," he breathes into my ear as I fall into a more relaxed state. Relaxed enough to know his hands are wandering and not to care.

"Rupe . . ." I trail off in a whisper as his caressing hand travels away from my belly and down to the region of my earlier concern.

"Shh . . ." he whispers. His fingers slide through my folds, and my hips jerk up at his touch. "That's it, love," he encourages. I turn my head to find his lips. His tongue dives into my mouth as his fingers do the same below. An unrecognizable sound echoes through my ears as he reaches deeper. "So lovely," Rupert mutters.

My hand joins his strong, purposeful one. "That's it; show me what you need," he eggs me on.

"I need you." I attack his lips aggressively while moving at the same pace with his hand.

Suddenly, my legs lock and my toes curl as the most delicious wave of pleasure surges through my core. Rupert kisses me harder as he continues to work me through this amazing feeling. Slowly, my body begins to relax, and the pressure from his mouth eases up. "So very lovely . . ." he says against my lips as I try to regulate my breathing.

"I suppose it was silly to make you turn around before," I ponder aloud.

"Not silly at all." He kisses my shoulder. "I'm rather impressed with you. Very bold, letting me in this tub with you."

"Yes, I don't know what that was about. I must've been possessed." I lace my fingers with his on my stomach.

"Clearly," he agrees as he squeezes me to him with his right arm.

"So, was that my first lesson in pedaling?" I crook my neck and give him a coy smile.

"Yes, love, and you passed with flying colors." He pecks my nose. I look forward again, feeling nervous. "What is it?" he asks.

"Hmm?"

"You're chewing on your lip. What's troubling you?" Another encouraging squeeze.

I take in a deep breath and slowly release it, trying to think the best way to ask him what I'm wondering. The only conclusion I've come to is to just ask. "Will we be continuing on with our lessons tonight or are we done?"

"Only you can answer that, love; everyone learns at their own pace." After a few seconds of silence, he clears his throat a little. "Would you like to continue with the lesson?"

"It's always best to continue when your student is thoroughly engaged, right?" Answering a question with a question always works for politicians—why not me?

"That is very true. Now lean forward so I can get you clean before I get you dirty." He lays a kiss on my temple, then pats my shoulder to get a move on. I smile despite my inner urging to act normal. Not that smiling isn't normal. I just don't want to come off as giddy. Does that make any sense? Oh, I don't know what I'm doing . . .

"Hand me that facecloth, please," he says as I give up on my thoughts and sit up. I grab it and pass it back his way.

"Can I call you Ru?" I ask as he lathers up the cloth.

"That's a random, interesting question," he points out as he starts to wash my back.

"Rupe sounds like I'm saying rope with a funny accent."

He laughs at this.

I love his laugh.

I love when I'm the cause of it.

"Only one person has ever called me Ru," he states almost apprehensively.

"Oh, does it bring bad memories?" I really don't know much about his past; we're always talking about mine.

"Actually, they are very good memories. My nan called me Ru. She got it from the *Winnie the Pooh* books. They were my favorite, and she loved to read them to me. It was our *special* time." He takes a break. "I haven't thought of my nan in a long time. That makes me sad. She was very important to me."

"I don't have to call you that. It's okay." I push it off since it seems to bring him some sadness.

"I'd love for you to call me that. I think she'd want you to. I'm half-sure she put the idea in your head herself." I can hear a smile in his voice.

"You think?" I look over my shoulder at him.

"Yeah. No-one's ever thought to call me that. I'd love for you to do so." He leans forward and plants a sweet kiss on my lips.

"Ru it is, then," I agree before facing forward and allowing him to continue bathing me.

There is something to be said about being bathed by someone you have feelings for. This has to be the most intimate experience I have ever experienced. I didn't even have this experience with Allan. I can't believe I'm having a "first" at six—*THIRTY* in the evening . . . at my age . . .

Shush.

Age is just a number, remember?

"Lean your head back so I can wash your hair, love," he commands gently.

"Oh, I don't want you to do that. I've just had it done this morning."

"Okay. Skootch up then."

I slide forward, and the water moves in waves as he stands up behind me and climbs out of the tub. I fight the urge to look over at him, desperately wanting to take a peak. "I didn't wash you," I say, deciding to distract myself by talking.

"This bath was for you." Out of my peripheral, I can barely see him wrapping a towel around his waist. "Up you go, now." He now holds a towel up for me.

"Oh, um . . ." I hesitate.

"Chop-chop, lollipop!" He shakes the towel in his outstretched arms as if to encourage me. I take in a deep, cleansing breath, trying to calm my nerves before I stand up and face him. "There you go." He's so calm as he wraps the towel around me. Of course, *he's* calm, he's not the one exposed. I grab his hand and climb out of the tub. "Are you having second thoughts?" he asks as we are practically nose-to-nose.

"I'd rather not talk it through. The more I think about it, the more nervous I get," I admit. "I'm so ridiculous." I allow my frustration to boil over.

He palms my face. "You are not ridiculous. You are not silly. You are perfect; that's all I see. Just tell me to stop if you become uncomfortable at any time. I'm okay with that."

"I am very comfortable with you. That's what makes me nervous. I know you are not David, but I can't help the way I feel, no matter how angry it makes me . . . allowing him to still have this power over me. It's not right, and it's not fair. And—it pisses me off!" I bite.

He pulls my face forward gently, angling it to fit his mouth over mine perfectly. He deepens the kiss with the slip of his tongue. I'm lost in the slow seduction. Too soon, he pulls away reluctantly, planting a few more kisses before completely straightening up. "Did you forget about him?"

"Who?" I knit my eyebrows.

"Good," he states quickly and lets his hands drop to mine. He laces our fingers. "Come now." He begins to walk backwards out of my bathroom, bringing me along with him. My heart is drumming so loudly, I wonder if he can hear it or see it. I try to concentrate on his handsome face instead of over-focusing on what's next. He's got a great head of hair; the splashes of gray give him a very distinguished look. His blue eyes are piercing. And his smile lights up my whole world. He stops walking but continues to pull me forward till we're toe-to-toe.

"I plan on tasting every inch of your skin," he announces.

"Okay," I breathe. Not a moment goes by, and my towel is unraveled from my body. My nerves spike up again. *Am I ready for this? Do I want to re-learn how to pedal?* "Do you have a helmet?" I almost shout.

A small laugh escapes his mouth. "Helmet?"

"To ride the bike," I explain. *Oh God, I sound like an idiot! Why couldn't I just say condom?*

"Protection?"

"Yes."

"I have no helmets with me." He bites back his smile. "But, I'm healthy. However, is there something you should tell me about . . . something that may have us on the front page of *The National Enquirer*?"

"What do you mean?"

"Are you still able to have children?"

"No! I don't think so."

"You don't think so?" He does the Maddie head tilt.

"No." I shake my head. I got a period last month, but that was probably the last time. I get them so randomly now.

"Sure?" he asks again.

"Yes. But you should still have something. I read a statistic that people our age have the highest number of people affected with STDs."

"Do you have an STD?"

"God—no!" I almost yell in disbelief.

"I don't, either. And since you can't get pregnant and me without a helmet . . ." he trails.

"What?"

"We'll be barebacking it, love," he answers. I mean, I think that's an answer, right?

"I don't think I know that position."

"Bareback means no condom," he informs me then does a little jerking of his head. He looks confused. "Love, I know it's been a while for you, but have you been under a rock for a few years?"

"I don't pay attention to stuff that doesn't affect me, so—yeah—I'm a little behind on the lingo." I get defensive.

"I'm going to come inside of you," he informs me in his usual calm manner. "It's probably going to be a copious amount as it's been building up for a while."

"Oh my God. That's not appropriate!"

"It's going to be an inappropriate amount, for sure," he agrees. Although, that's not what the hell I was talking about!

"Ru!" I yell, "Talking to me like that is *not* appropriate!"

"Why?" He jerks his head back.

"Because . . . because I'm a lady!" I straighten my gait, challenging him.

"You're my lady, and I'm over the moon about it . . ." he trails off with a sigh.

"Well . . . Well!" I have nothing—damn it!

"Well, what?" He smirks as he grabs my hips and pulls me ridiculously close.

"Nothing." I give up.

"I'm going to lay you on this bed now and reward myself with your taste," he gives me the play by play. *Play by play?* I'm not sure I even know what that means!

"What should I do?"

"Enjoy it . . . I hope." He brings me to my bed and lays me down. I close my eyes and concentrate on my breathing as I feel him opening my legs.

He bites at my inner thigh.

I jump to a full sitting position and stare at him.

He gives me a look.

It's a very commanding look.

I lay back down . . .

I feel hypnotized by the biting, the sucking of my skin. He licks near *there*. "No!" I jump up again.

"No?" He looks up at me.

"You can't do that."

"Why?"

"Because."

"That's not an answer."

"Because you shouldn't do that! It's . . . I." I think I may be hyperventilating.

"It's what?" he asks but licks up my center anyway, making me want to cry.

Stop!
This is very emotional for me.
Don't judge me, damn it!

"It's not right," I say.

"This is all wrong?" he asks before doing it again, but this time he teases me excessively.

"Ru!" I scream.

"Is this wrong, love?" he asks again before going back at it. I respond by fisting his hair and moaning like a twenty-dollar whore. Not like I know what the going rate is. I wouldn't know those things, of course.

I'd take his twenty.

I rock against his face as that earlier exquisite feeling comes over me. "Don't stop," I beg.

"It's wrong, though, love," he mentions midstride.

"No. Ohhhh, God, it's not," I moan.

"You sure?" he counters.

"Yes!" I practically scream as my toes curl.

Slowly, I come down. Rupert's ambition matches my decline. He works his way up my body and grasps my lips with his. I can taste myself on his lips. *Is this normal? Should he have brushed first or something? Maybe I should've talked to Shannon first.*

"What is it, love?" he asks.

"Nothing," I say quickly.

"You have questions?" He's so patient.

"No."

"Yes, you do. What are they?"

"I can taste myself on your lips."

"Best taste in the world . . ." he groans before attacking my lips again.

"Is this normal?" I ask as I pull away.

"Everything tonight is and will be normal for us and for most people," he answers.

"Okay."

"Yeah?"

"Yes."

"Good. I'm going to take you now."

"Where?"

"Here," he answers then thrusts inside of me urgently. My neck stretches and curves somewhat unnaturally.

He's . . . I . . . Oh God, pray for my lady spade. He's dusting away the cobwebs and the sorrow—I can tell you that much.

Chapter Twenty-Two

Blake

All in the Family

It's been two weeks since all the great events from two weeks ago: Julie getting the all clear, Cynthia's bizarre visit, and my heartfelt proposal that got shot down. Since these events, Julie has gone on a second interview for the internship and received it (she starts in January), Uncle Rupe is practically living with Cynthia, and I've hired Ethan. Very productive two weeks, I'd say.

Julie is still in the dark about her mother, but everyone else has now run into her. I'll give her this—her odd behavior (odd for her, that is) has been pretty consistent, so I am starting to believe that she really is trying to turn over a new leaf.

Speaking of oddly-behaving parents, my father has finally contacted me. I'm expecting his arrival any day now. The way he spoke to my godfather, we both assumed he'd be here a month ago. I just hope that when he arrives, he's in a good place. I'm tired of seeing him so miserable.

"I don't like the looks of this," my godfather interrupts my thoughts.

"The looks of what?" I resume wiping down the bar.

"You—thinking. It's scary, lad. You look as if you're hurting your brain."

"Shut it, old man," I groan. "What are you even doing here?" I wasn't expecting him as he's been spending all of his time with Cynthia lately.

"Moral support." He shrugs.

"Right . . ." I trail off, rolling my eyes.

"Alright, then." He sighs. "I feel a bit on edge."

"Why's that?"

"Well, I'm very happy at the mo. Your father is coming in today. I don't like it," he admits.

"He's your best friend—why don't you like this?" Honestly, I have no time for riddles today.

"I feel the need to lock Cyn away. I don't want to introduce them." He blows a big gust of wind through his lips like he hated to admit that.

"She's not his type." I try to reassure.

"She's not *my* type. That is, until now. He'll ruin it," he states very matter of factly. It's odd. I've never seen him react this way.

"What's this about, Unc?" Curiosity is killing the cat.

"Nothing. I just," he takes a deep breath, "I just don't want him trying to sink his paws in where they don't belong, that's all . . ." he trails off. "What can I help with?" He changes the subject

I shrug.

This is very confusing. But, with that said, everything is done. Just waiting to open. No busy work to give him to help him escape his thoughts. "Are you worried that Cynthia isn't true to you?"

"No," he answers sternly. "Your father just has a habit of going after what is mine."

"My mother?" I question.

"Right. Look here—menus aren't out!" he announces before grabbing them to place on the tables. That would be his cue to change my topic. Although . . . he's off, which means he's done discussing any sort of topic.

I always had a feeling . . .

I think I just got my confirmation.

I can't keep up.

It's beyond packed tonight; five hours have flown by like a minute. Honestly, I just can't keep up with this crowd. I've got four of us on the bar. I've called in the GEGs to help on the floor. Apparently, I've booked a band tonight that is very up and coming. This is fabulous, of course—if you have the staff. I, as we all know, am struggling in that department. But I shan't lie and say I'm not pleased this is happening on my father's arrival. On the contrary, it's the only thing keeping a smile lit on my face!

Ah! There's the right bastard now! I, of course, pretend not to see him, as I am so busy. I look over at my godfather shaking up a martini. He lifts his brow in a knowing way. My dad is his very best friend, but I trump that relationship most of the time with the insert of the Almighty's name in our acquaintance. I can see he's just as eager as I to show off my success. God, I love him. If it weren't for Uncle Rupe . . . well . . . let's just say I'm very grateful for his influence.

"Blakey!" my father yells.

I ignore.

I'm too busy, of course.

"Blakey!" He gets in front of me.

"Da!" I yell enthusiastically and yank him in for a hug before continuing with a drink order.

"What the bloody hell, son?" he yells as he looks around.

"It's a bit busy, aye?" I smile like I can't believe my own eyes, as well.

"Is it always like this?"

"Most nights!" I yell with pride.

He nods his head as he takes it all in. *Go ahead, Dad—tell me you're proud.* I hate that I am waiting for his approval. Honestly, what do I need it for?

He grabs my drink menu. "Good! You price your drinks cheaply!" he states as if that's the reason for this chaos.

I pretend not to hear him because, honestly, I want to take a shot at him. Instead, I walk over to my godfather's area of the bar. "Please swap with me," I beg.

"Of course," he answers swiftly and makes his way to my dad.

"Three Jolly Ranchers, two martinis—dry, one Malibu Bay Breeze, and one Coors Light," Julie rambles off to me.

"What?" I shake my head.

"Seriously?" she almost whines.

"Sorry, love."

"Okay, but I'm gonna need some extra tonight." She waggles her eyebrows then winks at me.

Mmmm.

I don't mind if I do.

I make the drinks and pass them off to her. I take a moment to appreciate her backside as she walks away. "Is that her?" my dad yells, interrupting my inappropriate thoughts.

"It is," I answer quickly before giving him my attention.

"You weren't kidding—she's gorgeous!" He smiles widely. He seems so cheerful. Suddenly, a thought occurs to me.

I lean forward, "Have you met someone, Dad?"

"Why do you ask?" His eyes light up.

"You have!" I yell and grasp him by the back of his neck to pull him forward and plant a big, wet kiss on his cheek. *'Bout bloody time!* "Did you bring her with?" I let go.

"She'll be in tomorrow." Bastard can't keep the smile off his face.

"That's fantastic news, Dad—really!" Maybe he won't be such a miserable git now!

"Carlos here?"

"Yes! Head back to the kitchen. He'd love to see you!" I jerk my head in that direction before focusing on the order being shouted to me.

"I can't get over the crowd you had here," Dad says as if he's in awe.

"I appreciate you helping us with the clean-up. It's been a struggle to get a good team here. But, it's starting to get better," I add quickly, never wanting to give him any fuel.

"Are you happy?" he asks.

"Very. I've always been my happiest here; you know that." I grab the broom and start sweeping rather than look at him.

"I'm sorry."

"You're sorry?" I look up. "That I'm happy?"

"No. I'm sorry that I've been such an arse about it all. I've never been one much for change. You're so much like my dad—it pissed me off. I tried to make you not be like him, always throwing gray clouds above your head. I just didn't want you to leave me, too. I pushed you away, though. I've pushed everyone away. Except for that arsehole over there," he points to my godfather, "can't bloody get rid of him, no matter how many times I've tried." He laughs a bit.

"Even stole his girl." I don't know why I mention it. Perhaps this random purging of feelings made me do it.

"Well, we all saw how that worked out for me. Besides, sounds like he's really happy. I've never seen Rupe so smitten . . ." he trails off.

"It's good to see us all happy." I smile before continuing on with the sweeping. Also, I'd like to avoid any questions about Cynthia. I don't really want my father to know that Uncle Rupe is with Julie's mother. It's bad enough everyone knows but her—a stranger knowing before she does may send her over the top.

Suddenly, thoughts of a future *Jerry Springer* episode with us as the cast crosses my mind.

Nah . . . I don't think we're at that level of fucked up, yet.

Oh, but we're getting there . . .

"Hey, dipshit, all your dishes are washed and put away. I'm done. Don't ask me to wash another fucking dish for the next five years, you got me?" CiCi complains behind me. As I turn around, she continues, "And don't be surprised when I call you in a couple of days to come wash some irate pussies for me. And don't ignore my phone call, either!"

I notice the look on my dad's face. "This is CiCi, Dad. She's a pet groomer. And what she's basically telling me is that she has a few cats in her appointment book that she's not a big fan of, so my payback will be to work a couple of hours for her, grooming the cats. Of course, she couldn't just say it like that because that would be normal. CiCi doesn't *do* normal," I add.

"Eh . . . hello, CiCi," Dad greets her.

"Your Royal Highness." She curtsies.

"I'm not royalty," he states.

"Oh, my bad. See, I thought you were since your son is such a royal pain in my ass." She shrugs.

"Ah . . ." he sighs as if it all makes sense, but it's followed by a moment of awkward silence.

"Really? That's what you've got?" I ask in shock. "You are slipping, my friend."

"Well, I can't be at my best when some asshole's had me peopling tonight—*I don't people, Blake; you know this!* Then you make me wash forty-two thousand dishes! I'm not even getting paid for this!" she says in defense.

"We'll call it payback for carving your bloody name into my table!" I yell, but it's a laughing sort of yell.

"Let's get something straight; that is our fucking table—accept it! Secondly, I wouldn't have to carve my name into shit if you would've gotten our couch like you were supposed to last year!" She points to the area they all decided their couch should go.

"This isn't Central Perk, and you are not a cast member of *Friends*! You don't get a bloody, fecking couch!"

"We require the lamp too, Blake," Maddie adds her two cents in.

"Right—and the damn fountain outside so you can spontaneously move the fecking couch and lamp in front of it to dance to your theme song! You're all a bunch of nutters!"

"'Bubblegum Bitch,'" CiCi states.

"What?" My dad and I both ask.

"That should be our theme song. It's by Marina and the Diamonds. We've been working hard on it," she informs us.

"Yes! We're going to perform it at your Halloween bash. We're going to be The Misfits . . . you know . . . from *Jem and the Holograms*?" Maddie adds with excitement.

"I'm very confused, boy." Dad looks to me as if he's stepped into another realm.

"I'd like to blame it on the late hour, but it doesn't matter what the hour is. Don't worry; you'll adapt." I let out a laugh as I remember my first encounter with these women. I must've had the same look on my face and fear in my eyes.

"Ceese, you ready, beautiful?" Kyle walks up. He stops and stares at all of us then shakes his head. "What did she say?" he asks, knowing his fiancée well enough, as we all do.

"Nothing! I can't help that his dad is a foreigner," she defends.

"He's British, Ceese." He smirks.

"Thank you, Captain Obvious. C'mon, I'm tired." And with

that, she yanks him along but turns to do the Queen's wave in our direction. Fecking nutter.

"Godspeed, mate!" Dad calls after him.

"That man doesn't need any form of speed—trust me," Maddie chides.

"Who's handing out speed?" Julie asks as she approaches us.

"Are you on drugs?" my father queries.

This night will never end, will it?

"Yes. I'm on Blakecocksine," she states matter-of-factly. Maddie snorts then goes into a fit of giggles. I just bite my lip, close my eyes, shake my head, and pray for this conversation to end.

"I've never heard of it."

"I'm happy to hear that, sir. It's done wonders for me." Very impressive how she manages to keep a straight face.

"How's that?" Dad clears his throat as if he's realized that he's gotten too personal.

"It regulates my hormones."

"Is it a pill?" *Oh, shut up, Dad!*

"It's an injection," she answers.

I walk away.

Check in on Maddie, will ya? She may be dying from laughter.

"Giving him a run, aye?" Uncle Rupert jerks his head in the direction of my father.

"I don't know if he'll make it out alive." I laugh.

"Is Maddie having a seizure?" He furrows his brows in concern.

"Dec!" I call out to him. He looks up from wiping down a table. "I think your girl's done for the night, mate."

"When did she have a drink?" He looks over at her, and his smile hits his eyes.

Oh, for fuck all's sake!
His smile hit his bloody, fecking eyes?

"What are you off about?" Unc asks.

"I've got a bloody, fecking pansy living in me head!" I complain

228

without much thought as to what that may sound like.

"I think you're spending too much time with this lot. I may need a translator to understand *you*." He slaps me on the shoulder and goes on about bringing glasses to the bar. I don't blame him.

Just then, Julie makes her way over to me. "You done torturing my dad now?" I smile and let my hands slide onto her hips.

"Yes. All that talk made me realize I'm due for my injection."

"Indeed, you are, missy." I lean in and grasp her lips. "Let's get out of here."

"Where's your dad staying?"

"Oh. Uh . . . shit."

"Seriously?" Her eyes go wide.

"He's been making his way here for *months!* I gave up thinking about it!" I try to defend myself.

"Well, ask him where he's staying without asking him."

"What? How the hell does one do that?" I ask in disbelief at this request.

"Jesus! Do I have to do everything around here?" she asks angrily as she grabs my hand and drags me over to my father.

"Sampson, we're ready to pack it up here. Where's your luggage so Blake can grab it to put in our car?" she asks.

"My name's Samuel, dear. Sam is just fine, though." He tries to smile, but I can see he's still unsure. "And actually, I've already put my luggage in the apartment upstairs, if that's alright? I don't want to be a bother to you two lovebirds."

"Samuel won't do. I had a boyfriend in high school named Samuel. He was a real dick. Saying Samuel could possibly bring up too many bad memories for me. Are you sure you want to stay here?" she adds.

"You could just call me Sam. Not really fond of Sampson, as it is *not* my name," Dad says this as politely as he can. I can tell because he's getting a bit red in the face.

"Sampson suits you!" She slaps his arm slightly. "Besides,

something could happen to me one day, and it will be so much more meaningful to you. You'll be like 'Son, remember how she always called me Sampson? It made me feel so special that she had her own name for me . . . you know . . . something that was just ours . . .'" Julie trails off in a daydream sort of state. My father stares at her as if I've stepped in the motherload of crazy.

Quite possibly, Dad.

"Right! So, yes, I'm perfectly comfortable here," he finally says. "Really . . . go on, you two!" he encourages.

"Well, as long as you're comfortable with that, we'll be on our way! Goodnight, Sampson!" She gives him a hug then kisses each cheek, forehead, and chin.

"Are you drunk, dear?" Dad asks.

"On love, Sampson."

"Right. Night then!" he says abruptly then turns to me for a hug. "We'll talk in the morn," he informs me quietly.

"I can't wait!" I say enthusiastically . . . in the most sarcastic-but-not-trying-to-show-it way.

Soon enough, we gather everyone to leave and make our way out to the parking lot. "Honestly, love, did you have to unload all barrels tonight?" I ask as we get into my car.

"Taking a page out of Ceese's book," she answers as she puts her seatbelt on.

"Let's take a moment and think about that declaration."

"Look, I'd rather your dad know my craziest. Blake, we're too old to pretend to be on our best behavior."

"It is perfectly okay to ease one into your crazy," I say.

"Did I do that with you?"

"No."

"And yet, here you are. Case closed."

"I'm a different—more accepting—generation," I remind her.

"Generation smeneration."

"Smeneration is not a word."

"Sorry, I didn't realize you took on a part-time position as the grammar police."

"I wear many hats, love." I wink at her.

"Speaking of asshats, that Ethan guy creeps me out. I can't believe you hired him," she says as she fastens her seatbelt.

"Oh no! I like him, and he's turning out to be a great employee! Do not put me off on him!" I beg.

"That's the same dude that was outside the comedy club. We had a strange encounter here a few weeks ago, and every time I looked up tonight, I caught him staring at me. He gives me the heebie-jeebies!" She shivers.

"Can't Maddie give you a pill for that?" I ask.

"I'm serious, Blake!" she snaps.

"All right. Let me see if I can somehow have a chat with him about it. See what he says," I concede.

"He'll say I'm crazy." She turns the heat on, making the windows fog quickly.

"He'd be right. You need to wait for the car to warm up a bit; you're only blasting cold air and making it difficult to see." I turn the heat down. She groans in frustration.

"Let's get you home; you're really in need of your hormone injection." I hit the defrost before slowly pulling out of the parking lot.

"Fat chance!"

"It is pretty fat, and your chances are excellent!" I smile broadly her way.

"Hmpfh." She crosses her arms and looks out her window, doing her best to ignore me.

We all know that won't last long . . .

Chapter Twenty-Three

Julie

Secrets, Lies, and Betrayals

LATELY, STARING UP AT THE CEILING INSTEAD OF SLEEPING IS MY new "thing." It doesn't matter the time of day or how exhausted I am; it never fails. I lay my head down and—poof—wide awake! There are various reasons for this: sex for me is like the equivalent to someone chugging back a couple of Red Bulls, whether or not I should reach out to my mom (am I ready to accept that she will never change?), and Ethan's creepy behavior around me. Tonight is D—all of the above. The Brit, as usual, has fallen into the man—I've just had sex—coma. Must be nice.

It was interesting to finally meet his dad. It's hard to see he and Rupert as best friends. They seem like polar opposites, but I don't really know him well enough to get a good gauge on that.

Speaking of best friends, it was a blast working with Ceese and Maddie tonight. They were acting a little strange at one point, though. You ever have one of those moments where you are talking about someone, and they pop up out of nowhere, and you have to play that shit off like you weren't talking about them? Maddie and Ceese did that tonight. I was about to call them out on it, but my table's order came up. Saved by double-loaded nachos. I'll grill their asses tomorrow about it; don't you worry!

Ethan kept trying to make small talk with me. That is, when I wasn't out of earshot, and he could just stare at me. It's a weird stare, though. I don't think he wants to fuck me—I just don't get that vibe. It's like he just wants to get to know me . . . be my friend. I know what you're thinking: *What's wrong with that, Julie? Don't be such a fucking snob!* I'm not being a fucking snob, so shut your pie hole! It's his approach; he's too eager and aggressive about it. It's weird. It's awkward. You know what else is awkward? He doesn't seem socially awkward with anyone else. Nope . . . cool as a cucumber. I'm gonna stick with being paranoid. It's always the oblivious, dumb fucks that get lured and killed by psychopaths.

No offense if you are an oblivious, dumb fuck.

We all have our roles to play.

Some advice: Don't investigate strange noises—run.

Ugh!! I need to get to sleep! Tomorrow's the round table. That's what I call our monthly Sunday dinners at the O'Brien's. CiCi just calls it her *other* monthly. Yes, Shannon and Happy like to keep up with our shenanigans. Everyone should have a Happy and Shannon parental unit figure in their lives. I've probably turned out so well because I grew up with a lot of surrogates. Basically—the "village" raised me.

Lights out, bitches.

I don't want to go there . . .

"Hey, boys, come and help me get another leaf in the table," Happy says as he pokes his head into the living room. "Shannon, our family's getting so big, we're gonna have to rent a hall to have these dinners," he tells her as he heads back to the dining room. All five men get up to help. One leaf—six men—sounds legit. Normally the guys aren't with us. At least not all five of them.

"Where's Caroline?" I ask Ceese in a hushed manner.

"With Preston," she answers, quickly looking at Maddie.

"What is going on with Caroline and Preston?" I turn my attention to Maddie.

"Please," she holds her hand up, "don't even get me started."

I wait.

One.

Two.

"She's leaning on him for moral support and attention—things her *husband* should be giving her—while my sweet, pathetic, love-sick brother is falling in love with her all over again and absolutely loving his new Superman complex," she states heatedly.

"Okay, let's not jump to conclusions that have been concluded years ago—he's always been in love with her. That's the only vagina he's ever wanted to smear his pap on, the only love-tunnel he wanted to stretch open to see, *thee* only cervix he was ever interested in checking," I remind her.

"What are you—the dad in *Grumpy Old Men*?" she snaps. Yeah, she's really pissed about this.

"I'm inspiring to be."

"Well, knock it off; it's not funny!"

"Psst," Ceese whispers in my ear, "I thought it was."

I mouth "thanks" to her before getting back to Maddie. "Hey, I'm just trying to lighten up the situation. I know it bothers you. It bothers all of us."

"You know what bothers me?" Ava asks. We all look at her. "Why the hell was Trent invited? Which one of you assholes did this to me?"

"That would be this asshole," Shannon answers from the doorway. "Charley's got everything ready. Let's go, girls. Ava, you and I will talk after dinner." She gives her a pointed look.

"Yes, Ma," Ava replies, straightens out her skirt, then quickly stands up. "Shall we?" She holds her hand out in front to let Maddie go. We all get up and follow Shannon like a zombie apocalypse due to her slow driving (she's on her scooter). It's a tough pill to swallow, seeing her in a scooter most of the time now. The only thing that makes me feel better is knowing that she is on some *great* drugs. Sometimes she throws us a pill or two if we're having a meltdown in front of her.

Shh . . . I didn't tell you that.

Also, only sometimes do we have a lot of meltdowns in front of her.

Shh . . .

"None of you could marry a contractor?" Shannon asks as she looks around the long table. "Jacccckkkk! HOW'S THE WEATHER DOWN THERE?" she yells to Happy.

"SHANNON, IS THAT YOU?" he yells back. *These assholes.* See why we love them? Seriously though, this table has eaten up the room.

"What do you want, Ma, an addition?" Mitch asks. "You know we'd do anything for you. Is that what you want?"

"Yes. I would like to have my entire family around this table . . . well, a much larger version of this table. I'd like to have Christmas dinner here." You can see the hope in her eyes.

"Mom, we'll do it, but there's no way we'll get it done for this Christmas," Kyle informs her.

"I just miss having it here." Her eyes fill up.

"We'll have it at my restaurant this year! I'll transform the whole place to cater to our family on Christmas Day. Next year, we'll have it here. The addition will be done by then!" Charley gives her quick solution.

"And you'll all come?" Shannon smiles, tears slipping down

her cheeks.

"Of course!" Trent speaks up. "We're all family, aren't we?" he asks, his attention on Ava, who chose to sit across from him rather than next.

"What addition?" Caroline asks as if she's in disbelief. We all bring our focus to her in the doorway.

"The addition we're all putting on your parents' house. You see, their family is growing, and since they love to have their family around them—in *their* home—it seems like the next logical step," I answer before anyone can get a chance.

"You're just as blind and ignorant as your mother," she says incredulously.

"What the fuck does my mother have to do with this?"

"Watch your language, Julie . . . goddamn it!" Shannon reprimands.

"You all may be fooled by the façade they keep up—still having your monthly dinners, I see." She looks around before continuing. "But, they need to be in assisted living! They need to sell this house, not build on it!" she yells.

"There is no façade here, Caroline," Shannon states calmly. "Yes, we still have our monthly dinners because I'm still the mother here. I want to know what's going on in my girls' lives. Don't mistake wanting to know from any of you that I don't already know when something is very off or something is very right."

"They are *not* your girls!" Caroline screams, pointing in the direction of us three non-related girls.

"You are ALL my girls! I know each one of you as if I gave birth to each and every one and not just the three of you that I have! I know when you are all happy. I know when you are all in pain. I KNOW WHEN YOU ARE SICK!" Shannon yells at an octave I'm not sure I've heard come from her before.

"Oh please," Caroline sighs defensively.

"Is it cancer?" Shannon's lip quivers.

"What?" Caroline gasps.

"Is. It. Cancer?" Shannon asks more sternly.

"Who told you?" Caroline looks to her sisters.

"No one had to tell me—I'm your mother!" Shannon screams. "You think I wouldn't know . . . couldn't see when one of my babies was sick? You think I can't hear you heaving at night? I'm your mother, Caroline! I know you. No matter how much you don't believe it—I know you." Shannon finally gives in to her apparent urge to sob. Caroline doesn't take much longer to fall apart.

"I think we should all step out," Maddie finally voices her words of wisdom. We all agree in silence and make haste.

I run to the bathroom because I need one selfish goddamn moment to myself. This is stupid. I'm a grown ass woman! Yet, here I am jealous of Caroline for having a mother who knows when she has cancer because she "knows" her. What the fuck is wrong with me? Seriously? Jealous?

They're probably smoking Medi-Mari together at this moment.

I have no one to smoke Medi-Mari with.

I'm perpetually five years old. I'm stuck. I'm always going to be on this stage till I just get the fuck off! How does a parent—how does *anyone*—have the ability to affect anyone like this? I've got to do something about this. I can't go on like this any longer. This isn't healthy. I've just said *this* way too many times! Don't go back and count. This conversation is about building the balls to move forward; stay with me.

There's a knock on the bathroom door. "Love? You okay? You've been in there for fifteen now," Blake informs me.

"Coming," I say softly before taking in a deep breath and a look in the mirror. Anyone else like how their eyes look after they cry? Don't lie—you look. Mine are going to get me laid so hard.

Look at me, finding the silver lining in things . . .

"Hi," I say once I open the door. I look up at him with the most vulnerable look I can conjure up. Well, I *am* vulnerable.

"Ah, love, let's go home." He cups my face in his hands.

"I think we should."

"Not yet," I hear Shannon. We both give her our attention.

"Are you okay," I ask quickly.

"Yes. Julie?"

"What?"

"Talk to your mother. It's time." Her eyes fill up again.

"You hate my mother. Why would you encourage me?" She's really caught me off guard.

"It's time. That's all I will say. I love you. Okay, now I'm done." She smiles.

"Look, I'm glad that you may have just had a breakthrough with Caroline, but that doesn't mean I will have one with my mother. You think *my* mother would know if I was sick . . . if I was *anything*?" *Ugh, God, what is wrong with me? I shouldn't be making this about me right now. Why am I making this about me?*

"Yes, she would," Shannon states firmly.

"She did!" Blake jumps in. "I don't know how she did, but she did!" His eyes are wide in amazement.

"What are you talking about?" I snap.

"Your mother came to our house, banging on the door and ringing the bell like a madwoman. When I answered, she was visibly upset. She wanted to see you. She gave me hell because that's the day you took my car, so she didn't believe that you weren't there. She started crying, wanting to know if you were okay. She begged me to tell her the results of your test. And she sobbed when I told her you were fine . . . you know . . . in relief. Uncle Rupe invited her in. I only stayed long enough for her to try to make amends with me. I really didn't know what to think of this whole encounter with her. It was odd, yet, I felt it was very sincere, which confused me even more, so I left." He shrugs.

He shrugs.

Are you fucking kidding me?

"See?" Shannon grabs my hand and squeezes it.

"Oh, I see all right!" I yell. "I see the man who's supposed to love and protect me shrugging over something *very* important like it was nothing! How could you keep this from me?" I scream in his face. "You know—you've seen—how torn up I've been over not speaking with my mother! Why would you keep this from me? Is this a control thing? Did you think if my mother were back in the picture it would make things harder on you?" I want to say more, but I'm so frustrated, all I can do is cry.

"I didn't do it to keep you away from her! I was confused—unsure if I should tell you. I haven't known her very long. I didn't want to give you false hope. You've been so vulnerable lately, Julie. I didn't want her to take advantage of that," he pleads with me.

"You told me not to contact her. Was that before or after she came by?" I try to calm down so that I can get my damn words out.

"After, but—"

"—No!" I cut him off. "I have been waiting my entire life for my mother to show up—*my entire life, Blake!* And when that moment finally happens, *you* take it away from me!" I poke him in the chest hard.

"I'm not the only one she has been running into or trying to make amends with!" he yells back.

"He's right, sweetie," Shannon interjects. "Your mom has been working really hard and making things right with a lot of people. She's becoming her old self again."

"How would you know who her old self is?" I ask in a snarky tone.

"Because they were once best friends," Maddie says, making me turn my head to the left to find the whole lot of them in the doorway to the hall, listening.

"We're still best friends, goddamn it. You don't throw away friendships like that. You wait for the other person to stop acting like an asshole. Sometimes you wait thirty years," she adds then gives a little chuckle.

"How do you know they were best friends?" I ask my best friend as I feel the frustration building up again.

Maddie looks visibly uncomfortable, like she's struggling to tell me something she can't. There's only one reason why she would hold back on telling me something. "I don't fucking believe you," I say through my teeth. "How long have you been working with my mother? HOW LONG?" I scream.

"Hey, don't yell at her! You know she has an oath to uphold to!" Declan defends her. Maddie just stands there, tears rolling out of her eyes, and I know she's dying to say something—anything.

"Who else knew? Ceese?" I feel like a wild woman.

"No. You know that none of us knew. You know Maddie would never betray a confidence. You also know that Maddie wouldn't do anything to hurt you." Ceese is oddly calm. Probably because she knows I'm about to lose my shit entirely.

"No. I was trying to help, Julie. I wanted to help you and your mom get to a place where you could enjoy a healthy relationship," Maddie tries to explain.

"Seems to me that just maybe you were getting tired of me being close to your mom. Maybe you feel I'm taking too much of her attention away from you." I know that's not true, but then again, do I really?

"That's what you think of me? You think I would go through all of this to have more attention from my mother? I can't believe you would say that to me," her voice shakes.

"That's enough!" Ava steps in front of Maddie. "I won't let you take your anger out on Maddie another minute. You need to redirect that shit right now!"

"Fine!" I huff. "Who else has had an encounter with my mother?" I look at all of them standing there like an army of traitors.

"She almost kicked the shit out of me the other day," Caroline says from behind me. I turn my head swiftly to see her standing by Shannon.

"It's true." CiCi gains my attention again. "I walked in and overheard her telling Caroline off. She also defended Charley and me. She said a lot of nice things about me, actually." Her eyes well up. "When she walked out of the kitchen and into me, she told me she meant every word and that she was proud of me. She is changing, Julie. I've seen it, Kyle, Mitch, Blake, my mom and dad—we've all seen it. You should be thanking Maddie for all of her hard work, not reprimanding her for it."

"Not one of you thought to tell me." I'm barely audible.

"Let's go home, love." Blake reaches forward and gently rubs my right arm up and down.

I bring my eyes to his and take in a deep breath. "You don't have a home with me anymore, Blake," I say calmly. The level of betrayal I feel at the moment is indescribable.

"Yes, I do," he matches my calm.

"You think I'm going to stay with somebody who betrays me?"

"Betrays you?" he raises his voice. "Nobody here has betrayed you, including me! I know this is all upsetting for you, Jules, but you are blowing it WAY out of proportion! None of us have told you because it is a delicate situation, and we all know how you have been struggling with it. Not to speak for everyone else but I feel pretty confident that we all had the same motive—to protect you! None of us knew what she was doing or if it was a hundred percent sincere. We were waiting it out to see what happens. You're taking this to a level it doesn't need to be at!"

You know that moment when you can feel yourself boarding the crazy train even though you're trying your hardest not to, and then someone says something brilliant like "calm down" or "you're overreacting" that catapults you right into first class on said crazy train? Yeah . . .

All aboard!!!

"You all have no idea. You don't understand—none of you!" I look around at all of them before I continue. "If I could unzip myself and walk over to your side of things, I would probably agree with you that it looks like I am overreacting. But I can't unzip myself. I'm trapped in here with thirty years full of these feelings . . . feelings of abandonment, of not being good enough, of jealousy, of loneliness, of not knowing why I was made to feel any of those things. That's a long time, and a lot of power wielded to one person," I cry. "So, maybe to you, I'm overreacting, but to me, I am just reacting. I've been waiting my whole life for my mother to show me what's she's been showing all of you. And I'm mad as hell! You weren't protecting me; you didn't trust me. You didn't trust me to sort out my own feelings. I—I . . . ugh, never mind! You can't possibly understand how I feel. You all have incredible families. You'll never feel what I feel."

"We're your family, Julie," Maddie says through her tears. I look around at all of them again.

"It's not the same," I say softly. Shaking my head, I make my way over to them and cut through.

"Julie!" Blake calls after me.

"Please." I put my hand up. "I need to be alone." And with that, I head over to the front door and swiftly leave.

Chapter Twenty-Four

Cynthia

Calling in the Reinforcements

"I DON'T THINK SHE'S COMING, LOVE," RU SAYS AS I STARE OUT THE front window again. I look down at my watch and see that it's 10:05 p.m. He's probably right. I don't think I'll be able to go to sleep, though. "Why don't you call Shannon to see if she's heard anything?" he suggests. I nod my head in agreement. Shannon's the one who called me several hours ago to tell me that Julie may be stopping by for an impromptu visit. She further explained what had happened today. This is not how I wanted things to happen. I didn't really have anything planned out, but I know this would not have been a runner-up for ways to reconnect with my daughter. "C'mon, now." He places his strong hands on my shoulders and squeezes gently. I crank my neck to smile up at him and pat the top of his left hand. He kisses my temple before letting me go. I head over to my sofa and grab the phone as I sit down.

"How did it go?" Shannon asks when she picks up.

"It didn't. She never showed up. Are you sure she was coming here?"

"I assumed. I really thought she would. Now I'm really worried." She lets out a big sigh.

"Why's that?" My heart beats just a little faster.

"Nobody knows where she is. She won't answer her phone. She hasn't been home at all," Shannon answers me truthfully.

"Has anyone checked with Judith? She probably went there," I utter optimistic bullshit. She's not at Judith's, not after what transpired between her and Maddie.

"No," she confirms my suspicion. "Think, Cyn. Where would Julie go?"

"Ha! I'm the last person who would know that!" I'm ready to fall apart.

"You're her mother. Think!"

I take a moment to really think about it. I gasp. "The comedy club! Julie would want to escape into laughter. I think . . ." Who am I to act as if I really know?

"Okay, stay put. I'm sending Mitch," she states.

"Why are you sending Mitch?"

"Because he's the closest to understanding what she's going through. Trust me; his dad makes you look like Parent of the Year."

"Thanks for the backward compliment," I snap.

"I love you, too. Sit tight." She hangs up.

"Shannon's on the case," I announce as I place my phone back on its charger.

"Good. Let's get you changed for bed." He holds his hand out to me.

"No. I want to be ready in case I have to go."

"Go where?"

"I don't know. Nobody knows where Julie is. Until she's found, I don't want to not be ready."

"Okay." He sits next to me. "Give me your feet."

"Why?"

"So I can be useful." He smiles as he leans down and grabs both of my legs to swing onto his lap. He pulls my socks off and slowly begins to give me a foot massage. I'm falling in love with him. How could I not? He is turning out to be everything I never thought I would ever find.

"How did I get so lucky to have you stumble into my life?" I lean my head against the sofa, smiling, taking the sight of him in. Have I mentioned how handsome he is? He's one of those guys that get better looking with age, like Sean Connery and Robert Redford.

"I was looking for a conquest to take on in my retirement, and there you were," he teases me.

"You certainly did conquer me, didn't you?" I give him a playful smirk.

"And every glorious night since." He leans over for a kiss.

"I really hope that when all is said and done, Julie and I will be in a good place and we can start doing things like family dinners with the four of us. Incidentally, I'm sorry we missed dinner with Sam and his mystery woman."

"You've already apologized a million times. I'm not sorry. What if I don't like her? It's not easy not liking the love interest of your best friend." He resumes the rubbing.

"On either side of the fence," I add to his thought, thinking back to how Shannon must have felt.

"I suppose. Luckily, I'll be here, and he's mostly there. If I don't like her, it shouldn't pose too much of a problem to cause a rift," he says thoughtfully.

"So . . . you are definitely staying?" I've wanted to ask him, but I didn't want to seem needy. At first, I was spending a lot of time preparing to say goodbye eventually. However, I learned a few weeks ago that he has dual citizenship. He doesn't have to leave after three months or obtain a visa as it is custom.

"I'm in love with you, Cynthia." He gives me a slightly

perturbed look and uses my full name. My guess is that he's not happy I even questioned whether he would stay.

"I love you, too." I palm his left cheek and lean in for another kiss. "Sorry I need so much reassurance."

"I understand." He gives me another quick peck. "Can I reassure you some more upstairs?" He waggles his brows.

"I can't, honey. I'm worried about Julie. I want to make sure she is okay." I pout a little.

"As soon as we hear that she's been found, we go up. I saw the knickers you put on this morning and I really must get them off of you. I've been waiting all bloody damn day," he says as if this is causing him pain. I can't help but giggle and give myself an inner high-five. Since Ru and I have been together, I have been treating myself to some sexier underwear and bras. Rupert definitely approves and appreciates my efforts, though, he'd think me sexy in anything, I suppose.

Julie

Misfit Toys

"Did anyone ever tell you it's not fun to laugh on your own?"

I look to my right just as Mitch sits in the seat next to me. "What are you doing here?" I ask in disbelief.

"The cavalry sent me."

"From the Island of Misfit Toys?" I ask with a roll of my eyes.

"Yes. They miss their fearless sidekick."

"Why did they send you?" I ignore his comment.

"Because I can relate to your feelings the best," he answers. I stare at him, waiting for some sort of reason they would think this. He takes in a deep breath and blows it out forcibly. "Did Charlotte ever tell you about my dad?"

"She mentioned that he wasn't in the picture," I say before bringing my attention to the stage as they announce the next comedian.

"He wasn't in the picture because drugs were always more important than my mom and me. He's been in jail most of my life. I know what it feels like to expect things—normal things—from the people you're supposed to be able to expect them from and to be let down on a consistent basis."

"You had your grandparents, though," I point out.

"And you've had four other mothers who've loved you as if they gave birth to you. We're lucky, Julie. I wouldn't be the man I am today if my grandfather hadn't raised me. I thank God every day for the man he was and for the man he helped me to become."

Damn, he's good. I don't even know what to say. To be honest, I'm not sure how I feel about anything, except that I feel confused. There's so much I don't know . . . so much I don't understand.

"I get why you got upset today. You were caught off guard. But you know none of us would ever do anything to deliberately hurt you. Everyone was just doing their best to protect you because they are just as unsure of your mother's new behavior as they are glad for it. Now, I don't know Cynthia well enough, but from what I do know, and from the consistent behavior she's been showing, I really believe she is trying to turn things around." He slaps my thigh gently before giving it a squeeze.

"Don't think just because I'm vulnerable and Charley's not around that you can have a go at me, Colton." I push into him to let him know I'm kidding.

"Damn it, McEvoy, I already rented a room for us. I should've worn my fancy pants," he groans, and I know that's a playful stab at Blake.

"Don't call me McEvoy—it's weird."

"It's weird that I didn't even know your last name until just recently. No one ever says it. It's like a big secret." He smiles.

"It is, and now I have to kill you." I laugh. Suddenly, I think about Blake. "Blake wants me to change my last name," I say without thinking.

"To what?" Mitch gives me a funny look.

"To his," I relay quickly.

"And you're scared?" he asks. I nod. "I almost lost Charlotte for the same reason. She never gave me a reason to be scared. It was me. It was self-defense. I didn't want to love and lose again. Not just that, but I didn't want to love another person again that would only disappoint me in the end," he admits.

"Does she disappoint you?" I bring my focus back to the stage, though it's all a bunch of white noise.

"Never. Not once. On the contrary, I've disappointed her on several occasions."

"Charley has the patience of a saint. She loves fiercely. She never gives up on the people or things she loves. She has a passion that should be commended." I look back over to him. "Mitch, every new relationship has its bumps, but she loves you harder than I've ever seen her love anybody besides her kids, of course. I've seen disappointment in my friend, and anything you've done doesn't compare. I think the great thing about you is that you know when you're being a complete shit and you own up to it right away. There's something to be said for that."

"Yeah—*this guy needs anger management.*" He laughs at himself.

"Nah, she gets it." I smile.

"Blake gets it, too," he says.

"Every time I can give it to him." I waggle my brows. *Shit*. "I was awful to him again." This almost makes me cry. I've come *so* far, and now I feel like I've taken a hundred steps back.

"Just give him anal; it'll be okay." He shrugs.

"I tried that, but it became exhausting chasing after him with a dildo." I let out a big huff of air. "He's just not into me giving him anal, Mitch. Is there a way I can coax him better? What does Charley do for you to calm you beforehand?" I'm very impressed with the straight face I am maintaining.

"She tells me to breathe." He chuckles. "Ugh, you crazy-ass girls." He puts his arm around me and hugs me to him like a big brother would. I kinda love this guy like a brother, I admit.

"Seriously, go home and talk to him." He lets go.

"I can't go home tonight. I have too much on my mind. I need to work it all out. I'm not even sure he'll be at my house after what I said today." I reach for my drink and quickly knock it back.

"Whoa! Slow down, slugger!" he practically yells.

"Dude, it's ginger ale. Slow your roll."

"What the fuck does that even mean?"

"I don't know—just go with it."

"Where are you staying tonight?" he changes the subject.

"Hotel, I guess."

"Here," he leans over to reach into his pocket. "Go to my house in Andover." He pulls out his keys and works one off the ring.

"That's like thirty minutes away," I complain.

"So what? I want you in a safe place." He resumes then hands me the key.

"I'm not running away from the mob or anything. Strike that—yes I am. Okay." I grab the key. "Do you think Charley will suspect anything?"

"Eh, well, Charley's suspected you to be an asshole a long time ago, so this will change nothing."

"Good to know. I wouldn't want to lose my 'asshole' status."

"Yeah. Speaking of assholes, this guy was really dull. You did a way better job than him." He shuffles his hand out toward the guy on the stage.

"How the hell would you know what the heck he is saying when you've been talking to me?" I swear my eyes are bulging out.

"It's my secret superpower: I know all that goes on around me." He said that like he was reading a fortune cookie.

"Does that superpower heighten when you are in your most brainless moments?" I ask.

"Hoyt!"

"What the fuck was that—your inner Suma wrestler?" I laugh.

"Pretty much. I gotta go. I'm fucking tired." He gets up. "Leave soon, please."

"Yeah, yeah," I sigh. "Hey! How did you even know I would be here?"

"Your mother said you would be. Maybe you've gotten so used to her not *showing up* that you can't even see her when she does." He raises his brows. "Night, Jules." He leans down and plants a kiss on my forehead before turning on his heels and leaving. Not only leaving the building but leaving me with many, very confused, thoughts.

I bring my attention to the stage where a new comedienne is trying her luck at getting the crowd going, but I don't hear one single joke.

It's all just white noise to my thoughts.

Cynthia

"What do you mean she never came home?" I ask CiCi.

"For the love of God, please don't ask me a question like that!"

It's a normal response to ask the question I just asked, but I know from others that questions like that drive CiCi crazy. "I just mean: where could she be?"

"She was supposed to stay at Mitch's house in Andover," she states calmly. "But I don't think she did. She's definitely not there now. She's not anywhere!"

"Okay, calm down, sweetie, we'll find her." I'm not sure if I'm saying that for her benefit or mine.

"Sweetie sounds much nicer than slutbag." Her voice snaps me back.

"I never called you a slutbag!" I almost laugh.

"You did in your head; I heard you," she accuses.

"Okay . . . maybe once or twice." I give in.

"I'm sorry I didn't live up to those expectations of yours."

"Really, you're such an underachiever," I play along.

"I know. Anywho, we're meeting at the pub in twenty to brainstorm," she informs me.

"Okay."

"We want you there too!" she says in an exasperated manner.

"Oh!" I practically jump in my seat. "Really?" My eyes well up.

"Yes. I mean, you knew where she would be last night. Not one of us had a clue. By the way, how did you know?"

"I'm her mother, that's all," my voice shakes.

"I'm really proud of you," she throws my compliment to her back at me. I can hear how sincere she is.

"Thank you. Okay. I'll be there in twenty," I confirm. I need to get off the phone before I start sobbing.

"Okay, bye!" She hangs up.

"What was that about?" Ru asks as he hands me my favorite mug full of coffee. I take a sip before placing it down on my kitchen island.

"That was CiCi. Julie hasn't been home yet. She was supposed to stay at Mitch's in Andover, but she didn't. Everyone is meeting up at the pub to try figure out where she could've gone," I fill him in.

"They called you as well? That's promising, love." He smiles widely as he palms my cheeks and pulls me in for a kiss.

"It is. However, this is not about me. It's about Julie. And the first thing I'm going to do is call her," I announce.

"I'm sure they've all tried that." His brow scrunches.

"But I haven't, and I'm the reason she's so upset. Perhaps she will answer or even call *someone* back if I call." I pat his chest before backing up and grabbing my phone.

I pull up her number and stare at it, excited and petrified all at once to be dialing her number. *I've missed her so much.* Finally, exhaling a deep gush of air, I hit dial. After a few rings, it goes to her voicemail, which I'm happy to hear she's changed it to a more professional one. "Hi, Julie, it's Mom. I'm just calling you to let you know that we are all worried about you. As a matter of fact, we're all heading over to the pub now, so we can work together to try and figure out where you are. I know what happened yesterday. I'm sorry. I'm sure it was terribly upsetting." I take a pause as I feel my voice begin to shake. "I have so much to tell you . . . when you are ready. But for now, we all really need to know that you are okay. Please call someone back. I love you, Julie, and I miss you . . . very much." My voice finally cracks. I hang up. Ru puts his arms around me, and I lay my head onto his chest for a little cry.

"C'mon, love, let's get dressed and head over." He kisses the top of my head.

"Okay," I agree as I wipe my tears away.

Chapter Twenty-Five

Julie

Check, please!

My mother's was the twelfth call I have received today. Hers was the only one I listened to. Honestly, I don't even know the woman who left me that message. There was not one mention of herself or how I was affecting her day poorly. It was all about me. It was the mom that everyone else has. Who was this person? I don't know. But, I am intrigued, yet scared at the same time.

And now I'm mad. I'm thirty-fucking-six, for Christ's sake! I shouldn't care anymore. I shouldn't care about falling into some false sort of trap. I should just expect it to be how it usually is. This isn't the mother I had wished for all my life. It's a phase she's going through. I shouldn't fall prey to it—I know better! And I'm mad. Because at thirty-six, I still want to believe she can be the mother I've always yearned for. *I'm so stupid for feeling this way.* What's wrong with me that I still need this person so much, that I still desire her approval and praise? Why? What for? I've gotten along just fine, haven't I?

She has so much to tell me? When I'm ready? What the hell does that mean? Is this a trick to get me to talk to her?

My phone vibrates. Looking down at it, I see that it's Judith, again. In her last voicemail, she was losing all sorts of patience with me. She threatened me with her wooden spoon. That's when you legit know that your friend's mother really thinks of you as their own—they threaten bodily harm when you piss them off. I ignore the call and watch some mindless TV instead.

I decided to stay at a hotel last night and booked it for tonight as well. I need space. I need quiet, so I can think. I'm still a little upset about yesterday. Mostly, I just feel as if I acted like a lunatic. It's embarrassing. Embarrassing because I know that as much as they want to understand how I'm feeling, they can't. Well, with the exception of Mitch. It was good to talk to him last night about things. I never really knew about his past with his dad. It makes me wonder about my own father. Maybe his death has something to do with how my mother parented. She was widowed at such a young age, and that couldn't have been easy. Even so, why haven't I seen my Nana? Maybe she passed away too, and it was too much for my mom to bear, never mind me. Maybe she thought I would forget about her in time and that would make it easier. Too many maybes. Too many questions. No answers unless I talk to her.

But first, I shall nap.

Don't look at me like that. This shit is exhausting!

BANG! BANG! BANG!

I practically fall out of the bed. *What the fuck?* I stand up and make my way over to the door and look through the peephole. There stands Kyle and Dec. I can see Kyle raising his fist like he's about to bang on the door again, but I unlock it and whip it open in time to stop him. "What the fuck is wrong with you two and how the hell did you find me?" I snap.

"I have my ways." Kyle pushes the door open all the way and they both barge with urgency. "Get your shit together; we've got to go," he states as he looks around like he's assessing the situation.

"Go where? I'm not leaving. Why the fuck can't you guys give people space when they need it. Jesus!" This is utterly frustrating.

"Your mum is in the hospital," Dec informs me.

"Oh, I'm not falling for this shit. You two need to leave." I go to reopen the door that Dec just shut.

"Julie, this isn't a joke! Get your things and let's go!" Mr. Belvedere orders. It's kind of sexy. I can see why Ceese couldn't chase him away.

"Why is she in the hospital?" I roll my eyes. My mother is as healthy as a horse. On a side note, I've never really understood that comparison. Are horses the healthiest beings on the planet? I mean, why a horse? Why not a goat?

"We don't know," Dec begins to explain as Mr. Belvedere starts packing my shit like he was given permission to do so. One thing is for certain—it'll be a neater job than what I would've done! "She came to meet us at the pub, started talking to Ethan, and the next thing we knew, she was on the floor, passed out. We couldn't get her to come to, so we called 911."

"You're her only family, and they'll need you to answer questions about her medical history," Kyle calls out from the bathroom.

"I'll call my grandmother." I grab my phone.

"We can't let you do that." He comes back out to the room. "Shannon said you're not allowed to call that woman."

"I don't know anything about my mother, Kyle!" I yell in a frustrated cry tone that drives most of us women crazy. You know what I'm talking about, right? You're frustrated, angry, or both and you cry because God was cruel when he wired us women.

"Get your shoes on, and let's go." He points to them, my bag in his hand, all ready to go.

"I'm in my pajamas!" *Damn it, stop fucking crying, Julie!*

"They're sweats. You'll be fine." Declan offers me a warm smile. I guess he's the "good cop."

"They are my pajamas!" I say through my teeth.

"Your secret is safe with us, Julie! Quit procrastinating and let's go!" he barks.

"Why do you even care? You hate my mother!" I accuse as I grab my chucks aggressively.

"I don't hate her anymore. I've actually grown fond of her."

"Fuck you!" I snap.

"No, I'm being serious. She's a completely different person now that she's had that stick up her ass removed."

"I think she knows you meant it, mate." Dec shakes his head slightly at Kyle like he's telling him to shut up.

"Let's go!" I huff, getting my right foot in before marching ahead of them and out of the door. I say nothing else to them as we make our way down the hall and to the elevator. I'm too busy now, wondering what the hell is wrong with my mother. *She's never sick.* Past medical history? *Good luck, seeker-of-information-I-haven't-a-clue-about!*

"We have to check you out," Kyle states.

"I'm already taken." I give him a condescending look.

"I don't know; a lot of things can change in twenty-four hours," he mumbles.

"Shut up, Kyle!" Dec says forcefully.

"What? What do you mean by that?" I feel as if the wind has been knocked out of my sails. We've just arrived at the front desk, and he chooses to engage the person behind the counter rather than answer my question. He tells the woman that I've had a family emergency, that I'll be checking out a day early. She looks at me, and I'm sure I look visibly upset, because I am. I can barely see her through my pool of tears, and I can feel that my nose is starting to run. Apparently, she can too, since she's just handed me a few tissues. She cancels my reservation for tonight and wishes me well. I just nod before following the guys on autopilot. *Has Blake finally come to his senses, realizing that I'm not what he really wants or needs?*

Before I know it, we're at Kyle's car. Dec holds the passenger door open for me. I decline, opting to go into the backseat for two reasons: Dec is six-three, and I want to be left to my doom and gloom thoughts.

How am I going to survive Blake leaving me? He's the love of my life. I can't live without him. Why did I have to be such an idiot? God, he's so patient with me. I broke him. I relied on that patience too much. I took advantage of it. *I'm such an asshole. I'm a stupid fucking asshole!*

"I'm sure she'll be okay, Julie," Kyle speaks softly. I look up and see that he is looking at me in the rearview mirror. I ignore his comment and wipe away my tears. Men are so stupid when it comes to women, I swear! Honestly, he basically just told me not to expect Blake to be my "plus one" to anything ever again, and he thinks I'm crying about my mother? *Fucking idiot.* "God, look at this traffic!" he groans. "You couldn't stay closer to home? You had to stay in Boston?" he complains.

"Sorry the location of my short sabbatical—where I wanted to be left the fuck alone—is inconveniencing you, Kyle. Perhaps you could save yourself a lot of grief next time by keeping your fucking nose out of things that aren't your business!" I yell without crying. That deserves a female-only wave.

"Ah! This will make you happy!" Dec turns a little to look back at me with a smile. "Blake's just texted me that he will meet us at the hospital. He was afraid you hadn't eaten today, so he's gone off to get all of your favorite snacks and a Chai Tea from Starbucks."

"He's bringing me snacks?" I ask in a hopeful, yet, confused tone.

"He's been so worried about you, Julie."

"Kyle made it sound like he was done with me." I'm pretty sure I sound as vulnerable as I feel.

"I didn't say that!" he states defensively.

"Uh . . . yeah, you did, asshat!"

"You sort of did, mate," Dec agrees with me. I really love this guy. *Good choice, Maddie!* The sudden thought of my dear friend Maddie reignites my anger toward her. I understand why she had to keep this from me. I just don't understand *how* she could keep this from me. I mean, how long has this been going on? Did my mother approach her or vice versa? How much of the stuff my mom *really* needs to tell *me* does she already know?

"I didn't mean for it to sound like that. I meant for it to make you think about what you put him through. I know you've really done a lot better, Julie, but there are times you still disconnect from him. He's on eggshells around you more often than not. It's not a confidence builder, I can tell you that much." He takes in a deep breath and lets out a sigh like he wants to say more but probably shouldn't. "He loves you more than anything. Every inch you give him, he treats it as if you've given him a hundred yards."

"Funny you should say that; every inch he gives me, I act as if it's a hundred yards." I give a playful smirk and waggle my eyebrows. Laughter erupts from both of them. The tension (that I was probably the only one feeling) seems to have lifted. I understand where Kyle is coming from, and he's right. However, don't expect me to admit that to him.

Before we know it, the traffic on I-93 breaks up, and we pick up our pace. I finally bring my thoughts to my mother, wondering why the hell she passed out. It is odd. Like I said, she's as healthy as a nagging goat. Pah! *I'm so clever!* Why doesn't Shannon want me to call my grandmother? Never mind; she's right. My mother may have had a stick up her ass, but my grandmother has a titanium rod that I believe may be welded in there. I'd choose my mother over her any day! I wish you could blame it on her losing my grandfather to Alzheimer's, but she was even like this when Pop-Pop still had all his wits about him. As a matter of fact, he was the only one to be able to get her out of her hard-crusted shell from time to time. Suddenly, a memory pops into my mind. It was during the time I had stayed with them when my mother was away. I woke up to laughter I had heard coming from downstairs. I didn't recognize the voice and being a curious five-year-old, I got out of bed and followed the sound of it. I sat on the stairs as soon as my grandparents were in view. Grandmother was sitting on Pop-Pop's lap, and it looked as if he was tickling her. *"Now, Theodore, you must stop!"* She smacked his shoulder. *"There's no one around, Louisa. No need to be formal."* He smiled warmly up at her. My grandfather's smiles were always so warm. *"Teddy, really, we mustn't wake Julie,"* she pleaded in a softer tone. *"And then she will see that you are the sun in my life, filling my days with happiness and warmth. What a tragedy if she were to discover that,"* he teased her. *"I wouldn't sparkle, much less shine, if it weren't for you. I love you, Teddy,"* she declared before she kissed him. I remember feeling so happy to see them happy. I also remember wondering why Pop-Pop called Grandmother his son when she was his wife. Funny how kids think, huh? I just don't get why she only acted like this when she thought no one was looking. So odd . . .

Soon enough, Kyle is taking the Derry exit. There are a lot of mixed reviews about Parkland Medical Center, but none of us have ever had an issue there. I think its small size is less intimidating, to be honest. "Is she still in the ER?" I ask.

"As far as we know, yes. They were running tests on her when we left," Dec answers.

"How long did she pass out for?"

"Several minutes, which is why they are doing a work up on her."

"Why do I need to be there, though? If she's come to, then she can answer all the questions about herself." I throw my hair up in a hair tie just as Kyle parks the car.

"Jules . . ." Kyle trails off like he's unsure of what he wants to say. He shoots Dec a look.

"What? What are you not telling me?" I demand.

"Well, her speech is garbled, and she's got some right-sided weakness."

"Are you saying my mother had a stroke?" I can barely get the words out.

"They are running tests," he reiterates before opening the door to get out. Dec and I both follow suit. We make our way to the ER entrance. Oddly, I'm practically jogging. My adrenaline has kicked in, and it's sort of pissing me off. But, I can't help it. She's my mother and no matter what—I love her.

The waiting room seems almost packed. My flock of dysfunctional weirdos accounts for about ninety-five percent of the crowd. "Why the hell are you all here?" I furrow my brows at them.

"Trying to make up for you not being here," Shannon counters quickly, submerging me in the pool of guilt that only a mother could conjure up. Shannon looks pretty worked up; she's red in the face and her eyes are puffy. Perhaps it's best if I don't engage.

"Jules?" I hear Blake from behind me. I turn to face him and his arms immediately open wide. I walk quickly to him and the safety and warmth of his embrace. How did I ever function before he came along? "C'mon, I'll take you back." He kisses the top of my head.

"Who's with her now?" I look up at him.

"Uncle Rupe."

"Uncle Rupe?" I jerk my head back. "Why the hell is he in there?"

"Uh, well . . . eh, remember that redhead he fell in love with at the coffee shop?"

"*No!*" If my eyes bulge out any more than they are at this

moment, they may burst.

"Afraid so."

"And you've known how long?" I inquire.

"Please, I don't want to argue about this. I was sworn to se- crecy." He turns us to begin walking down the hall to the double doors. "I was wholeheartedly against it when I found out. But then I saw them together and the transformation in both of them. I've never seen my godfather so happy before. They're really good for each other."

I don't know what to say. I don't want to argue, either. However, I can't say that it doesn't bother me about everyone else knowing everything I should know first. She's *my* mother, damn it!

Just as we walk in, the doctor looks up at us. "Dr. Owens, this is Cynthia's daughter, Julie," Blake introduces us. I try to pull my attention away from my mother for a moment to greet him. It's un- nerving to see her lying so still, eyes closed, hooked up to IVs and monitors. She's still beautiful, but I can suddenly see her age. The reality hits me: my mother is getting older. Mortality is not her su- perpower. Okay, she's not ninety-five, but she is at an age where medical hiccups begin to happen even for the healthiest person.

"Do we have any results, yet?" I ask as I let go of shaking the doctor's hand.

"Yes. Your mother has had a series of TIAs."

"Well, who should we eliminate from her life?" I ask.

"I'm sorry?" The doctor looks confused.

Blake chuckles. "T as in Tom, love. She's having TIAs, not PIAs."

"Oh, mini-strokes?" I ask, ignoring Blake.

"Exactly. We have your mother on an anticoagulant now to help. I'll also be prescribing a statin such as Lipitor to help lower her cholesterol and the plaque build-up. She'll need to follow up with her regular doctor as well as a cardiovascular doctor," he in- forms me.

"I don't understand how this has happened. My mother is wound tightly, but high cholesterol? She's healthier than I am." For real—this woman could run laps around me.

"Sometimes a healthy lifestyle is not enough. Genetics play a big part. If your mother didn't lead the healthy lifestyle she did, she could've possibly been in this predicament or worse years ago."

"When can she come home?"

"We're in the process of admitting her right now, and she will probably be here for at least two days. Do you have any other questions?" he asks.

"No. Thank you." I bring my attention back to my mother, making my way over to her. I grab her hand and kiss her forehead. Her eyes flutter open, and she gives me a closed-mouth, exhausted-looking smile (well, as best as she can. It's lopsided. I'll be sure to imitate her when she's better). "Everything's going to be okay," I assure her.

"Julie," Rupe interrupts us, "Since she's going to be here a few days, I may as well run home and get her some things she'd want."

I stare at him.

"Oh, right!" he states as if he's just remembered he's forgotten something. "Julie . . . your mother and I—" I hold my hand up as he attempts to inform me of what I am already aware of.

"It's okay, go ahead," I say. A small, grateful smirk crosses his lips.

"All right, darling?" Rupe looks to my mother. She nods. He walks over to her other side, leans down, and plants a kiss on her lips. "Won't take me long," he says before giving her another quick kiss. Me? Oh, just staring at them like I'm watching a Hallmark movie.

"See?" Blake whispers into my ear. I shrug with indifference.

"I'll be back soon. Do you need me to call anyone to handle the pub for you?" he asks Blake.

"Nah. Dad's covering for me."

"That's astonishing! Who is he anymore?" he jokes.

"Right?" Blake laughs.

I take a seat next to my mother as Uncle Rupert leaves. I'm not really sure as to what I should be doing or saying. This is very awkward. I don't want to push aside the last year, but somehow it all seems irrelevant right now. "Can I get you something—a drink of water?" I ask her.

"No," she barely voices.

"Okay, Cynthia," a young, cheerful nurse pops in on our side of the curtain, "we've got a room with a view for you!" She smiles.

"Fantastic!" Blake boasts at this news.

"It won't be if the view is her roommate's ass," I chime in.

"Ever the optimist, love!" he teases.

"Somebody has to bring the sunshine and rainbows." I shrug. "What room will she be in? I'll go and let our ridiculously large tribe out in the waiting room know."

As soon as she gives us the room number, I make my way out of the room. *I probably shouldn't have left her alone. Damn it. This moral shit is going to kill me one of these days!* "Blake," I turn on my heels, "You go tell them. I'll go with my mom."

"All right, love." He gives me a kiss on the cheek, then continues on.

Just as I walk the several feet back, my mom's bed appears. I walk up to the side of her and take her hand as the nurse pushes her along. I don't look over at her because I can't. She's squeezing my hand in a way that is making me feel very emotional—*it's pissing me off.* Look, I understand that she's been doing some sort of moral overhaul, but I'm not ready to forgive and forget. I had finally taken a stand, damn it! Suddenly she's been doing all this sort of stuff that's making me feel like my grudge should lose all its steam. That's not fair! Right? I mean, we're talking about a lifetime of bullshit here!

"Julie," she whispers. "I'm sorry."

And I really can't look at her now because I hear her crying. *I'm so mad!* I'm mad because I want to comfort her. Because that's who *I am!*

And just like that—I realize . . .

I'm the one who *shows up.*

Because she taught me how painful it is when no one does . . .

She taught me that.

"I'm here, Mom," I say as I squeeze her hand and finally bring my eyes to hers. "I'm here," I repeat.

By the time we make it to her room, it's full. Everyone's here except Ava and Trent. Mom starts crying again once she sees them all waiting for her. I feel like I've just been transported through some strange vortex that placed me in the Land of Opposites. These people have *never* smiled willingly when my mother has appeared in the past. I let go of her hand as the nurse continues to move her bed in place. Choosing to stay by the door, I watch everyone greeting her.

"Are you okay?" Maddie asks as she literally bumps into me. I glance down at her and give a little shrug as my answer. "It's a lot right now, but when you're ready, we should really talk about everything. Sometimes silence can do more damage to friendships than saying hurtful things."

"Got it, doc," I say coolly.

"Julie," she sighs. I can hear the disappointment in her voice. Oh well! Did she really expect me to be over it? She should've told me. It's not like I would've reported her!

Rather than continuing any conversation with her, I listen in on what Shannon is saying to my mom about getting matching handicap license plates that say *Best Crips*. "That sounds gangsta—you guys should definitely do that," Ceese chimes in. "Just make sure to keep one pant leg up so people know you're ready to break a hip."

Maddie and I both snort at this. She gives me a hopeful glance. I roll my eyes.

Declan strolls over and holds his hand out to Maddie. "Let's go, sweetness. You need to get some sleep," he says. She nods, practically on the verge of tears. He opens the door for her and lets her go out first before shutting the door behind himself.

I chew on the inside of my cheek.

Damn it.

I yank the door open and run after them. "Maddie, wait!" I call to her. She stops and turns. "I'm . . ." I trail off into a big huff.

"It's okay. We'll talk when you're ready." She smiles.

"It's not okay for me to act like a petulant child."

"You have every right to feel the way you feel. And you have the right to feel that way for as long as you need to. It's perfectly healthy."

"Ugh! I hate when you get all shrinky-dink, but thanks for saying that."

"You're welcome. Don't hesitate to call me. This isn't easy to emotionally navigate through." She swirls her hand around for emphasis.

"Okay," I agree.

"I love you, Jules."

"Love you too, Captain." I smile before going back into the room. However, Blake rushes me back out. "What's the matter?"

"Nothing. Let's get a bite to eat while she's occupied." He pulls me along in the opposite direction Maddie and Dec went.

"Can we go to Maryann's Diner?" Ridiculous request—we shouldn't be gone for that long.

"Perfect. Uncle Rupe is on his way back. She'll be fine." He laces his fingers with mine. "It'll give us time to touch base."

"One track mind you have," I tease.

"Yeah, something like that." He winks. God, he's so handsome. He's one hell of a boyfriend. Great friend, too. He's funny. Smart. Forgiving. Kind. Always knocks it out of the park in the bedroom . . .

Why do I get so scared of this?

Of us?

"I'm sorry about what I said yesterday," I blurt.

"I don't recall any nonsense that came out of your mouth yesterday in regard to our relationship."

"Well, with my head spinning and all, it was probably tough to focus on the verbal portion of my crazy."

"Indeed." He laughs as we make our way outside.

It's a cool, crisp day, and I fill my lungs up to full capacity, then exhale. This is my favorite time of the year, when summer and fall are battling it out with each other for center stage. You get perfect, sunny days where the wind gives you just the right amount of chill and the leaves on the trees rustle in a calming way. And suddenly, I feel like everything will be alright.

Then again, I did just take in an obnoxious amount of air and could quite possibly be lightheaded.

Chapter Twenty-Six

Julie

And then there were two . . .

Quietly, Blake and I slip back into my mother's room. Rupe gives us a little wave but then puts his finger up to his mouth for us to keep quiet. I look over at my mother to find her asleep. "How's she doing?" I whisper.

"Better. She's regained full function of everything."

"When did everyone leave?"

"About a half hour ago. I want her to rest because your grand-mother is on her way," he mentions.

"There's not enough rest in the world, or wine, for that matter, to prepare for that visit." Crap. I wish Shannon were still here. I could use a pill or two.

"I didn't even tell her for fear of her stroking out again."

"Nice, Ru, very nice." Mom musters up the energy to speak.

"Hello, darling." He rises out of his seat and gives her a pro-longed kiss on the lips. My stomach should be churning right now, right? I kind of like them together, though. Perhaps my mother's problem was that she had a stick up the wrong hole. *Dear God, Julie—shut up!* Quickly, I rub at my temples and try to imagine anything other than the image that is trying to climb into my brain. We both know that once it gets in there, there's no bleaching it out.

"Do you have a headache, love?" Blake rubs my back. I wish I did. That would surely keep that image out.

"I'm okay." I stop rubbing my temples.

"Now that I know my mother is coming, I suddenly feel a headache beginning to start, as well. Does this happen to you every time I come over, Julie?" Mom smiles, and I can see she's trying to slice through any tension that may be in the room.

"It's why I buy Ibuprofen in bulk."

"Glad that Costco membership is working out for you then," she states, and after a moment of silence, we both start laughing.

"Are we missing something?" Blake asks as he and his godfather look at the both of us and to each other with confusion.

"No. Just one of our many silly arguments," Mom addresses the question.

"I got a membership, and she told me I was wasting my money," I add.

"Well, nothing's changed, Cynthia. She still likes things in bulk-sized." He waggles his eyebrows. I smack him in the arm, giving him a horrified (but I'm sort of laughing, so my repulsed response loses its thunder) look.

"I don't want to know about that!" She waves her arms in dismissal, and I laugh some more. Who is this woman?

"Like mother, like daughter, I say," Rupe adds in his two cents thoughtfully.

"That must be terribly disappointing for you then, Mom," I tease Uncle Rupert.

"What's disappointing?" I hear my grandmother behind me. The smile leaves my mother's face. Good God, it's like an epidemic in my family. A domino effect—passed down to each generation. I wonder if Grandma had a difficult relationship with her mom too?

"That I'm going to be in here for another day or two," my mother answers quickly. "Mom, you didn't have to make the trip in tonight." Like my grandmother would've waited a day to get all the gossip to tell her bridge club or whoever the hell she hangs out with. No, she needs to know what is going on five seconds before it even happens. Eighty-six years old, and she hasn't mellowed out a bit.

"Nonsense. I would've been here hours ago, but nobody seemed to care enough to inform me." She pulls off her gloves in a passive-aggressive way.

"Well, I was a little busy having and then recovering from a stroke. Sorry to inconvenience you," Mom says through her teeth with a fake smile in place.

"I understand the condition you were and are in, Cynthia, but there is no reason for my own granddaughter not to call me. I had to learn about you being here from Janice. How embarrassing." She huffs.

"I didn't call you, Grandma, because I didn't think it would be best for her to have you around right now," I state without hesitation.

"And why is that?"

"Because you stress her the fuck out!" I yell.

"Julie!" Mom gasps.

"How dare you speak to me like that? After all I've done for you!" Grandma is about to flip her wig. Her face just took on a shade of red I've never seen before.

"After all you've done *for me?* The only thing you've ever done for me is turn my mother into a narcissistic bitch, like you! Yeah— thanks a lot for that, Grandma!" Every bit of rage I've been feeling is boiling over the top. I can't even stop; my adrenaline is pumping like crazy. I actually feel a little light-headed. Probably karma for screaming at a little eighty-six-year-old woman like an animal.

Blake grabs my arm. "C'mon, love, I think it's time for us to go."

"If it weren't for your grandfather and me, you and your mother wouldn't have half the life you have had! You think you know everything, don't you, Julie? You know nothing, my dear, delightful granddaughter!" Her tone is condescending . . . and creepy. Like horror flick creepy.

"Mother, please don't," my mom pleads. I look over at her to find her suddenly exhausted again with tears streaming down her face. Uncle Rupe is looking at me as if he could throttle me.

"I should tell her the half of it, Cynthia, and then she wouldn't be so quick with that smart mouth of hers," Grandma threatens.

"The half of what? What is she talking about, Mom?" I ask and watch as her eyes well up to the point where everyone in the room is probably a blur to her. She finally blinks, and more fat tears run down her cheeks. Her breaths become rapid, and the monitor beeps as her blood pressure spikes.

"That's it, Louisa, you're out of here!" Uncle Rupe yells at my grandmother. "As a matter of fact, I think you all should leave."

Just then, we hear a knock on the door before it opens. "Is this a bad time?"

"Yes!" most of us yell as we look to see who's coming in.

"Ethan? What are you doing here?" Blake asks.

"I wanted to check in on Cynthia . . . make sure she's okay. I am the reason she passed out." He makes his way into the room and looks around at all of us. "Oh, this really is a bad time, isn't it?"

"Come a little closer, dear," my grandmother speaks so calmly to him. Man, she can flip that switch quick. He takes few steps toward her but looks at us as if he's unsure. Unsure? I'm unsure as to why he continues to want to creep me the fuck out. Why not just ask Blake at the pub or text him to see how she's doing? He's got a weird thing for me, and if Blake doesn't see it now, there's no hope for him!

"Ah, yes . . . Ask and ye shall receive." My grandmother smiles as she stares up at Ethan. "I am going to leave now, but, before I do," she turns Ethan to face our direction, "I'd like you to meet your brother, Julie . . . the other half of it."

My mother takes in a big gasp of breath.

"What?" Either I heard her wrong, or she's fucking delirious.

"Don't you see the resemblance?" She raises a sharply penciled eyebrow at me as if to say "checkmate." But this isn't a game. *This is not a fucking game!*

"I want her out of here, Ru!" Mom cries.

"Right! Out you go, Louisa!" he barks at her.

So many thoughts—so many feelings—are running through my brain. Nothing makes sense, yet, some of it does. "Are you thirty-one?" I ask him.

"Yes."

I turn to my mother, who is visibly beside herself. "Is he the reason you left me with her for several months?"

"Yes. You remember that? You've never mentioned it before." She wipes away her tears quickly as if she's ready for whatever I've got to unload on her.

"I recently remembered it. It was the first time you didn't show up for me. I had a recital. I spent the entire time on stage looking out in the crowd for you." My chin begins to quiver as I try to fight off that God-awful feeling that has stayed with me my entire life since that day.

"Oh, but I was there, Julie!" She reaches for my hand. "I came back to see you. I was very pregnant, though, and couldn't let you see me. I was so proud of you. It was really hard for me not to run up front to wave at you. I was there." She squeezes my hand, tears regaining their momentum.

"I'm so confused. I don't understand. Why would you give Ethan up? Daddy was still alive then."

"Yes, I'd like to know the answer to this, myself," Ethan mentions.

"She was protecting you, Ethan," Rupe speaks for her. "Your father was an abusive prick, among other things."

"What? No, he wasn't! He was a great man. Tell him, Mom!"

"And that's how she protected you," Rupe speaks for her again.

"What? But, I have nice memories," I argue. Okay, I have some memories of hugs and being called his little Irish princess. I stare at my mom. She frowns through her tears as she shakes her head slowly. I look back over at Ethan. "How long have you known?"

"I've always known I was adopted. It wasn't until my mom passed away that I knew who any of you were. I'm an only child, and well, now I'm a family of one. I thought there'd be no harm in seeing if maybe I could rejoin my original family, if you'd have me. I'm potty-trained and all now, so that's a plus." He sticks his hands in his front pockets and rocks onto his heels nervously. "Before you make your decision, I think it's only fair of me to mention that I have a tendency to ask life-changing questions at the most awkward times. It's a bad habit, and I'm desperately working hard on correcting that."

"You're a funny little ginger, aren't you?" I mean, he totally passes in the funny department, doesn't he? He must be my brother!

"Dude, we're the same height!"

"Dude, don't call me dude!"

"Don't call me little ginger!"

"Deal. Don't expect me to call you big ginger, though!"

"Why would I expect that? That's just weird."

"It is weird."

"Right," he agrees.

"Okay, then . . ."

"Does anyone understand what's going on here?" my grandmother asks with exasperation.

"Yeah," my mother starts, "they're acting like brother and

sister." She squeezes my hand and holds her other one out to Ethan. He walks up to that side of her and grabs it. "Look at you two. I never thought I'd see this day. Both of my children." Another squeeze. "Can we keep him, Julie?" she asks me.

"Jesus, Mom, you're such an asshole," I say through a laugh. "He's not a dog in a shelter."

"Although I do play fetch really well," he mentions.

"You two have the same sense of humor. I'm going to have my work cut out for me." Mom beams.

"You're welcome, dear." Grandma taps the foot of Mom's bed.

"I need you to leave," Mom speaks harshly to her.

"You never like to give credit where credit is due." Grandma shakes her head disapprovingly and pulls her gloves back out of her purse.

"You have got to be friggin' kidding me!" I raise my voice again. "You know what? I'm taking you out of my will! I don't want to bother with you anymore!"

"Julie, dear, I am eighty-six years old—why would I be in your will?" She rolls her eyes at my threat.

"Because bitches like you never die!" I snap. "Now please leave!"

I think she may have just growled, but she's leaving, nonetheless.

"Julie, you shouldn't have said that to her," Mom whispers loudly.

"Why? She pisses us all off."

"If we don't keep her around, who will take care of our funeral arrangements?"

"Pah! That was good, Mom!" I laugh.

"Right? It came right to me!" She smiles widely.

"Smile!" Rupe calls out, and we all look toward the foot of the bed.

"Oh, no, Ru! I look like hell!" Mom complains as he takes a pic

273

of us three.

"Shut it! You're beautiful, darling." He winks at her.

"Knock, knock," someone announces. "Just coming in to see if you need anything." It's Mom's nurse.

"Her monitor was peeping like crazy several minutes ago. Her blood pressure went high," I inform her.

"Sorry, I was on break, and there was an emergency down the hall. She seems to be stable now," she says as she looks at the monitor before checking her IV.

"Well, we got rid of the source." Rupe gives a quick nod as if he's agreeing with himself.

"That's good. Given the day you've had, Cynthia, I think maybe you should send some more folks home, so you can get rest," she advises.

"That's a brilliant idea. Right, love?" Blake rubs my back.

"Yeah, we probably should go. Will you be okay, Mom?"

"I think I'll be better than okay. Besides, I'm sure I won't be able to chase this guy out." She jerks her head in the direction of Uncle Rupe.

"Not a chance!" He smiles.

"Can I come back tomorrow?" Ethan asks Mom.

"I'd love that."

"I want to go to Maddie's," I announce as I call her on my phone.

"Eh, you sure?" He looks over at me.

"Yes," I say just as she picks up. "Hey, tell the Viking to put his sword away. I'm coming over."

"Everything alright?"

"Some shit went down tonight, and I have questions. Don't worry. I'm not feeling hostile. Actually, I feel like I'm in a pretty good place, which I'm certain is not normal given the circumstance." I crank the heat on, to Blake's dismay.

"Okay, I'll put on some tea."

"Oh, look at you, being all prop-pa and what not," I say in my dreadful British accent.

"Did Shannon slip you something?" Maddie laughs.

"No, but I wish that she had. Okay, see you in a few!"

"Bye!"

"Why do you want to go over tonight? Why can't you just come home and talk all this through with me?" Blake turns down the heat.

"I will. I promise, babe." I grab his hand and lace my fingers with his. "I just need to talk to Maddie first. She has insight that neither one of us have. This is a lot for me to work through. I think I understand a lot of things, but I'm not sure. I'm not sure about the stuff with my dad. I didn't want to press my mom tonight about it, but I'm really confused. Has your godfather told you anything?"

"No, he hasn't. Which I'm glad for," he adds.

"Why are you glad for that, because it was less for you to keep from me?"

"Yes, but not entirely." He releases a quick chuckle. "You know how my dad is very chipper these days?"

"Because of his new love?"

"Yes. So, I met her today before all of this happened."

"And?"

"And it's Uncle Rupe's younger sister, Aggie."

"Oh. My. God! What? How is he going to handle this? Will he be cool?"

"I don't think so. He's very protective of Aggie."

"But they're grown adults to like the second power! How can he be upset?"

"To the second power?" He laughs. "What does that even mean?"

"They're so old, they could've reached adulthood twice. No, I'm wrong; it's to the third power. They're old enough to have reached adulthood three times."

"Your brain is frighteningly entertaining." He brings our hands up to kiss the back of mine. "Anyway, he can't get mad at me for withholding information when he's done the same."

"And if he gets all nutso, throw him off with information he wasn't expecting," I recommend.

"Like what?" His lips curve up into a smile.

"Tell him I'm pregnant."

Blake steps on the brakes. "Are you?" He looks over to me.

"No, but I will be at some point. I've decided to procreate with you."

"How lovely."

"Isn't it? So, when we do have a baby, what number will they be in line for the crown?"

"Eh . . . that would be the number zero." He starts driving again.

"Well, that's a start."

"No, it's not really."

"Of course it is. You can only go up from zero."

"Of course, love, what was I thinking?" He bites his smile back.

"Such a pessimist." I sigh. Blake turns onto Maddie's street, and within a few seconds, he pulls into her driveway.

DECLAN IS LEANING AGAINST the island, watching me like a hawk. "What?" I finally ask him.

"She doesn't need you yelling at her anymore. I hear it once, and you're out of here," he states firmly.

"Hey, mate, it's all right, promise," Blake defends me.

"Blake, this has gutted her. She couldn't even tell *me* that she was seeing Cynthia. This has really brought a lot of unnecessary stress down on her. Just remember that, Julie."

"I understand, Dec. I promise," I say just as Maddie makes her way out of the bathroom.

"Sorry. Hey, sweetie, Hunter needs help with something." She walks up to him and toes up for a kiss.

"What does he need help with? He should be going to bed."

"That's exactly what he needs help with." She smiles and gives him another peck.

"You're such a pushover, Mum," he teases her.

"I'm supposed to be. It's in my job description."

"Hmm." He gives her another quick kiss and heads off.

"You two are fucking adorable." I grab a cookie off the plate in front of me and toss the whole thing into my mouth.

"We're adorable, too," Blake defends us. "Especially when you eat like a rabid pig. *Extremely* adorable!"

I give him a wide, toothy grin full of cookie.

"Our children will adore you . . ." he trails off and stares at me in a new strange sort of way. A good strange. The kind that could get a girl a little verklempt.

"Are you pregnant?" Maddie asks with excitement.

"No, but I think he just made me," I answer truthfully.

"I have super sperm—just ask her lady doctor." Blake winks at me then leaves us to our own devices.

"You two are in a good place, huh?" She sits across from me.

"Yeah. I really kind of love that Brit."

"I'm really happy for you." She takes a sip of her tea.

"So, I have a brother," I announce. Maddie spits out her tea, spraying me.

"Was that a 'holy shit, I didn't know that' spray or a 'who finally fucking told you' spray?"

"Door number one!" She grabs napkins to wipe down her mess.

"So, you didn't know?"

"Jesus, Julie, *no!*" Her eyes bulge out. "How do you know you have a brother?"

And so, for the next hour, we go through about three cups each of tea as I tell her what happened today and how I found out.

"Your grandmother takes the fucking cake on narcissism. You know she only did that to put herself back in a better light. What is her damn problem?" Maddie shakes her head in disbelief.

"I don't know, but it backfired on her. Maddie, it's so weird."

"What is?"

"My reaction to it all. I mean, I've been losing my shit every chance I got the past two days. Then, this big bombshell drops and I'm all like, 'hey, bro! Long time no see!' Am I in some sort of strange denial? What the fuck?" I aggressively throw my hair up into a messy bun.

"I think the reason why you acted the way you did is because things finally started to make some sort of sense to you. You know, it just . . . how can I put this?" She stops for a moment to think. "The burden of feeling that something is your fault for not being right can be crippling. And I think that while this was all beginning to unfold, it did in a way that made you realize that you were never at fault. It wasn't you. It was life. It was what your mother was dealing with. I think that the fact that this came from your grandmother is the reason why it went over so well. Not intentional on her part, but she took away the villain costume from your mom. Does that make any sense?" She does the infamous Maddie head tilt.

"Do you mean that I was too busy being mad at my grand-mother to be mad at my mother?" I crinkle my nose unsure.

"Eh . . . no, but that could be part of it. I think you've been working out some things on your own without even realizing it. And I just feel that it helped that Louisa tried to put all your blame on your mom. For some reason, I think you just knew that wasn't right. I don't know." She takes another sip.

"I think you're right. No, I get it." I bring mine up for a sip as well. "Do you know about my dad?"

"Yes, but I think you should ask your mom."

"Okay. Not a hero, though?"

"Not even close."

"Okay."

"Everything will be. You know that, right?" She reaches across the table for my hand.

"I think I do. I mean, I'm sure there's a lot that I don't know yet that will bother me . . . piss me off, more than likely. But I feel a change in the air—a good one—you know what I mean? I may be speaking prematurely. I haven't processed everything yet." I try to catch myself from falling right into the wishful thinking ways that I have always easily fallen into when it comes to my mother.

"No, I don't think you are. Listen, Julie, the best thing you ever did for yourself and your mother was walk away from her for a while."

"It's been almost a year," I remind her.

"Yeah and look at all you've both accomplished apart. That's what you guys needed. This was not something you two could figure out together. The reason why everyone talked to your mom before you did was because that's what she needed to do. I knew that she needed to work on herself and her relationship with others before she got to the most important one . . . you. I didn't want her to fail, Jules." She tears up.

"That must've been hell for her," I joke to lighten up the mood.

"The struggle was *for real*! But, it got easier with each success. I've seen your mom blossom in ways that I've never seen before. It was like she was finally coming up for air."

"This must've been awkward for you."

"Awkward cannot even describe how fucking awkward this was for me. I was more concerned that you would find out before she finally got to you and that you would hate me." Her chin quivers.

"I'm so sorry, Maddie. I was an asshole to you. You know . . . above the norm. Can you forgive me? Also, your eyes are a real sexy green when you cry."

"Random compliments are not necessary; there's nothing to forgive." She smiles.

"You're dying to look at them, aren't you?"

"Yup." She laughs. I grab my purse and rummage through it to find my compact, handing it to her as soon as I do.

"Well, damn."

"See?"

"Yeah."

"I'm sort of getting a lady boner."

"I'd be flattered, but you get a lady boner about everything." She rolls her eyes.

"What can I say? I'm hitting my sexual stride."

"You've been hitting it since you were sixteen."

"Practice makes perfect."

"Yes, we should all strive to be the perfect whore," she states in a wishful manner.

"Kick your friend out, sweetness, and I'll help you strive a little harder," Declan offers from behind us.

"Hey, no soliciting here, buddy!" I warn.

"How's it going out here?" Blake makes his way in.

"Great. I was about two seconds away from getting laid until you two interrupted us," I complain. Both of them stop and stare at us. Not because they are shocked by what I said (but you all knew that). It's more like they are imagining it. "Let us know when you're done, gentlemen, so we can take our turn imagining you two going at it."

"Aarghhh!" they yell in disgusted unison.

"Why did you have to say that and ruin the bloody moment?" Blake gives one last shiver.

"Am I not good enough for you, Blake? Do you not find me . . .?" Dec takes a moment to act upset, "attractive?"

"Oh hush, now, buttercup. You know I do! Especially when you wear your hair so pretty in that man-bun," Blake plays along.

Dec acts bashful and dramatically bats his eyes at Blake.

I turn back to Maddie, "I think they've been around us too long."

"*Way* too long!" she agrees.

"Incidentally, you're my number one-point-five."

"I know." She smiles.

"You know?"

"Yeah. I'm everyone's one-point-five. I like that I am."

"You do?" I never thought about this before tonight, but I guess Maddie isn't anyone's number one bff. Shut up; you number your best friends, too. And, their rank changes depending on what's going on in both of your lives. It doesn't mean you love any of them more or less than the others. Free yourself from the guilt!

"Yes. It means I am never the second fiddle to anyone."

I raise my cup up to take a sip, contemplating this thought.

"I'm the fiddle in the middle," she states calmly, and I inhale my tea rather than drink it. That fucking bitch waited for me to take a sip! So evil.

"I like to fiddle in Maddie's middle," Dec says because I'm clearly not choking hard enough.

"Hey, diddle, diddle," Maddie flirts.

"You two are obnoxious!" I argue as I try to stop laughing. I take in a deep breath and finally calm down. "All right, we're going to head out now. I've got my own diddle to fiddle with." I jerk my thumb in Blake's direction.

"She's going to sit on my tuffet," he joins in on the pornographic massacre of nursery rhymes. Okay, they are not quite massacred yet, but it could get to that point extremely fast without any one of us batting an eye.

"I don't think I'll ever be able to read a nursery rhyme again without my mind going into the gutter," Maddie confesses.

"I've never been able to read them without hearing the sexual undertones."

"What sexual—nope! Never mind. I don't want to know." She shakes her head adamantly as she mirrors me getting out of my chair.

"Alright, shortstack, well, thanks for letting us come over. And thanks for helping me through some of this." I walk around the table to give her a big hug.

"No problem. I'm so happy that everything is working out. Just promise me one thing." She pulls out of our hug, looking up at me.

"What's that?"

"Don't stop spending time with my mom. I need you to spend time with her. I mean, she really enjoys that time with you."

"As long as you continue to spend time with my mom."

"Of course I will—she pays me to." She one-ups me.

"Solid burn, shortstack."

THE RIDE HOME IS A QUIET ONE. I can't help but replay today's events in my mind over and over again. Also, Maddie's take on the situation. She's always so clear-minded when it comes to these things. It amazes me.

I have a brother . . .

That's mind-blowing. I have thirty-one years of torturing him to catch up on. He seems cool, now. Glad he worked through that creepy stalker phase he was going through. *So awkward.*

I still don't feel like I'm processing all of this correctly. Shouldn't I be like one of those chicks on *Bridezilla*? Maybe it is like Maddie said. When I think back on this past year, I realize how much I've grown as a person, a girlfriend, a friend, and maybe I'm ready to grow as a daughter. It just wasn't possible until recently.

They always say that a mother can sense different things about their child, that they're going through something. Maybe it's the same for a child. Maybe we can sense when our parents are going through something. Maybe I sensed my mom changing, gaining freedom from the prison she trapped herself in. Maybe that's why

I've felt ready to talk to her. Maybe I could start one thought without saying the word maybe . . . *just maybe.*

I have a million and one questions for her. There are things I can't just simply let go of. I want to know what happened to my nana. However, I know that a lot of these topics will be very difficult for my mom and me, so I'm going to wait until she gets the "all clear." There are things that shouldn't be explained in haste or get interrupted while explaining. Yes, it's best that we talk when she gets home.

It's amazing how life can change in the blink of an eye, isn't it? Only thirty-something hours ago, I was pissed off at the world (meaning: my friends), feeling like the inner loneliness I've been warding off for years was busting out at every seam. And now, after a crisis, some due explanation, and the undying support of the people who love me, not only has the loneliness simmered down, I don't feel it at all. I certainly don't feel uncertain about my future and the possibilities that are in my reach. I look over to my left at Blake, and silently study him as he drives. His kindness and patience go to depths that, sadly, seem unhuman. Not that he needs help in this department, but it makes him hotter than just by his looks alone. Though, his looks *definitely* do it for me. I bite my lip as I watch his hand grip and ungrip the steering wheel as if he's stretching his fingers while waiting for the light to change. My mind wanders to all the wonderful things he does to me with that particular hand. My thighs squeeze together tightly.

Dear AT&T,
I'm gonna reach out and touch this sexy-ass Brit tonight.
You're welcome.
Love,
I can't remember what the fuck I ate for breakfast, but I can
remember your ad from the 90s.

"Julie, your sudden, labored breathing tells me I'm going to be one very lucky man tonight. Am I right?" A little, satisfied smile graces his lips just as the light turns green.

"You have no idea. I'd be a little scared, if I were you," I warn.

"Bring it, Red," he challenges.

"Oh, I'm gonna bring it. I'm going to flip it. I'm going to twerk it. I'm going to do some gold medal-worthy shit with it."

"Don't oversell it, love. It overwhelms you when we finally get to *it*." He brings the particular hand down and pats my thigh.

"You're right." *He totally is.* "This will be the worst sex you have ever had in your life. You'll wonder what you are even still doing with me."

"That's the ticket!" He chuckles a little. "God, I love you." He smiles over at me.

"Good because you're stuck with me now." I grab his hand and lace our fingers.

"Can't imagine a better person to be stuck with."

"Me neither." I sigh.

"I'm hoping that you meant you couldn't imagine a better person than me to be stuck with, as well," he clarifies.

"Oh yeah—that too!"

"What am I going to do with you?" he asks, his voice full of mirth.

I'm sure he'll figure it out.

He always does in *THE END*.

Epilogue

Cynthia

One Year Later

TUESDAYS AND THURSDAYS ARE OFFICIALLY MY NEW FAVORITE days of the week. Not that I was ever partial to a specific day, but now I am. I get the honor of being in the company of one Reagan Louisa Spencer for most of the day—all by myself. She's four months old, and she is the queen of all our hearts. Yes, that whole time Julie was worried about having a baby, she was pregnant. Apparently, it all made sense to her. She told me about the pressure and uncertainty she felt, the battle inside of wanting something she didn't think she should have.

It made me sad to hear that, knowing she questioned her ability to be a great mom because she didn't have much to go by. I am very proud to say that she no longer feels that way. So much has changed this past year—all for the good. Both of us are happier than we ever knew how to be.

It wasn't easy.

No, it took a lot of working through many things to get to where we are now. There's a lot I'm still working on. When you spend a substantial portion of your "good" years with someone who drains every confidence and every inkling of self-worth, it's hard to wake up one day and suddenly think you're fantastic. Even after you push aside behaviors that were only the fault of that person, there is a part of you that wonders what was wrong with you in the first place that made you fall for such a person. It's not an easy thought or concern to get rid of. Looking back, you realize that all the signs were there. However, Maddie reminded me of my age when I fell for David. She reminded me of the circumstances, as well. Losing Allan put me in a very vulnerable state. I had absolutely no control over losing Allan. When David came along, I was charmed—for sure. But I was also susceptible. You see, David knew Allan. I didn't know this until after we were married for some time. Anyhow, that's how he landed me. He knew Allan enough to mimic his character. *I was so naïve.* So much so that I didn't listen to my best friend when she told me things were "off" about David. I just wanted to be happy, you know? I didn't want to cry anymore. I wanted what Allan had promised me. David seemed to fit the part.

When David forced himself on me, he told me I had been leading him on. I assumed he was right because he acted so much like Allan. I had missed Allan so much, it seemed plausible. Allan was my first *everything*, so it made sense to me that I led David on. I forgave him . . . because it was my fault.

I became pregnant with Julie. David asked me to marry him. This was only because Edie made him. The day I signed my marriage certificate is the day I truly lost what was left of "me."

There are two different types of people you can find yourself depending on: those who should never be depended on and those who would dodge a bullet for you. I picked the first option, though I didn't know it at the time. Strike that—I didn't want to believe it at that time.

Being married to David was like serving a sentence for bad karma I should've never been serving. You know those cases you hear about in the news about people that are falsely accused of a crime, they serve many years in jail until it finally comes out that they've been innocent the entire time? That sums up my marriage to David.

Trying to explain everything to Julie was awkward. I didn't know where to begin, how to explain my thought process. I'm not even sure her father ever really loved her or whether he put on the façade of a loving, doting father just to piss me off. I couldn't stand any minute Julie was near him, and he knew it. He used to say, "Don't worry, Cyndy, I don't have to brainwash her into thinking you're a useless idiot, she'll figure that one out on her own." He was the only one who ever called me Cyndy. To this day, I cringe whenever someone asks me if I'd like to be called that.

Going into detail about how awful he was to me was so difficult. She obviously didn't know about his drinking and gambling. If it weren't for the fact that direct deposit didn't exist then, we probably would never have had groceries in the house; as soon as I deposited my check, he had it spent. He, of course, could never hold a job longer than a month or two. It was his mother who pulled me aside and told me to give her some *mad money* every time I got paid. I didn't understand what she was talking about, so she explained that mad money was the secret stash you hid away for safe keeping. That was the day I had learned Edie and I had something more in common than our married names. Apparently, David's behavior was a learned one. So, I took to the art of couponing to make the money stretch. I stretched it well enough to cover the increase on David's life insurance policy through my company. I knew one day something would catch up with him. I just didn't know if it would be his health or his gambling.

Before I even had enough money saved up to leave, I decided to. I just couldn't take it anymore—the drinking, the gambling, the random women in my bed, but mostly—the abuse. I confronted him about everything when Julie was spending the night at Edie's. I told him I was leaving, that I wanted a divorce. He went into the worst rage he had ever gotten into. He screamed in my face, telling me nobody else would ever want me. Suggested I was jealous of the women he brought home because they knew how to please him right. I told him I was perfectly capable of handing him a beer as well—it wasn't rocket science. I may have mentioned how lousy he was, that he couldn't even keep it up more than a minute. My last concern, at that point, was pleasing him. I couldn't stomach the idea of him touching me. His first concern, though, was to prove me wrong. And he did. It was God awful, and I don't want to talk about it. Only that Ethan was conceived then. And I couldn't . . . I just couldn't bring him into a house I was trying to get Julie and me out of.

David never knew I was pregnant. When I got to the point that I could no longer hide it, I asked my parents to take Julie. My mother said yes without any hesitation. "You're doing the right thing," she said. I was shocked. I didn't even explain the circumstances in detail. It was the first time I truly felt my mother's presence on my side.

A week after Julie's recital, David was murdered. He owed a lot of money, and I wasn't there to foot the bill. It wasn't until several years ago, when my dad's illness started getting to the point where he was unable to make better judgments, that he spilled the beans. It was my mother who informed the loan sharks of where David was, as he usually had the same three hiding places. Not truly believing the words that came out of his mouth, I called my mother about this. The only thing she said to me was this, "I was reading an article the other day about a child that was run over by a car. He was stuck. Without thinking, his mother went to lift the car up off of him, and she was successful." And then, she hung up.

"She lifted a car for you," Julie said, smiling through her tears when I told her.

"I guess she did."

"What happened to Nana?" she asked me. I knew she would, though I hoped she wouldn't.

"We had a falling out. You see, she thought I was the one who had tipped them off. They murdered him in her home. She found him. Even though she knew her son was an evil prick, he was still her son, and it was devastating."

"Poor, Nana."

"Yeah. I tried to keep connected with her but had to cut ties. We got into too many arguments over it, and I was afraid she would reveal to you what had happened. Julie, I didn't want you to know that you came from that type of home. You were so young. You had nice memories of your dad. Being raised by a single mother is hard enough, I didn't want to take those idealistic dreams of a happy home away from you. I wanted you to have pride about where you came from," I tried to explain.

"You were enough."

"What?"

"You were enough for me to be proud about. I'm proud of you now." She grabbed my hands. "Sure, I'm sad about not having a legit awesome dad, but I had an awesome mom that sacrificed everything for her children, and I wasn't even given the chance to know I had it. Instead, you projected yourself the way you thought a strong woman should be and it was all wrong. I wish you knew how strong you really were, then you wouldn't have felt the need to try so hard. Most of the time, it made you look or sound like an asshole, Mom." She said the last bit as if she was exhausted.

"Really, Julie, please don't hold back," I teased.

"I'm serious."

"I know. But you have to understand . . . he made me feel so weak. I still feel so weak, though it's getting better."

"I hate him for many things, but mostly for that. Us women

are so hard on ourselves—we don't need any help with that. It's not easy to realize this when it's happening to you, but usually, when someone degrades you so, it's because they know you are better than them and they will never measure up, so they try to beat you down. I'm so sorry this happened to you." She pulled me in for a hug.

It was the best hug I've ever had in my life.

There were things I didn't tell her that day. One in particular, was that her Nana was still alive and well. I also didn't tell her that I take care of all Edie's medical needs: financially as well as advocacy. Though I distanced us from her, it wasn't without explanation to her. I have always been in touch, whereas I send her updates and photos about Julie. It wasn't until about five years ago that I took on the role of Power of Attorney for her. She had no one else. I didn't mind at all. When I met with her and the lawyer to go over every-thing, we even laughed. Edie had managed to put away a lot of *mad money* over the years. She even had an account for Julie. However, that money had run out a year ago. She's been in assisted living the past four years. If you have any idea how much a place like that can cost, you'd understand how she quickly outlived her money. I han-dle the bill there every month, and her social security takes care of the rest.

On Julie's birthday, I gave her the best gift ever—I gave her nana back to her. I told her that I had been volunteering at an as-sisted living, and I just needed to pop in to give one of the residents something I had been promising to drop off before we went out for her birthday dinner. I grabbed some of my Girl Scout cookie stash just to look legit. Julie was far along in her pregnancy by then, so the cookies weren't a long shot. Truth be told: they're not a long shot even when she's not pregnant.

When we got to the community and then to Edie's room, I shoved the cookies in Julie's hands and encouraged her to go first to deliver them. Julie's keen on the elderly, so she didn't falter at all. She looked at the nameplate next to the door before knocking. I knew she wouldn't recognize Edie's last name because it was her maiden one. She had changed it back after David had died.

"Go ahead and open the door; she won't mind," I told her.

Julie shrugged then opened the door. "Mrs. Reagan, Girl Scouts calling!" she called out. I nudged her forward. Just as we made our way into the living room, Edie walked in.

"What did you say, dear?" she asked.

"Girl Scouts . . . Nana?" Julie gasped.

Edie looked up at her. "Grasshopper?" I had forgotten she called Julie that when she was little because she always had such long legs.

"Nana?" Julie cried. She looked back at me, and I nodded.

Edie had her hands up to her mouth as if in admiration. "Look at how beautiful you are," she said to Julie before opening her arms up for a hug. Julie wasted no time. She sobbed into her grandmother's neck. I think they held on for a good five or ten minutes.

We visited for a while, and Edie came out to dinner with us. Julie has said since that this was the best birthday present she had ever received. They've been as thick as thieves ever since.

When Reagan was born, no one was more shocked than my mother that Julie gave her the middle name of Louisa. Okay, I was extremely shocked. Still, my mother almost fell over in Julie's hospital room when she heard.

"I don't understand her name," my mother stated, seemingly a little beside herself.

"If she's to be an amazing woman someday, I wanted her to be named after two amazing women," Julie simply stated.

"I still don't understand." My mother's voice shook a little.

"Reagan is the maiden name of the woman who saw the reality of the situation she could've easily bathed in denial over. Louisa is for the woman who is the sun in my Pop-Pop's world, the same woman who lifted a car to rescue her daughter. Spencer, because

that's the last name of this hot Brit over here that knocked me up."
She jerked her thumb over at Blake. To that, we got a flash of Blake's
brilliant smile.

"May I hold her?" My mother sounded so full of emotion that I
had to look at her to make sure it was still my mother in that room.

"Of course you can." Julie smiled and handed Reagan over.

My mother melted like butter, holding this little baby in her
arms. It was surreal to see her like this. "She looks just like you,
Cynthia." She looked up at me, her eyes full to the brim with tears.
"You were so beautiful, and I promised you the day that you were
born, that I would never let anyone hurt you and get away with it.
I haven't been the kind of loving mom I should've been, but I kept
my promise, Cynthia."

"Yes, you did, Mom, and I am so grateful. I love you," I said
before giving her an awkward hug. Well, she was holding the baby.
Also, all hugs with my mom are awkward. At least, they used to be.

Yes, a lot of things have changed for the good this past year.
Ru and I married six months ago. He is all the things I had once
known that love is about. I forgot for a very long time. I often tell
him that I had wish we met back then, that he was the father of my
children. He always tells me that it's just as well we've found each
other now because my children are now his and he doesn't have to
change a single nappy.

Julie, of course, sees him still as Blake's godfather, but Ethan
looks at him as a dad. This makes both of us happy. When I chose
Ethan's adoptive mother, I chose a single one. It spoke to me. Not
so much as to the fact that I was plotting to leave David, therefore,
making me a single mom, but choosing to be a mom, though single, spoke volumes to me. I knew he would always be priority in her
life. According to Ethan, I was right. Unfortunately, Karen died of
pancreatic cancer about five years ago. This explains why her year-
ly letters completely stopped. Still, I wish she had told me. I may
have been more prepared to meet Ethan. At least I knew who he

was right away because of the photos she sent over the years. Ethan and Julie have some resemblance, but he mostly looks like my dad, which I am grateful for. Their personalities are almost twin-like. They certainly keep us all laughing with their banter.

Having Ethan in my life has made me happier than I had ever dreamed I could be. I hated to admit that I was jealous of Karen because she had all the big moments in his life. Maddie told me that my feelings were completely normal, especially since I gave him up because I wanted to protect him, not because I didn't want him.

I have many things to be grateful for now, but I am most grateful for Julie's strength. If she hadn't had the courage to walk away from me two years ago, I may never have had the urgency to change things . . . to self-reflect. She did the right thing—for both of us. Because of her, all the pieces in my life puzzle are coming together. My family has grown (not just the biological kind), my friendships have grown, but most importantly, my confidence has grown (the real kind, not the pseudo version I had before). Yes, I did the work to obtain this all, but Julie's action was the seed, and I never forget that.

I don't just live my life anymore.

I show up for it.

Other Books

About the Author

I am a domestic engineer (born and raised in New Jersey) whose sole responsibility is guiding three young, impressionable kids into becoming phenomenal adults. This challenging yet rewarding work requires a lot of love (coffee), patience (wine), and determination (periodic exorcisms). And so far—I'm nailing it! I used to work all of this magic from the beautiful state of New Hampshire but am now blessing North Carolina with my brand of harmless crazy. You're welcome, North Carolina.

Before becoming a domestic goddess (not really), I spent over a decade working in the medical field, where I wore more hats than the queen.

I have loved the written word and the great escape it provides since I was a little girl. When I wasn't reading about people and the places they lived, I created my own characters and adventures. Finally, I started putting a pen to paper and allowing my characters to come to life. When I don't have a pen in hand, you can often find me laughing at the conversations my characters are having in my head.

Acknowledgments

I would like to thank my kids for always putting up with a tired mommy, especially around deadline time. I couldn't ask for better, more understanding kids.

My proofreaders, Mel Henry (see note about semi-colons below) and Theresa Sederholt, for always being honest and blunt. And all around great friends!

My editor, Claire Allemdinger, you poor thing. Lol. Oh, how we laugh at the language barrier! English really is the toughest language. It's even harder when you deal with someone who is fluent in Jacanese. Ha-Ha! Thank you for putting up with me. Some people lose weight; I lose 300 semi-colons and 100 ellipses. You're a great friend. On second thoughts (see what I did there?), you're a fantastic friend, and I am blessed to have you in my life!

My formatter, Stacey Blake (Now you've had 2 of my characters named after you without me even trying! Lol), there's a magic you have that is undeniable. It goes far past the patience you show me and all the other authors. Thank you! Also, I wear more skirts now because of you! Lol.

Wendy Shatwell, you've been with me from day one. You have helped me, guided me, and put up with me more than anyone else in this book world. Thank you from the bottom of my heart for always being there, even when I'm a shit and don't check in as much as I used to! I love you, lady! I'm honored to call you my friend.

To all of my readers who have stuck with me: Thank you! I love you guys so hard! I'm so sorry this book took so long to get into your hands, but I hope it was worth it to you! Your friendships and kind words over the years have really kept me plugging along! Oh, I'm not supposed to say "plugging" anymore because it has a whole new meaning now. Well, we don't wear our capes for nothing now, do we? ;) Love you guys! Thank you!

Lastly, I want to thank my mom for getting better at showing up. I work a lot of hours, go to school, write, and travel for signings. I couldn't do all of that without her help. So, thank you, Mom; I love you.

www.ingramcontent.com/pod-product-compliance
Lightning Source LLC
Chambersburg PA
CBHW021505240626
47154CB00002B/506